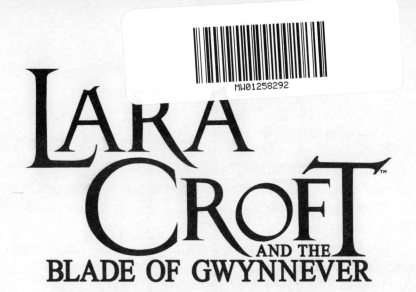

LARA CROFT™
AND THE
BLADE OF GWYNNEVER

Other Novels by Dan Abnett and Nik Vincent

Dan wrote the *Tomb Raider* novel *The Ten Thousand Immortals* in 2014. His latest novel *The Wield* is published this year from Gollancz. His comics *Aquaman, Titans, Earth 2* and *Guardians of Infinity* are currently available. Dan has also written the game *Alien Isolation* and contributed extensively to the *Shadow of Mordor* games.

Nik's latest novel *Savant,* written under the name Nik Abnett, is available this year from Solaris Books. Nik's short story *The Twa Corbies* is available in the *Out of Tune vol II* anthology from JournalStone.

LARA CROFT™
AND THE
BLADE OF GWYNNEVER

NEW YORK TIMES
BESTSELLING AUTHOR

DAN ABNETT
& NIK VINCENT

Lara Croft™ and the Blade of Gwynnever

Copyright© 2016 Prima Games, a division Penguin Random House LLC.

Published by Prima Games®

6081 East 82nd Street, Suite 400
Indianapolis, IN 46240

www.primagames.com

Prima Games® is a registered trademark Penguin Random House LLC.

Tomb Raider © Square Enix Ltd. 2016. Square Enix and the Square Enix logo are registered trademarks of Square Enix Holdings Co., Ltd. Lara Croft, Tomb Raider, Crystal Dynamics, the Crystal Dynamics logo, Eidos, and the Eidos logo are trademarks of Square Enix Ltd.

ISBN 978-1-4654-4141-6

0 9 8 7 6 5 4 3 2 1

001-286779-Sept/2016

Printed and bound in Great Britain by Clays Ltd, St Ives plc

Dedication

To the dort and her boyff: The three musketeers and
D'Artagnon... Oh thank you very much.

Acknowledgements

Dan and Nik would like to thank Chris Hausermann and the team at Prima Games for their help, advice, and forbearance during the writing of this book.

Foreword

This year we're celebrating 20 years of *Tomb Raider*. The franchise has always been about the spirit of discovery, the thrill of the unknown, and the promise of adventure. At its center is the iconic Lara Croft, and we're incredibly pleased to feature her in a new novel as part of the celebration.

When given the opportunity to work with Dan and Nik a second time, we jumped at the chance. Their work on *Tomb Raider: The Ten Thousand Immortals* demonstrated their understanding of our beloved character, and a dedication to faithfully representing Lara in novel form. We knew they possessed a desire to craft a pitch-perfect story.

Of course, we couldn't make things too easy. Dan and Nik were now comfortable within the modern survival-action of *Tomb Raider*, but when we first began the process of outlining the second novel, we knew we'd want one that celebrated the 20-year milestone. So we asked them to shift gears and deliver a nostalgic Lara Croft experience—one that would transport fans to multiple locations around the world, and was filled with high-spirited action, intrigue, and otherworldly forces. At the helm: the dual-pistol-wielding, confident Lara Croft who has a quip for every dangerous situation. Writing a novel like this would warrant a different style and tone. More importantly, it required a deep understanding of the traits that make the two versions of Lara distinct, as well as the core character qualities they share.

The good news was that this novel imposed fewer restrictions than the previous one had, given this outing would exist as a somewhat standalone adventure. Dan and Nik didn't have to take specific preceding events into account, nor did they need to ensure Lara ended up at a certain point. While this certainly offered creative freedom, it also meant there was far more room to potentially veer off-course. Sometimes too many options can be just as difficult as too few. However, Dan and Nik had earned our trust, and we were incredibly excited to see where they would take Lara, given the open road in front of them.

They certainly did not disappoint.

Dan and Nik have successfully tackled both sides of the *Tomb Raider* universe, the modern and the nostalgic. They've delivered two distinct yet equally high-quality experiences for our favorite archaeologist, first showcasing her as a relatively inexperienced young woman dealing with the aftershocks of a traumatic survival ordeal, and now as a confident, globe-trotting adventurer who greets anything the world can throw at her with a pair of blazing guns. No small feat, and a testament to the heart and effort they both poured into this new adventure.

As always, the team at Crystal Dynamics dedicates this book to our fans around the world, many of whom have been with the *Tomb Raider* franchise since its debut 20 years ago. To those long-time fans, as well as our new ones, we thank you for your incredible support and passion. We hope you enjoy the adventure you're about to embark upon with Lara Croft.

Rich Briggs
Brand Director, Crystal Dynamics

LARA CROFT

AND THE
BLADE OF GWYNNEVER

PROLOGUE:
THE HEART OF SERENDIP
Southwestern Sri Lanka

The ruined temple, and the rainforest gorge it stood in, were called Tapyantore. In a lost language that had been dead for fifteen hundred years, the word meant "green death."

Lara Croft knew with complete certainty that it was about to live up to its name.

Four hundred metres below her flailing, free-kicking feet was the lush, mist-swathed canopy of the rainforest. The plunge into it was going to break her neck and her long bones. The branches and rope vines would rip off her limbs. Broken wood would stab and skewer her. And if she weren't dead enough by then, the forest floor beneath the canopy would definitely finish the job.

Above her, the 20mm-thick steel-kern, nylon-mantle climbing line was as tight as a gallows rope. Between Lara and the creeper-wrapped Tapyantore bridge—a stone pier that connected the eastern wall of the gorge to the rocky pillar of the ancient temple—stretched six metres of the taut line, and it was frayed half-through around the midpoint of that stretch. Despite the sweat in her eyes, she could see the sturdy fibres separating, one by one, under the weight of her suspended form.

Lara's grip was keeping her from an instant plunge into the canopy—that and a single loop that the fall had pulled as tight as a tourniquet around her left wrist. Her grip was so frantically tight it was drawing blood from her palms.

How long did she have? A minute before the last fibres snapped? Less than that? Anyone else might consider just letting go and falling, with resigned grace, into the bosom of the jungle, his arms spread wide in acceptance. Not Lara Croft.

For any normal archaeologist it would be a fitting death: to perish in one of the ancient, lost corners of the world that he had dedicated his life to exploring. The eternal jungle would embrace him, enfold him. It would shroud him in leaves. His body would lie, unmourned and unmarked, and quickly decompose, returning to the earth, into the great cycle, feeding the forest's vigorous growth. Tapyantore would make him one of its secrets. Not her. Lara Croft was not just any archaeologist.

The only response that fit Lara Croft's character was to fight. She was never more alive than when she was faced with adversity, confronted by danger. Adrenaline was her friend, her buzz.

Lara Croft had never let go of any lifeline, metaphorical or otherwise. She was a fighter: born, bred, and raised. The hazards of survival might overcome her one day, but she would do battle with them today. She would do battle and she would win.

It was hot—stupidly hot—and murderously humid. The air was like soup. The sheer effort of Lara's struggle made it hotter still. Her shirt and cargo pants were soaked with sweat and rain. The socks in her army boots felt waterlogged. Even her old leather bomber jacket seemed lank with moisture.

Lara was breathing hard. Sweat streamed down her face and her spine. It poured down her arms under her sleeves. Her palms were sweating, too, burning her skin where salty sweat met the raw rope burns.

"Sarap!" she yelled. Her voice was hoarse. "Sarap, for God's sake!"

Sarap appeared on the ancient stone bridge above her and peered down through the fringe of liana and honeysuckle. He was a Sinhalese adventurer, about forty-five years old. In the six days he and his two companions had spent guiding Lara through the tropical rainforests of southwestern Sri Lanka to find the Tapyantore Gorge, they had become friends.

Or so she had believed.

Halfway across the causeway bridge, with a sad smile and the politest of apologies, he had turned and shoved her off the edge.

"Pull me up!" she commanded.

He shrugged sadly.

"So sorry," he replied.

"Sarap! You bastard! Pull me up!"

There was a chance that if she were commanding enough—and Lara could be very commanding—he might just help her. On the other hand, he'd pushed her off the bridge in the first place. He had to have a motive, and a good one.

As she had plunged, her training had kicked into gear, and old habits had saved her from instant death. They had pegged the kernmantle climbing line along the edge of the narrow, precarious stone arch. The structure was festooned with thick, wet vegetation. As Lara had crossed, she'd looped the line around her left wrist, a seasoned climber's habit. When Sarap shoved, the loop had caught her, almost wrenching her arm out of its socket, but she'd hung on, gone with the fall, relaxed.

She had presumed it to be just a stupid, clumsy accident. She'd shouted.

Then, as she'd dangled from the loop of climbing rope, she'd seen Sarap tut in disappointment—and take out his piha kahetta dagger. He had leant down and patiently sawn through the super-tough line with the blade's razor edge.

The kernmantle line had parted with a whip crack, and Lara had lurched and fallen again, swinging out and wide under the ancient bridge like a pendulum. Only one end of the line was then secure.

She'd seen Sarap tut again, and edge his way along to cut the other end.

Then his smartphone had rung.

The ringtone was the theme to some action movie, an ominous, dramatic soundtrack to her latest adventure. Hilarious.

That damn phone. Sarap was so proud of it. He was always going on about its features and apps, forever chatting to his buddies and girlfriends as they trekked through the sunlight-slanted glades of the rainforest.

All that time, he'd clearly been chatting with someone Lara should have known about. That was his motive.

"Whatever they're paying you," Lara yelled, "it won't seem like enough when I hand you your arse, Sarap!"

"It's enough," he called back, his singsong voice floating down to her through the clammy air. "And you'll never get out of there alive, so my arse will be fine, thank you."

Money always talked. Sarap liked his bling. He liked his tech. Money spoke to him, and he liked what it had to say. He was a mercenary. That's why she'd hired him, after all.

"Double!" Lara yelled. "I can get myself out of here and hand you your arse. Or we can do this the easy way. Give me a hand and I'll pay you double."

"I honestly would like to oblige," Sarap replied, "but I am very sure you would kill me in a rage even if I pull you up. And no cash reward is worth that, let me tell you."

"Double!" she snarled. The pain in her wrist, shoulder, and hands was almost unbearable. She focused on the easiest solution first. "Double, and no questions! Pull me up, and we'll forget this misunderstanding ever happened!"

"Misunderstanding..." Sarap echoed. "I like the word. It is conciliatory." He was thinking about it. That put strength back into her; maybe this would be easy, after all.

"The Heart of Serendip is very precious," Lara called out. "I understand that people desire it very much."

"Indeed," he replied.

"Who made you the better offer, Sarap?" she called up. "Who was it?"

Her desire to fight, her sense of justice had got the better of her. She regretted it. Rookie psychological mistake. Sarap was a mercenary, but he didn't like that fact to be acknowledged. She'd just straight-out declared he was murdering her for financial gain. She had offended his dignity and his twisted notion of honour.

Above her, Lara saw Sarap's face darken in annoyance and withdraw from view.

Dammit!

From above, she heard him talking. Was he chatting with the other two, Putra and Bapanni? Were they horrified at his actions? That couldn't be it. They'd be down with it. Sarap would have cut them in. They were his boys.

No, he was on the damn phone again.

"Hello? Hello? Yes, I... No, please say that again. I said, 'Say that again,' please. Reception here is very bad."

Silence.

Lara reappraised the situation. The pendulum effect of her plunge was still swinging her in a lazy circle under the bridge. Okay, so she'd do it the tough way. She flexed her arms to increase that swing. She just had to swing herself close enough to the wall of the gorge, or the sheer face of the temple pillar. She just had to time the swing to leap clear... Then she just had to land well enough to grab a handhold...

Three variables: the arc of the swing, timing, and the landing. It was down to her body and the math. Okay.

She swung, pumping her arms and bicycling her legs as though she were in some nightmare spin class. She gained some momentum, increasing the arc of the swing.

She heard the ringtone. The heroic anthem of that damned movie.

"Hello? Yes, we were cut off. Yes, well, that is the situation. I see. Well, I should think three times that. Yes. Good, then. Goodbye."

Sarap reappeared. He smiled down at her.

"Terribly sorry," he said. "They raised their offer."

He reached down with his piha kahetta and began to saw through the line.

Swinging hard, Lara said, "Well, once a mercenary bastard, always a mercenary bastard." She wasn't going to let him break her concentration. He might have heard her. She didn't know and she cared even less.

Sarap hadn't been offended. He'd used her offer to leverage a better fee. Fine, she still had the option of handing him his arse.

"Your turn of phrase is not very polite," he told her, sawing away urgently. "I would have expected better manners from a finely educated lady of good breeding like you."

So, he *had* heard her.

"You think my words aren't polite, wait till you meet my fists!" she said. She was swinging wide, but was still a long way from either the gorge wall or the face of the pillar.

But the action of Sarap sawing was actually helping. It was pushing at the line and amplifying the arc.

The creeper-swathed rock face of the temple pillar loomed in front of her, but she was falling away from it again before she could reach out and find a handhold, swinging across the deep gorge. The gorge wall was coming closer now. Lara reached out her right hand, stretched, grabbed, and came away with nothing but a handful of torn leaves and tendrils.

Sarap was nearly through the line. Lara could feel it giving way. The sheer face of the temple rock rushed towards her. No choices. No waiting for a better opportunity.

The blade sawed through the line. The line cut like a pistol shot.

Lara threw herself clear, arms and legs wide, reaching, stretching, grabbing...

She hit the rock face with stunning force.

The air was punched out of her. She had slammed into the thick cover of creepers and hanging moss. She was blind. Sap and fibres filled her snarling mouth. She was sliding, slithering, falling. She grabbed, kicked, scraped, clung. Vines tore, branches snapped, leaves ripped. Disturbed insects billowed around her.

Her eyes scanned, and she threw out an arm.

She stopped falling.

She blinked, shook her head, spat out bits of leaf and mould. Her legs were swinging free over the drop. She'd slid about ten metres down through the rock-face overgrowth. She'd managed to snag her right arm in the crook of a tough creeper trunk and hooked it there, arresting her fall. The lashing, severed line had done the rest, tangling in an obstruction some metres above her.

The whole vertical mass of vegetation creaked and stirred. Lara knew it could tear away from the rock at any moment. She moved, gingerly. She found footholds and took some of the weight off her arms. The line had yanked so tight around her left wrist, her hand was numb. Flies and bugs buzzed around her. Something crawled across her cheek and she twitched it off.

Lara began to haul herself upwards, one foot, one hand at a time, testing every branch and ledge for stability. She heard voices from the bridge. Had Sarap and the others seen her improvised salvation? She couldn't tell. Maybe they'd heard the splintering crash of vegetation and presumed it was her swan dive into the canopy.

She couldn't tell, and she didn't care.

Lara climbed.

The Temple of Tapyantore was a third-century ruin of the Karasagor culture. There was no trace of it except in the most esoteric books. The Karasagor had been so secretive, almost every scrap of their culture and legacy had been lost to history. The temple was red basalt, carved out of the top of an eerie rock pillar one thousand metres high and six hundred metres broad. The pillar rose from the floor of the Tapyantore Gorge, an eighteen-mile-long canyon choked with rainforest, and the canyon sides rose to even greater heights above the walls of the temple precinct. Water vapour fogged the throat of the gorge. The air was full of birdsong and the percussion of a trillion insects. Every move Lara made was accompanied by the rustle of foliage, the snap of twigs, and the sound of loose clods of dirt and stone tumbling away down the precipice under her.

It was going to take hours to climb to the lip of the temple wall. Lara knew that her limbs would not last that long. There was nowhere to rest, nowhere to stop that didn't involve being in tension and clinging on. Nothing would stop her attempting the ascent.

She felt something through the foliage as she reached for her next handhold: a corner, a carved edge, geometric.

Lara pulled the creepers away, raking the leaves aside. She found a sill, the bottom of an aperture. A window or drainage chute was cut into the cliff. It was small, barely half a metre square.

Lara smiled. This was her way off the cliff.

She squirmed up into it, headfirst. The hole was choked with wet dirt and vines. Lara had to grapple with her numb, bloody hands to get any kind of secure purchase. She crawled, forced to fold her arms around herself and wriggle forwards like an earthworm into the slender chute.

It was pitch-black. The air stank of organic rot. Daylight was a pale green square behind Lara's scrabbling boots. She inched on, panting. She felt cobwebs as thick as heavy silk drape across her face, and pulled her way through them. She felt things scurry over her hands and arms. The red-tail huntsman spider could kill from a single bite in twelve seconds. Then there were the snakes: the krait, the yellow viper...

Well done, Croft, Lara thought. *You've discovered a brand-new place to kick the adrenaline up a gear.*

Something ran across her hand. She smacked it away. In the gloom, her dark-adapting eyes made out a centipede almost forty centimetres long. Lara made a fist and mashed it into the stone of the chute, immediately smelling the dead-fish stink of its spattered ichor.

She crawled on, through thicker cobwebs that made her sneeze and choke. Lara spat them away. She flicked a large, inquisitive borer beetle off her collarbone.

Then she smelt something new, something unexpected.

Fresh air.

With renewed energy, she elbowed on, and suddenly the mat of vegetation under her gave way.

Lara fell, and landed hard.

She had fallen into gloom, but not pitch darkness. There was a cold stone floor of red basalt and a damp smell. The air was almost chilly, cooled by the depth of the chamber and the thick rock. Her sweat-soaked body shivered. Lara rolled and sat up. The cut rope was still wrapped around her wrist, drawing blood. Both ends of it trailed back into the chute from which she'd fallen. She unwound it and then nursed her wrist and rotated her seized, pulled shoulder. There were leaves matted into her hair. Lara finger-combed them out and found something else. Her hand came away from her hair with a large, black spider dancing across the knuckles.

She flipped it away. Another spider was advancing up her chest. She flicked that off too and got up fast. She brushed herself down vigourously. The last thing she needed right now was a poisonous bite or sting.

Lara thought about ditching the rope, but she had no pack or other kit, apart from her utility knife. The line had saved her, twice: her lucky rope. She drew it out of the chute and coiled it up.

The chamber was deep. Pale daylight shafted in through tiny slit windows high above her. It was an offertory of some sort, or perhaps part of the storage cellars used for ritual items. Lara was sure Tapyantore followed a common architectural scheme favoured by the Karasagor culture. All their temples followed it. She'd suspected it from findings she'd made at another ruined site at Kalangahl, and it had been corroborated by the insane scrawled maps the eighteenth-century explorer Sir Hubert Morris-Moses had left in a notebook she'd punched out a Hungarian mercenary in a bar fight to obtain. The world was full of mercenaries, and they all seemed to be working for people who had a grudge against Lara.

Morris-Moses had been quite a character, and the world authority on Karasagor culture, a field of study so abstruse, the rest of academia had been pretty sure there didn't need to be a world authority on it. His works had been derided by the Royal Society, and by Sri Lankan scholars (scholars of Ceylon, as it had been then).

He had persisted. He had continued his explorations of the interior and written six more books, none of which had found publishers. Morris-Moses had been a fighter, like Lara. He'd never given up, but key elements of his work could be found only in his personal notebooks.

They'd never found his body. He had vanished on an expedition to find Tapyantore. Were his bones down there in the gorge, resting in the secret peace that had tried to welcome her, too? Had the Green Death taken him?

Lara and Sir Hubert Morris-Moses could have spent eternity together, tranquil under the vines and moss, swapping campaign stories and trade secrets. From his notebook, Lara was sure she'd have liked him.

He had been a fellow maverick.

Following her memory of his sketch maps, she climbed the steps and crept along the offertory passage, a stone corridor that led to the well chamber. The smell of rot was stronger here, rot and wet.

Lara hoped there was still time. If Sarap had been paid to dispose of her, then the intention was to prevent her reaching the Heart of Serendip, said to rest in the shrine of the temple. That meant someone had paid him to get it for him or her instead.

The Heart, said to be a gold-and-ruby effigy of a civet about a foot high, in which the ancient Karasagor stored their primordial wisdom, was a precious object in its own right. If it possessed legendary properties, and Morris-Moses claimed it did, it was beyond monetary worth.

Lara heard footsteps. She ducked into cover. Putra, Sarap's right-hand man, strode into view. He was carrying the short-pattern M1 assault rifle he had assured Lara was "excellent for jungle hunting" during the trek to the gorge.

She waited until he had passed her, then threw herself onto his back. Surprised, he lurched forwards and smashed his forehead against the passage wall.

Putra fell. Lara was on top of him. He rolled, blood dripping down his face, and blinked up at her in honest surprise.

"You?" he gasped.

"Yes," Lara said. "I made it."

She punched him on the jaw, bouncing the back of his head off the paved floor.

He was out cold. She got up and helped herself to his precious M1. One clip in place, safety on. She found a second clip in his bandoliers.

Lara hurried down the corridor, up a further flight of steps, and entered the vast and echoing vault of the shrine.

Two huge, deep, stone-cut sacred pools filled with brackish water flanked a stone platform that led to a breathtaking altar of limestone inlaid with silver. Pitch-dipped torches burnt in wall brackets around the chamber, filling the shrine with a dappled, moving orange light. The flames glinted off the water and reflected off the golden idol perched on the magnificent altar.

The golden effigy of a civet. The Heart of Serendip.

Bless your lost bones, Morris-Moses!

Lara was about to step into the open when she saw a figure walk down the stone platform to the altar. It was a woman, tall, strong, blonde, wearing high-laced boots, camo shorts, and an army-surplus canvas jacket.

Lara knew the walk, the saunter, the arrogant stride.

It was Florence Race...Florence bloody Race.

Race was a stunning woman, Lara had to admit. She was about as fit as a person could be, lean-limbed and athletic. Despite the heat and filth, despite the unglamorous conditions and lack of makeup, Race managed to be staggeringly beautiful. She had high cheekbones, a slender neck, and hair like spun gold. In her forties now, Race had been a *Vogue* cover model, a famous painter's muse, a rock star's girlfriend, and a war photojournalist, all before she had turned to the shadier profession of treasure hunter.

Florence Race was damn good at that. She was damn good because she was utterly, murderously ruthless.

As Lara watched, Race gazed at the Heart. Then, she slowly lifted it in her hands, raising it triumphantly.

"I win!" Lara heard her say to herself.

Lara stepped out of cover, the M1 held at her hip, and aimed at Race.

"Not today, Flo," she said.

Race turned, the golden treasure in her hands. To her credit, she only slightly blinked at the sight of Lara Croft.

She smiled, as if they'd met at the opera at Glyndebourne.

"Lara bloody Croft!" Race exclaimed, laughing. "Alive and kicking. You are a piece of work, Lara."

"Alive, despite your best efforts and cold hard cash," said Lara. "The Heart, hand it over."

"No, no, dear, this is mine. I win this time. No hard feelings, sweetie."

Lara raised the rifle to her shoulder.

"Now, Flo," she said. "I have had quite a morning, and my finger is so tired, it's getting twitchy."

Race smiled more broadly.

"I'm sure we can come to some arrangement," she said.

"Such as?"

"Drop that gun for a start," said Race.

Lara felt a double prod in her back: gun barrels.

She turned slowly, lowering the M1.

Sarap and Bapanni faced her, weapons ready to fire.

"Drop it, if you please," said Sarap.

Lara tossed the rifle. They led her up the platform between the sacred pools to face Race.

Race was packing the effigy into her rucksack.

"Lara, dear, I'd love to stay and natter, but I have a buyer waiting in Colombo. I'd take you along, but I have to travel light."

Race looked at Sarap.

"No witnesses, please," she said.

Sarap glanced at Lara.

"Now!" Race ordered.

Sarap hesitated.

"I think," he said, "perhaps a little extra consideration for the dirty work you suggest?"

Always the mercenary, Sarap.

"You want more?" asked Race, zipping up the rucksack. "I've raised your fee already, and you didn't perform as required for that bonus. She survived."

"Even so," Sarap began.

"No deal," said Race. She'd bent to take a 9mm automatic from her rucksack. Rising, she casually shot Sarap in the chest with it.

With a look of confounded surprise on his face, Sarap toppled backwards and fell into one of the sacred pools. His body began to sink. There was a burbling sound, and then Lara heard the distorted ringtone theme from that movie bubbling out of the water.

There was a sudden, frenzied thrashing in the water. Lara recoiled. An immense mugger crocodile, larger than any she had ever seen, had risen from the depths and taken Sarap's corpse in its fat jaws. It thrashed, rolling. The water frothed red.

Race looked at the shocked Bapanni.

"Any questions about the fee from you?" she asked.

Bapanni shook his head.

He was too late raising his gun and turning it on Lara.

Lara Croft heard Florence Race's question and knew that it was all over if she didn't act fast. She took one step back, turned, and lowered herself into the pool.

Bapanni aimed at where Lara had been standing a moment before. Florence turned back when she didn't hear a shot. Both were just in time to see the faintest ripple on the surface of the water as the top of Lara's head disappeared.

"You're a fool, Bapanni," said Florence, firing her 9mm into his chest at point-blank range. He dropped at her feet. Then Florence looked out at the pool. "And you're a bigger fool, Lara Croft. A bullet would have been a lot less painful and a lot more dignified than being eaten alive by a dumb croc. And at least you would have left a beautiful corpse." She picked up her rucksack and walked away.

Lara sank further into the murky darkness. The water was like oil. Still and calm, she watched the lurking shape of the croc through the algae and silt. It was moving in figures of eight through the water, trailing clouds of blood.

She'd been under for maybe twenty seconds, and she didn't know what was happening. She'd heard the shot, assumed Race had killed the other mercenary. Florence could be waiting for her. She had to play dead for long enough to convince the woman to leave.

The croc had eaten. If she was still enough, it might not know she was there.

The croc turned in its figure-of-eight pattern, and swung back in Lara's direction. She waited for it to continue in the pattern, but it just kept coming. Another second and she could see its teeth protruding out of its lower jaw. Another and its nostrils appeared to flare. Another second, and Lara could clearly see the croc's eyes, wide open and looking right at her.

Lara had one chance. She yanked the coil of rope off her shoulder. As the croc came in, she dived away from its strike, and lashed the climbing line around its snout.

The massive croc powered away with a smash of its heavy tail. Lara held on, and the thrust pulled the looped rope tight, clamping the monster's snout shut. It began to thrash and churn, struggling to get its jaws out of the rope snare.

Her lucky rope indeed.

Her breath nearly spent, Lara surged to the edge of the pool and broke the surface. She rasped in a lungful of air. There was no sign of anyone on the platform above her.

Cautiously, expecting a gunshot at any moment, Lara clawed her way up and rolled out onto the platform. Behind her, its snout now freed, the mugger crocodile surfaced and snapped jaws the size of a trouser press at her. It missed.

Dripping, Lara rose.

Bapanni, dead from a gunshot wound, lay on the platform nearby, just as Lara had suspected.

Florence Race—and the Heart of Serendip— had gone.

"So, Florence, you think I'm dead? Well, that's one way to give me the upper hand," said Lara. Some you won, some you lost, and she hated the latter kind. This was a draw. She'd get another chance at Florence Race, and the woman would never see her coming.

Dan Abnett & Nik Vincent

CHAPTER ONE:
NECESSARY DISTRACTIONS
London

Carter Bell still wasn't answering his phone.

Lara was getting tired of hitting redial. On her first day back in London, she'd tried him three times. When he hadn't picked up or returned her messages, she'd assumed he was busy, or underground at the dig site and out of range.

By the third day, she'd become annoyed. She'd been hitting the redial more frequently, so frequently she could mimic the words and intonation of his answer message. She'd tried email and even looked for a likely landline.

Lara had only come back to the UK because Carter had asked for help. After the mess in Sri Lanka, she'd been tracking Florence Race, but the treasure hunter had gone quiet. Lara had been tempted by an expedition in South America that was asking for people with her skill set, but she still wanted to keep tabs on Florence and didn't want to overcommit her time and resources.

Then Carter had called. Lara had been at her hotel in Colombo, packing her case. Carter, usually so confident and laconic, had sounded anxious. He was working on a dig in London. Strange things had turned up. He told her he felt a little out of his depth, and that she was the only person he could think of who would take it seriously. When was she going to be in London next?

"I'm on the next plane," Lara had told him.

Helping out a trusted friend, that was the distraction she needed. Helping out a colleague who had the same instinct for the world's buried secrets as her. Helping out someone who sounded as if they were in trouble—or were going to be very soon—someone who had found something strange. That would distract her.

She could help out Carter, and still keep tabs on Florence Race. When the woman made a new move, Lara would know about it.

On her third day back in London, Lara decided to go and find Bell. She was tired of waiting for a call to arrange a meeting, and she knew where he was supposed to be. Besides, she was beginning to be concerned about him.

London seemed to be in a bad mood. She loved the city, perhaps more than any other city, and she usually found the time she spent there stimulating and refreshing. Coming home to England after a trip was grounding. When Lara had left three months earlier, spring had made the streets seem vigorous and alive.

But summer had brought an uglier mood. There was industrial unrest, strike action, anti-austerity protests, and rancorous debate in Parliament. Despite the sunshine and glorious weather, London felt like it was in an angry slump and spoiling for an argument.

The mood perplexed Lara. She'd only known London to seem so unfriendly once before, a long time before, back when she was just a kid. The city had been a threatening place, full of shadows in the shadows and suspicious faces in every crowd.

Back then, though, that had been her. She'd come home after a tough time at school, before she'd made a friend, and she'd been projecting her loneliness and mistrust onto the world around her. London had seemed ugly because she'd seen it that way.

Now it just seemed ugly all by itself.

Crossing town on a busy, sunny morning, Lara reflected that it might still be her. She wasn't a kid anymore. She was older and a lot more experienced. She took the knocks and setbacks of life in her stride. But the business with Race in Tapyantore had been nasty, and it had veered from the professional to the personal. No, Lara decided. The animosity she felt was towards Florence Race. London hadn't done anything to her.

A rally in Hyde Park had clogged the West End with traffic. A strike by London Transport had culled the number of buses and tubes running, and that had put more cars on the streets. A separate strike by refuse collectors had turned pavements into obstacle courses of unwholesome rubbish sacks spilling into the gutters. And people just seemed angry with life. The native politeness had evaporated.

Lara had given up on public transport, and the idea of getting her car out of secure parking was laughable. She had a mountain bike, but she hadn't used it in six months, and she couldn't be bothered to get it out and check it over for a ride across town. She'd opted for a Boris Bike instead, hiring one of the utilitarian share-scheme machines from a public dock.

With characteristic energy, Lara powered into her journey, standing on the pedals for most of the way, weaving in and out of the backed-up traffic, and sprinting every clear stretch she found.

Candle Lane was in the city of London, right in the heart. The backstreets were a maze of turns and corners, part of the oldest surviving, unplanned parts of the capital.

Candle Lane itself was an old Underground station that hadn't been operational since the late fifties. The street was narrow and closed to traffic. The buildings on either side were derelict and boarded up, awaiting redevelopment. Lara cycled in past the hazard barrier, dismounting as she came to a halt, and left the bike leaning beside one of the six yellow skips that half-blocked the street.

There were high fences around the site, which enclosed one of the older buildings. Lara noted site equipment under green tarps and stacks of duckboards. On the fences were big notices announcing and explaining the Crossrail project and describing the redevelopment that was going to take place aboveground. There were also a number of notices that read "keep out" and "authorised personnel only."

Crossrail was a big deal, a massive engineering project that rivalled the Channel Tunnel. A major rail link was being put in to run under the city laterally, finally linking rail access between the north and south edges of the city.

The project was huge, and it was going to take years and billions of pounds. It wasn't an extension of the Underground rail network; it was a massive tunnel to take fast, aboveground trains. Immense boring and digging machines were chewing a path through the core of the old city, hundreds of feet below street level.

It was impossible to dig through the cellars of a city like London without finding things. London stood on many, many previous Londons, an archaeological layer cake. Because of the potential disruption and the listed nature of so many buildings, archaeologists seldom got to take a look at what lay beneath.

But like the Channel Tunnel project before it, the Crossrail link had been commissioned to allow for the finds made along the way. Every hundred metres or so, something new was uncovered, and work was stopped to allow fast-moving teams of professional archaeologists to explore, remove, and preserve the data. So far, the work had uncovered Tudor foundations, Georgian basements, Norman wall lines, and Roman floors. Vital surgery was being performed on the city, and historians were being allowed to make the most of the incision.

Candle Lane was in the path of the proposed tunnel, and initial work there had revealed Tudor and Roman remains. Carter had told Lara that the government had given the London Archaeological Institute a ten-week window to recover what they could before the giant borer machines went through. In the case of really significant discoveries, the precise route of the tunnel might even be altered.

Lara crossed the lane to the site entrance. The cage door in the wire fence was padlocked shut. There were no lights on in the shells of the buildings that straddled the dig, despite the skeins of heavy power cables that ran out of the site entrance to the large generator trailer parked close by on the lane's south side. The generator was locked up and silent.

Lara peered through the chain-link. She called out a hello. Time was of the essence. Why had everybody taken a day off?

A laminated notice hung on the cage gate, flapping in the breeze on its cable tie. She pinned it flat and read it. "Candle Lane site. Crossrail regrets the site is currently closed. No admittance."

Lara frowned.

Between this and the lack of response from Bell, she knew something was wrong. She decided to take a look. The chain-link fence would be easy to get over, especially if she scaled it via one of the rubble-laden skips.

"Can I help you?" asked the security guard.

Lara wasn't sure where he'd come from. He was wearing the uniform shirt and trousers typical of a private security company, but there were no tags or logos on it. He was also a fairly young, fit, bulky man. He looked toned. In her experience, private security firms hired ex-military or ex-police, middle-aged and a little less fit than they had once been.

This man didn't look "ex" anything.

"I'm supposed to be on-site," she said. She was glad he hadn't caught her halfway up the skip.

"Site's closed," he replied, eyeing her. No "luv," no "miss," no "ma'am." All the condescending over-familiarities that she usually found so abrasive were missing, and the lack of them seemed sinister. The guard was terse and surly, like the rest of London.

"No, I'm supposed to be here," Lara said gently. "I was invited."

"Site's closed," he repeated, "as you can see."

"Can I speak to the project leader?" asked Lara.

"No one here."

"Then Carter Bell? He's working here and—"

"No one here," said the guard.

"I see that," Lara replied. "How do I contact them? Can I reach them through the Institute?"

The man shrugged, not as if he didn't know, but that he didn't care to answer.

"Is there a number I can call?"

"No," the guard replied.

"Okay," Lara said. She turned to walk back to her bike.

"Who do you work for?" she asked, turning back for a moment.

He was standing, watching her, waiting for her to leave.

"Security," he said.

"Right. Which company?"

"Security," he repeated.

"Thanks," Lara said. "You've been very helpful."

He knew he hadn't, but he didn't rise to her obvious sarcasm. His expression didn't change. Lara had seen a stare like that a few times. Not ex-military. Military.

She got on her Boris Bike and rode out of the lane into the unfriendly city.

CHAPTER TWO: HANOVER CARE
London

Parking herself in a coffee shop on St. Martin's Lane, Lara did some searching on her smartphone. The London Archaeological Institute's website had a link to Crossrail dig projects that fell under the L.A.I.'s purview, and halfway down that list, she found Candle Lane. The project head was listed as Annie Hawkes. Lara hadn't seen Annie Hawkes for years, but she knew her and respected her work. She was old-school and methodical, and an excellent excavator.

Lara called the Institute and asked to speak to Hawkes. Not possible, she was told. Ms. Hawkes is on leave.

"Since when?" asked Lara.

"Since last week, I think."

"When will she be back?"

"I'm sorry, I don't know."

"Can I speak to anybody involved with the Candle Lane project?" Lara asked.

"I'm sorry, no. That site's been suspended."

Lara tried calling a few acquaintances that she knew were friends of Annie Hawkes. None of them had seen her in a while. She tried directory enquiries for a home number, but Annie Hawkes was unlisted.

Lara ordered a second flat white and started to run Annie's name through every search engine she could think of, using a few filter tricks she'd learned over the years. She ignored any obvious mismatches and discounted any listings that clearly weren't the right Annie Hawkes.

Frustrated, Lara launched a search app that a friend in the NSA had told her about and went for a dip in the Deep Web.

The Deep Web was a troubling, uncharted place: the vast, unseen, murky realms of the web, far away from the well-lit commercialised surface waters where most people surfed. This was a clandestine world, secret and encrypted; home of government agencies, illegal commerce, and grimly obscure special interests.

Anne Hawkes was listed on the patient register of a place called Hanover Care, a private hospital in North London.

Lara drove to North London that evening. The traffic was lighter, and she figured that if the hospital had visiting hours at all, they would be in the early evening.

It was still light when she parked her roadster on a leafy square. The long summer evening was quiet and peaceful. Lara walked along a terrace of grand Edwardian houses and found Hanover Care, a large Victorian villa with modern annexes. It looked expensive and exclusive.

There was no access for visitors.

Lara strolled around the perimeter, passing strong modern fences that edged the grounds, and found a service entrance. Two delivery vans were parked on the chequered waiting area: a food-service truck and a lorry that bore the logo of an industrial laundry service.

Two women in overalls were unloading ready-to-microwave food packs from the truck and transferring them to trolleys. The back of the laundry lorry was open, the loading hoist lowered. Three high-sided carts of fresh bedding sat waiting to be wheeled into the service wing. Lara walked up alongside the lorry, keeping it between her and the two chattering women unpacking the food. She reached into the laundry carts and rummaged in each one until she found a stack of white coats. She pulled one out, checked the label for size, and stripped it out of its plastic wrapper.

Lara put it on. Apart from the pressing creases, it looked okay. She buttoned it up and strode confidently towards the entrance. The women looked over at her. She smiled at them as though she knew them. They smiled back and went back to their task.

Act like you're supposed to be here, Lara told herself. *Works every time.* She walked through the loading bay and turned into a corridor, passing hurrying orderlies and workers pushing trolleys. A look at a glossy wallboard told her the layout of the various departments, and that Hanover Care was a specialist psychiatric facility.

Lara helped herself to a clipboard from a wall rack—a prop to make her disguise more convincing—and then headed to the area's reception desk.

"Hawkes," she said to the staff nurse on the desk. The woman looked at her.

"Annie Hawkes," said Lara. "Her charts are supposed to be here for me."

"Oh, sorry," said the nurse. She checked her screen. "No, not here. Sorry. She's in 307, right?"

"I thought it was 308," said Lara.

"No, it says 307 here," said the nurse. "Her forms will be up on two, at the night station."

"Thanks." Lara smiled and gave the nurse a "what are you going to do?" shrug that got a friendly smile back.

Lara went upstairs. She used the stairs, not the lifts. Even thirty seconds in a closed lift with someone was enough time for curiosity to take root.

The second floor was quiet. Lara could hear a TV playing nearby, distant beeps from monitor systems, and the occasional chime of the elevator bank. An orderly passed by wheeling a warming trolley of meal trays. Lara looked at room numbers.

Room 307.

The door was closed. Lara tried the handle and went straight in when she realised it was unlocked.

The room was plain, almost stark, but not crude. There was a bathroom cubicle with a toilet and shower, a modern hospital bed, a bedside cabinet, and a rolling bed table. No pictures, no TV, no flowers in the plastic vase. An orthopaedic armchair was positioned in front of the single window, and a woman in a housecoat sat in it, staring out through the reinforced, unbreakable glass at the private lawns.

"I don't want any dinner," the woman said, without looking around.

"I haven't brought dinner," said Lara. She realised she'd made a mistake. This wasn't the right Annie Hawkes. Annie Hawkes was a short but robust woman, and this lady was elderly and frail.

"And none of the drugs either," said the woman. "I don't want any more of the drugs."

There was something about the tone of her voice, though.

"Annie?" Lara said.

The woman looked around at last. She seemed to have difficulty focusing on Lara. She seemed puzzled. Lara had expected Annie Hawkes to be a little older, because it had been a few years since their last encounter, but what she saw was a shock. Annie Hawkes hadn't got old, but she was pale and very thin, as if she had been on starvation rations for a month. She had a wild, haunted look, and her fingers were picking nervously at the arms of her chair.

The vitality and genial enthusiasm Lara remembered had long gone.

"Who are you?" asked Annie.

"It's me. Lara Croft."

"Are you new? I don't want the meds. Do you understand? I don't want the meds. I told the other doctor that."

"I'm not a doctor," said Lara. "Annie, do you remember me? My name is Lara Croft."

Annie frowned and said the name to herself a couple of times. Then she looked back at Lara.

"Lara Croft?" she said. "Oh, God. They didn't get you too, did they?"

"You remember me?"

"Of course I do. I'm not mad. It's been ages. How long has it been?"

Lara moved closer and crouched down, facing Annie.

"Six years, at least," she said.

Annie looked frightened.

"I've been here six years?" she whispered.

"No," said Lara. Clearly, whatever meds the hospital had put her on were making Annie's mind wander. "It's been about six years since I last saw you. I think you've been in here for a week or so."

"Seems like longer." Annie sighed. She picked at the chair arms. She'd plucked the fabric away to the foam. "When did they get you?"

"They didn't get me," said Lara, calmly. "I came here to see you."

"You did?"

"Yes. Annie, who's 'they'?"

Annie frowned again, as though it was hard to think, or as if the thoughts were painful.

"They closed the site down," she said. "They just walked in and closed it down. I suppose they had to, after what happened, but it was so abrupt. I argued, of course, but they said I didn't get to decide."

"Carter Bell asked me to come," said Lara.

"Carter? That dear chap. Is he here?"

"I don't think so. Do you know where he is?"

Annie shook her head.

"He asked me to come and help at the dig," said Lara. "It sounded important."

"Important!" Annie giggled. There was a worrying darkness to the laugh.

"Can you talk to me about Candle Lane, Annie?"

Annie looked out of the window and fell silent for a moment.

"Annie?"

"Wonderful Roman layers," she said. "Wonderful. A whole mosaic floor, hypocaust. The floor needs preserving. The tesserae are very fragile. We need to get the chaps on that."

"It was a Roman find, Annie?" asked Lara.

"Well, under the Blitz stuff. So much rubble infill. Wartime. And the plane."

"The plane?"

"Dornier, I think. German bomber. Came down in an air raid and had sunk when the rubble subsided. Right through the Tudor stuff. So much to work through. So much to process. Of course, I asked for a delay. An extension. It's an important site."

She fell silent.

"Annie? What else happened?"

Annie looked at her.

"I know you. Lara. Lara Croft."

"That's right, Annie. Annie, what else happened at Candle Lane?"

Annie shivered. Her fingers picked at the chair arms.

"We dug up the ghosts," she said. "We shouldn't have. We should have respected their peace. But we dug them up."

"What do you mean?" asked Lara.

"We should have let them sleep."

Annie looked out of the window again, as though she was expecting to see something or someone out on the lawns.

"Down in the lowest level. Near the stone. I never expected to find that. I mean, it shouldn't have been there. Not like that. I had to look. I mean, we had to dig. It was such an incredible find."

"What did you find, Annie?"

"The Son of the Sun. His marks, right there. The symbols. Absolutely incredible. But we shouldn't have touched it. They didn't like it."

"Who didn't?"

"The ghosts. They warned us off, but we kept going. Blindly! We were such fools. We opened up the whole shrine. Ritual site. So marvellously preserved. The stone, the table, and the blade. But the ghosts came out and chased us away."

"Annie, what were the ghosts?" Lara asked.

"What are you doing in here?"

Lara looked up. The door had opened, and a man was glaring at her. He was wearing green scrubs.

"What are you doing in here?" he repeated.

Lara stood up.

"I was just seeing to Ms. Hawkes's meds," she said.

"I don't know you," said the man, stepping forwards.

"Meds," Lara said again.

"I don't want any meds," said Annie.

"She's not due any until ten," said the man. He was studying Lara hard. "Who are you?"

"Look," said Lara, "I'll go and get the charts. We can sort this out."

She started to walk towards the door. He blocked her.

"Where's your tag?" he asked.

"What?"

"Your ID tag? Show me some ID."

"Calm down," said Lara. "You're getting worked up over nothing. I'll get the charts and—"

"Show me some ID right now," said the orderly.

Lara tried to walk past him. He grabbed her arm.

"Let go," said Lara.

"ID now," the man demanded. His grip tightened.

"Get your hand off me now," said Lara. She looked him straight in the eyes. "Right now."

"Not until you show me some ID," the man spat.

Lara sighed. She reached for his wrist. He tensed and blocked her. The shift in his weight allowed her to loop her arm under his and apply enough force to turn him away. A simple, swift, non-violent technique. His grip on her broke, and he found himself taking a couple of unexpected steps towards the bathroom cubicle.

Lara headed straight for the door. She had no intention of hanging around while trouble piled up.

The man grabbed her bodily from behind. Her deft technique would normally have disorientated a person for a moment, and certainly would have put most people off further engagement. But he came at her.

The impact propelled her forwards into the half-open door, which slammed shut. He had a choke hold on her, an expert grip. It was professional. It was military.

He wasn't talking anymore. He was simply going all out to subdue her.

If Lara resisted, he'd tighten his grip, and she'd black out fast. Lara went limp instead, forcing him to bear her weight as she slumped back, and making his grip a little slacker.

This took him by surprise. Natural instinct was to resist. He tried to recompose his grip.

Then Lara resisted.

She slammed an elbow back into his gut. The man barked in pain, and his grip lost focus. Lara reached up and wrenched his arms away with her hands. She turned to face him fast and found him already coming at her. She placed two forearm blocks in quick succession, which deflected his blows, and then jabbed a punch that caught him in the cheek.

He shouted something. The noise of the altercation was going to bring others. Annie had drawn her feet up onto her seat cushion and was cowering in the armchair, looking on in distress.

The orderly swung a punch, which Lara dodged, and then rotated into a kick.

"Kickboxing. Okay," said Lara, "if that's where you want to go." She grabbed the ankle of the leg that swung at her, pivoted, and threw. The orderly hurtled away, bounced off the side of the bed, and fell on the floor. He got up, spitting curses, and she let him get on his feet before she demonstrated how kickboxing really worked.

The spin-kick took him hard in the chest and threw him into the door of the bathroom cubicle. The door smashed open, and the man fell awkwardly between the toilet bowl and the hand basin.

He started to get up again. It was time to leave.

Lara ran out of the room. In the hallway outside, members of staff had begun to approach, both curious and concerned.

She pushed through them and headed for the exit. No one tried to get in her way.

As she hit the stairs, she heard the orderly's voice behind her, yelling.

"Stop her!"

CHAPTER THREE: UNDERGROUND
London

Lara fled down the stairs. She heard the doors bang open above her, and the orderly shouting. She banister-slid the last flight and exited into the ground-floor hallway.

Someone must have pressed a silent alarm. She saw two uniformed hospital security men milling around the nurses' station. No going out the way she'd come in, not without creating an even bigger scene.

Lara headed for the main entrance, dashing along the hallway, trying to look more like a doctor in a hurry than a person fleeing. Nobody paid her particular heed. There was a general bustle.

The scrubs-clad orderly burst out of the stairwell and looked both ways. He saw the back of her hurrying off along the hall and yelled out, giving chase. The two security men by the station heard the cry and began to run after him. One reached for the radio set clipped to his shoulder.

Lara glanced back, saw them in pursuit, and broke into a run. Now people noticed her. Tall, athletic, and extremely fast, she sprinted down the hallway, and heads turned.

The orderly was no slouch. He was almost gaining.

Lara wondered why the hell they were after her. Apart from the obvious—she wasn't supposed to be there—the effort was fiercely specific. The orderly was no orderly. His manner, his decent training, and his fitness in a sprint spoke of current or recent service activity. He was anonymous military, just like the unhelpful guard at the dig site. If someone was employing private contractors, they were first class.

What were they protecting?

And what the hell had poor Annie Hawkes seen?

Lara reached the foyer. The double glazed doors were dead ahead of her. Staff jumped out of her path in surprise, and a nurse with a file cart was forced to swerve.

Between Lara and the exit, two more uniformed security men ambled forwards to intercept her.

"Right, then, Miss," one began, holding up his hands to herd her back. He was big, but chubby and slow. Lara dodged him easily. The second man, younger, lunged for her, and she skidded into a sidestep, deflected the lunge of his outstretched arm with her shoulder, and barged him away. Winded, the man stumbled, fell into the nurse's cart, and overturned it. It fell with a crash, spewing patient notes and files across the tiled floor.

The orderly, still running at full stretch, vaulted the fallen cart with a bound, and caught her at the doors. Lara had her hand on one of the brass handles, and was pulling the heavy door open when he slammed into her, pressing the door shut again. The orderly grabbed for her, and got hold of her white coat. Lara turned inside it, letting it pull free and drag off her arms. He tossed the empty coat aside, and threw himself at her.

Lara slapped his grasping hands aside, backing away fast. The heavy glass doors were right behind her. The orderly threw a punch, and she ducked hard. His fist hit the glass with a dull impact like a muffled gong. The plate glass appeared to flex, but did not break. The orderly's hand, however, was not so durable. He howled in pain, and dropped to his knees, clutching his broken fingers.

Lara flung open the doors, and raced outside. The security men were still giving chase, but she was much faster than they were. She leapt down the front steps, and sprinted up the drive towards the gate. Voices behind her yelled for her to stop.

Lara ran out into the street, stopping hard to let a black cab go by, and then ran behind it as it sounded its horn and took off down a side street opposite.

At the end of the road, she doubled back, and ran into the square where she had parked her roadster. The keys were already in her hand.

When the security men, out of breath and struggling, entered the square, they were in time to see the little roadster pull out of its parking space and roar away.

It was one in the morning when Lara arrived back at Candle Lane. The night was hot and still, the sky an orange glare of sodium lights. She'd driven home, prepared some kit and changed her clothes, and then gone out again by cab.

Candle Lane: if she was going to get any answers, it would be at the site.

Lara asked the taxi driver to drop her off a street away and then covered the final distance on foot. There was a bustle of activity around the entrance of a late-opening club, but otherwise the area was quiet.

Lara had put on black boots, black combat pants, a dark T-shirt, and a black leather bomber jacket. She'd pinned her hair up and was carrying a small, black, nylon rucksack.

Just shy of the lane, she pulled black gloves and a dark beanie from her rucksack and put them on. Then she rummaged to take out a pair of good-quality night-vision goggles, but thought better of it. She wasn't going for all-out stealth. The street was poorly lit, but not pitch-dark, and she hoped that her plain attire would keep her as anonymous as possible to any CCTV. The night-vision goggles would be a dead giveaway, and they were in the rucksack if she absolutely needed them.

The lane was shadows, with a pool of light cast by the single street lamp that was still operational. Lara hugged the shadows along the walls until she reached the skips, and then climbed up and moved across the backs of them to the wire fence. She checked that she was out of range of the cameras, and put on the goggles. The world changed to a pale green underwater scene. Using the goggles, she checked for the beams of laser sensors and the heat of pressure pads. Nothing. The site had been secured, but conventionally so.

She swung over the fence and dropped down the other side, landing on rubble. It was quiet, apart from the distant thump of music coming from the nightclub half a street away. She heard water dripping.

She moved around to the site entrance and used the bolt cutters in her rucksack to remove the padlock from the weather doors. She went inside.

Lara was on the ground floor of a derelict mail-sorting office. Duckboarding along the floor and a string of lamps showed her the route to the site along a side corridor. The air was dry, but she could smell a persistent damp.

At the end of the corridor was the mouth of the site, an excavated pit about ten yards square. It was lined with scaffolding, and ladders led down from one platform to the next, deep into the ground. Empty spoil trays and specimen cartons were stacked up on shelves beside the pit, and benches were piled with equipment: plastic bags, brushes, lamps, hand tools, and water bottles.

Lara clambered down the scaffolding ladders. The smell of damp was stronger below ground level. The dig had sliced clean down through the depot's basement structure into the sub-soil and the layers beneath. Heavy reinforcement posts had been put in to hold the pit up and open.

Three ladders down, Lara took off her goggles to preserve power, put them away, and switched to a flashlight. The powerful pearl-white beam probed the way ahead of her.

She went down about twenty metres and found herself in an artificial cave, a dug-out cavity of considerable size. More site equipment was stored here, with sorting tables, heavier tools, and racks of hard hats.

Following the beam of her torch, Lara entered the main tunnel.

The tunnel was wide and lined with duckboarding. It sloped down. About twenty metres along, a side shaft opened to her right, and she peered into what was clearly part of the abandoned Underground station. She saw white tiling and the remains of a platform bench. Lara pushed on and soon felt a draught on her face. She was passing under one of the vent shafts constructed to keep the air circulating.

Beyond the vent, the tunnel opened up into a broad chamber that showed extensive excavation work. The floor had been dug to various levels, revealing old postholes and timbers. The area had been gridded out with coloured tape attached to pegs. There was more equipment here, and more strings of lights.

To the left of the chamber, metal ladders led down into a larger chamber twenty feet below. Lara passed an area of mangled wall that was partially wrapped in heavy plastic sheeting. She saw traces of metal through the sheeting, heavy, dark, and angular. Was that the buried plane wreck Annie had mentioned? It didn't look like much, just a layer of compressed, time-stained wreckage sandwiched between layers of earth and rubble.

The lower chamber was more impressive. The floor had been dug away, and Lara's torch beam revealed traces of tiles that had once formed a Roman hypocaust, the under-floor heating system. Then she saw the floor, a tiled mosaic. It was beautiful and almost complete, a scene of Imperial domestic life created from thousands of tiny tile shards. Household gods and a benign paternal face looked up at her from the floor. It was one of the best Roman survivals she had ever seen on the UK mainland, as important as anything at Fishbourne Palace, or Dernavorum, or Ilchester Villa.

Lara looked at it for a long time, studying the flow and composition by the light of her torch. This kind of relic was the reason she did what she did. It was beautiful and fragile, a direct connection to the past. It had been hidden from human eyes for eighteen hundred years.

Annie's team had done an amazing job exposing and preserving it. Why had they stopped?

Lara froze. She thought she heard a noise. She waited, but no one appeared and nothing stirred.

She felt a breeze again, like a soft sigh. There was another excavation beyond the Roman floor. She followed the duckboard walkway around the mosaic and found the head of another metal ladder. It disappeared down into an earth-cut shaft.

Lara started the descent. Two rungs down, she froze again. She kept hearing noises. Was there something down there with her?

Nothing.

Just her imagination, perhaps. And if it wasn't her imagination, she'd deal with whatever it was. With Carter Bell missing, and Annie Hawkes incapacitated and held captive in a psychiatric unit, Lara was spoiling for a fight.

Lara continued down. The walls of the shaft were stone after the first few feet of earth: old and well-worked slabs that suggested to Lara something ancient, really ancient.

It looked like a cyst chamber, an ancient tomb cut into the earth to take a burial. It looked almost Neolithic.

If that were true, the deepest parts of the site weren't eighteen hundred years old. They were more like three or four thousand years old. Annie Hawkes's team had stumbled upon something very rare and truly incredible.

The shaft was deep. A single ladder wouldn't reach all the way to the bottom, and a second one had been lashed to the first. Lara moved from one ladder to the next carefully, aware of how directional her light was and how easily one misstep could end her visit disastrously.

She wondered, again, whether she was alone. It was as if there was someone or something right there with her, as if something in the shaft was clinging to the wall behind her in the darkness. She wasn't given to paranoia; it wasn't in her nature.

Lara shook off the feeling, and panned her torch around. There was nothing but bare stone.

"Come out, come out, wherever you are," she said into the darkness.

At the bottom of the ladder, Lara found herself in a broad, low chamber lined with stone slabs. It was eerie, and her slightest movement made odd, reflected sounds. It was damp and hot, and the air was stale.

The chamber was incredible. They had discovered a Neolithic cyst buried deep under the heart of London. This was perhaps the earliest evidence yet of occupation or habitation in the tract of river basin that would one day become one of the most famous cities in the world.

Lara moved around the chamber slowly, taking it all in. The stonework was extraordinary, perfectly worked by hand and antler tool and perfectly fitted together. She wondered if it had been a tomb, but there was no sign of graves.

Then she saw the altar.

It filled the far end of the chamber. A stone plinth, rectangular and made of what looked like sarsen stone, was set in front of a single standing stone about nine feet high. The plinth was clearly what Annie had called the table. There was a long, shallow groove in it, perhaps for offerings. Numbered markers had been left where objects had been found and removed.

The standing stone was even more extraordinary. It was engraved, cut with bas-relief figures, and the shape, very geometric, was—

Lara stopped. She took a deep breath.

What she was seeing was impossible, unbelievable.

She took a step closer, and played her torch beam up and down the stone.

It wasn't a Neolithic standing stone at all. The shape, construction, and design were unmistakable, as was the style of the inscriptions covering its face.

The standing stone was, in fact, an obelisk of the Egyptian New Kingdom period.

Almost trembling with astonishment, questions whirling in her head, Lara took out her compact digital camera and began to take pictures of the obelisk from all angles. No wonder Carter Bell had been so troubled and concerned. This object had absolutely no business being here. Who had made this crypt? It couldn't be Neolithic. Had some secret society of Victorian eccentrics dug the place and furnished it with a relic they had shipped back from Luxor? It was a confection, an artificial creation put together by the idle and the rich. It had to be. The ancient Egyptians had never come to the British Isles. They had never been guests of the Neolithic Britons.

Lara thought she heard movement again, and then quickly remembered the intense disquiet she kept feeling, the sensation that she was not alone.

But this time it was real.

Powerful torch beams caught her. She turned, blinded, and half-saw two or three silhouettes behind the glare.

"Raise your hands," a man's voice ordered.

"Who are you?" Lara asked, squinting.

"Raise your damn hands."

The torch beams pinning her did not waver. She heard the click of safety catches sliding off.

"Raise your hands now, or we fire," said the voice.

Lara Croft raised her hands in surrender.

CHAPTER FOUR:
IDENTIFICATION PURPOSES
London

The room was small and very plain: brick walls, a cast concrete floor, a single door, and a small barred window, high up. The single fluorescent-light fitting emitted a harsh glare. Two chairs sat on either side of a simple metal table.

Lara sat on one of the chairs, facing the table, waiting. She figured she was still somewhere in the central London area. The drive in the plain van had only lasted fifteen minutes.

The anonymous men in dark clothes had left her waiting in the room for three times that long.

A man stepped into the room and closed the door behind him. He was just under six feet tall and solidly built. Lara estimated he was in his late thirties. He was dark-haired, and quite good-looking, if you liked the rugby-player thing. He had a small scar running down from the side of his nose to his upper lip.

The man was carrying Lara's jacket and her rucksack. He put them down on the table.

"Who are you?" Lara asked.

The man did not answer. He unzipped the rucksack and spilled the contents out onto the table.

"Where am I?" Lara asked.

Again, the man didn't reply. He moved the items that had fallen from the rucksack around, sorting through them: flashlight, penlight, a fold of notes and some loose change, digital camera, utility tool.

He picked up the utility tool, slid it open until it was in its knife format, and then slowly began to cut out the lining of Lara's bomber jacket.

He did it skillfully. He'd done it before.

"That was a nice jacket," Lara said. She made no attempt to stop him. She sat back and watched.

The man cut the lining out of the body, turned the sleeves inside out, and then inverted all the pocket linings. He felt the coat carefully for concealed pouches or hard objects. He put the jacket down. Then he took the knife and slit the rucksack apart with similar efficiency, like a butcher jointing meat. He finger-searched each seam. Then he put the gutted rucksack down too.

Holding the knife, he looked at Lara.

"What are you going to cut up next?" she asked.

The man clicked the utility tool shut and set it on the table. His fingers lingered over the flashlight and the pen torch, and then picked up the camera. He switched it on, pressed playback, and scrolled through the stored pictures. There was nothing on it except shots of the Candle Lane site. Lara had fitted a packet-fresh memory card on her way out last night.

Disappointed, the man went back through the pictures, deleting each one in turn. He switched the blanked camera off again and put it down.

He looked at her.

"No ID," he said.

She shrugged.

"You probably have to assume that was deliberate," she replied.

"Because you thought you'd be caught?" he asked.

"In case I was caught," she said.

"Do you know how long it will take us to identify you?" he asked.

"No. I suppose that depends who you are," said Lara.

"Name?" he asked.

"That's what I'm asking," she said.

He stared at her, his gaze unwavering.

"What is your name?" he asked.

"I'm assuming you're military," she said. "Or ex-military. What are you, private security?"

The man was wearing black fatigues. He wasn't wearing his sidearm, but he and the three men who had detained her in the cyst chamber had been equipped with matte-black Sig nines. Their clothing and demeanour, even their haircuts, had been uniform.

"You don't seem to be grasping the principle of interrogation," the man said.

"And you don't seem to be grasping the basic principles of detention," Lara replied. "I have rights.

You need to identify yourself and your authority. You need to tell me if I'm charged with anything."

"I don't need to do anything," he said. "And you need to start cooperating."

She raised one eyebrow.

"Or?" she asked.

"Again, the questions here are flowing the wrong way," the man said.

"Not a very deft interrogator, then, are you?"

"Why were you at Candle Lane?" he asked.

"Why were you?"

The door opened. One of the other men entered and handed an iPad to the man with the scar. Then he left again.

The man with the scar looked down at the iPad.

"Lara Croft," he said, reading off the screen. "British passport. Archaeologist and explorer."

"Nice," she said. "Pulled that by face-rec software? So, military or more than military. Police? No."

"No. We figured it was you; you're a known person. We just like to be thorough."

"Policemen follow rules," said Lara. "They read a person her rights. They understand the parameters of detention."

"You've met some very nice policemen," he said.

"I've always found them charming," she said, "if I want to know the time, or ask directions."

"What were you doing at Candle Lane, Miss Croft?"

"Well, now," Lara said, making a display of pretend deep thought. "I'm an archaeologist and an explorer. I simply cannot imagine."

"Do you think you're being amusing?" he asked.

"No, I think I'm annoying the hell out of you. Once you're annoyed, you'll make a slip, and I'll start to learn things. It's a very simple interrogation technique."

"Really?" he asked.

Lara nodded.

"You've already moved from fact-oriented questions to more emotional observations. 'Do you think you're being amusing?' That's just borderline aggravated, and not germane."

He continued to stare at her.

"Of course," Lara said, folding her arms, "you could cut through the games by talking directly and identifying yourself."

The man pulled out the other chair, sat down facing her, and looked her in the eyes.

"My name is Cryer," he said.

"Am I charged with something, Mr. Cryer?"

"Breaking and entering."

"I didn't break. Well, not much. I entered."

"A prohibited site," he said. "If we brought charges, they would carry a stiff penalty."

"I doubt it," she said. "Besides, I was invited."

"Invited?"

"To join the Candle Lane dig."

"When?"

"About four days ago."

"You were in Sri Lanka about four days ago."

"I was. The invitation came during a phone call."

"From?"

"A member of the dig team. A friend. He wanted to recruit me. He needed my expertise. I came to London and went to the site. The place was closed."

"But you decided to enter anyway," said Cryer.

"Archaeologist and explorer, Mr. Cryer," she said. "I'm not sure why that's giving you so much trouble. I have a great curiosity. It's in the genes. I look for answers... particularly when I'm being stonewalled."

"The Candle Lane site was closed, Miss Croft. The excavation was wound up."

"By whom?"

"By us."

"And who is 'us,' Mr. Cryer?"

"Division Eleven," he said.

Lara opened her mouth to answer, but hesitated for a split second.

"Ah," he said. Was that a smile? "A response at last. Discomfort. Some of that bravado gone, has it?"

Lara recovered neatly.

"Ministry of Defence," she said. "I was close, then. Division Eleven was a rumour. Unconfirmed. A bit of a myth, I thought, but here you are, and Theresa Johnson has a lot to answer for."

"Leave the Minister of Defence out of this," said Cryer.

"Actually, given my line of work and the fact that you do, apparently, exist after all, I'm amazed our paths haven't crossed before."

"Maybe they have," said Cryer.

"Nice." Lara smiled. "You're that good, huh?"

"We have our moments."

"Division Eleven, so the rumour goes, is Special Operations. Artefacts. Unusual circumstances."

"We prefer the term 'exotic issues,'" Cryer said.

"I'm sure you do. Why was the site closed? What did Annie Hawkes find?"

"I don't think that's a conversation we're going to have, Miss Croft."

"Well, then, you're missing out," said Lara. "You've got my file on that tablet. I imagine it's quite extensive. Extensive enough to show you that I could offer a great deal in the way of special assistance."

"Not necessary. It's all in hand."

"Really?" she asked.

Cryer sat back slightly, but his gaze did not leave her for a second.

"Division Eleven has a great deal of latitude in its operations, Miss Croft. A very great deal. Legal latitude. We are not bound by the usual regulations. It's a small addendum to the Anti-Terrorism Act, actually. We can do just about anything we like. Hold you without charge, for instance. Hold you indefinitely. Withhold legal assistance. Withhold your opportunity to contact anybody or inform anybody of your whereabouts."

"Mr. Cryer," Lara tutted. "Is this the part where you threaten me?"

"That wasn't a threat," he said. "I haven't got to the threat yet."

"I'd say finding Annie Hawkes sedated and held against her will in a psychiatric hospital was all the threat you needed," she said.

"Ms. Hawkes is ill," said Cryer. "The Candle Lane site made her ill. She was one of a number of individuals from the excavation team who had to be placed in care for their own good. They are receiving the highest level of medical support. We're not monsters."

"Monsters always say that," said Lara.

Now he smiled.

"What did Annie Hawkes find?" Lara asked. "What made her ill? What made her team sick? Why was Candle Lane closed? Why is the M.O.D. involved?"

"Miss Croft—"

"Let me help you, Cryer."

"Let me help you," he said. "You're seeing something that isn't there. You're fired up by a mystery that doesn't exist. Blame that curiosity on your genes. There's nothing sinister going on."

With a slow and mocking roll of her head, Lara looked at the room around them.

"I beg to differ," she said.

"All right," he said, amused. "Let's do this. You saw the site."

"And it's an extraordinary site. It needs to be opened and fully detailed."

"It deserves it, yes," he agreed.

"If you delay or cancel the dig, a priceless site will be lost to Crossrail."

"No, it won't," Cryer said. "The Crossrail route is going to be altered slightly so that the Candle Lane site can be left undisturbed. The alterations to the project are being arranged right now. I wish I could tell you that it's because of the quality of the finds there. Truly splendid things, I completely agree. In this case, however, the decision rests on a simpler issue. The site is contaminated."

"It's what?"

"Contaminated," he said. "You saw the plane."

"Yes, briefly. And Annie mentioned it. World War Two. Luftwaffe."

"Correct," Cryer said. "One of six brought down on a single night during the Blitz. April 1941. A modified Dornier Do 17. Achsbach Division, reserved for special duty by Oberkommando Der Luftwaffe—Extraordinary Flight Operations. One night, one raid. Six planes downed. It was believed, at the time, that the wreckage of all of them had been recovered, but that aircraft lay hidden in the rubble and was subsequently buried."

"That happens. What are we talking about? Is it still carrying its stick of bombs, or had it managed to ditch them?" Lara asked.

"It had not dropped its payload. The payload is still there, in the wreck."

"So defuse it."

Cryer smiled.

"The payload wasn't a bomb, Miss Croft, not conventional explosives. It was experimental. The weapon on board was designed in haste and desperation by the Nazis to end the war with Britain quickly. Thankfully, the plane was brought down and the weapon did not detonate. It was a nerve agent."

"Chemical warfare?" she asked.

"Extremely unpleasant material. Utterly monstrous. It's been lying in the ground under the city for seventy years. Leaking into the sub-soil, in fact. The composition has changed over time, reacted with groundwater, et cetera, but it is still lethal. Ms. Hawkes's team disturbed it, unwittingly. Over a period of days, the nerve agent began to affect most of the team members exposed to it. Symptoms ranged from skin irritation, headaches, fever, stomach upset, to anaemia, and, in one instance, a seizure. It also provoked memory loss, paranoia, and hallucinations. In the worst cases, Ms. Hawkes included, the brain damage may be irreversible. We're treating all the cases. The site is closed, and will remain closed until we can find a secure and comprehensive way of clearing the nerve agent and cleaning the site. That may take years."

"I see," said Lara.

"Which is why we didn't want anybody going in there," said Cryer, "or a panic spreading, if word got out. Given your credentials, I'm sure you can appreciate the sensitivity of this situation. I'm sure you can be trusted to keep this information to yourself."

"I'm sure I can," said Lara. "You could have led with that."

The door opened again, and another man came in. He handed Cryer a sheet of paper.

Cryer read it.

"The nerve agent has a very unpleasant effect on the human mind," he said. "Depending on the degree of exposure, it causes massive delusions, leading to psychotic breaks, irrational behaviour, self-harm, and violent outbursts. We didn't know what your exposure level was, Miss Croft. If it had been high, you would not have dealt with this conversation well. You would have denied the truth of it. We've found this in several cases. Ms. Hawkes is one of them. She became convinced the site was haunted, and that supernatural events had been taking place. She becomes agitated and even violent if any attempt is made to explain the actual situation to her. She is in Hanover Care for her own well-being and for the public good."

Cryer gestured to the piece of paper.

"Your exposure levels, we have ascertained, are negligible. You are not contaminated. You are not at risk, and you are not a risk to others."

Lara nodded.

"So I can go?"

"Yes, Miss Croft. You can go, provided we have an understanding about the confidentiality of this situation, and that you sign a release to that effect. I'll give you a phone number to call if you experience any ill effects in the next few weeks. Please use it if you do."

"All right."

Lara got to her feet.

"That site needs to be cleared," she said. "The finds are too important to lose. The Roman level is very significant indeed."

"I agree," Cryer said.

"But it's nothing compared to the cyst chamber. That's probably the most important find I've ever seen in this country. It rewrites our understanding of Britain's prehistory. It is vital for it to be properly excavated as a soon as possible, and—"

"Miss Croft, there was no cyst chamber."

"Whatever you want to call it. The chamber with the obelisk. Where you found me."

"There was no obelisk," Cryer said. "No obelisk, no cyst chamber."

"I saw it," she said.

"I believe you believe that."

"I took pictures of it," she began, and then looked at her camera.

"Exposure during your brief visit was enough to affect your mind, Miss Croft. You're clean now, but you were hallucinating. It was your imagination."

"No," Lara said.

"I'm sorry. Did you feel paranoid or disturbed underground at the site, Miss Croft? Did you feel you heard sounds and movements?"

"Yes," she said.

"And you believe you saw an obelisk?"

"Yes," she said.

"We found you in the lowest level, an old drain culvert. Not a cyst chamber. It was the poor air and the residue of the nerve agent. You were hallucinating."

Lara looked at Cryer.

"Was I?" she asked.

"I'm afraid so," said Cryer. "But everything's all right now."

CHAPTER FIVE: HAUNTED
London

Under old stars lay a forest. The forest was old, too, a dark stand of tall, ancient trees, their canopy a starless black, their structure invisible except for the way it blocked out the speckled night sky.

The forest creaked and whispered in the night breeze.

An owl, not the only hunter awake that night, called through the gloom. Somewhere, further away, a fox barked and yapped; a fox, or something that made the hard, human pain noise of a fox.

Beneath the trees, the glades of the forest were bathed in a silver haze. Starlight, clearer than Lara had ever seen it, transmuted a lingering, slow night mist into ghost haze. Tarnished smoke drifted lazily between the black uprights of the tree trunks.

The mist was not empty.

Lara walked forwards, each step as quiet as she could make it. Bracken and soft, damp soil sponged under her bare feet. Somewhere, some night beetle or nocturnal bird cracked and snapped at bark, a muffled pistol shot.

Who was out there in the smoke? What was out there?

She saw a shape that loomed from the mist as she approached it. A man... No, a hooded, shrouded woman... No, a stone: a standing stone, soft-shouldered and rising to a rounded tip. Other stones, once upright, leant and rested in a nest of brambles at its feet. The stones had been brought here a long time ago, and their structure, and their purpose, and their very meaning had been forgotten because it was a time before there was a language that could be written.

Lara walked up and stood facing the stones. Mist drifted around her, like the white fumes of a spent bonfire. She examined the surface of the stone, the grey and green lichen, the old swirls and lines of carvings that millennia of rain had smoothed to faint tracks.

The fox yapped again, closer. Undergrowth rustled, but it had not been stirred by the breath of the breeze.

Lara turned. There were other stones standing in a circle around her, vague shapes in the mist.

But they were not stones. They were men.

They were grey and silent. They were motionless. Heavy robes swaddled them against the night chill. The flat faceplates of their ancient helms reflected the starlight as a flat glare with simple slits for eyes and frowning apertures for mouths.

They were so still. Perhaps they were stone, too. Ancient statues...or ghosts.

The slow, faint swirls of breath clouded from their mouth slits. Not statues. Not ghosts.

"Who are you?" Lara asked.

There was no reply.

One figure slowly uncurled an arm. It was holding a long-hafted axe with a beaked blade.

It wasn't an axe for splitting wood or clearing timber.

It was an axe made for parting flesh and bone. It was an axe made for war.

There was a rising howl, a guttural wail no more or less human than the yapping of the fox out in the darkness. It came from all the figures, rising in their throats, echoing from their graven faceplates.

They rushed her.

Lara leapt back with a cry of terror.

The coffee mug shattered across the kitchen tiles.

She looked down at the smashed mug and the large star splash of blood-black liquid, the shards of china twinkling like stars.

She realised she was shaking.

"What the hell...?" she murmured.

Lara was in her kitchen, at home in the manor. She was alone. The clock on the wall said four. The banks of elegant designer lights over the marble countertops were on. It was quiet. Heavy rain pattered against the glass doors that led out onto the terrace, and beyond, acres of parkland between her and her nearest neighbours.

Lara walked to the garden doors. It was late afternoon, but the sky was prematurely dark. The clouds over the park were bloated and grey. The rain was torrential and fell like a veil. It was as if she were seeing the landscape through glass smeared with Vaseline.

She cleaned up the spill, swept away the broken mug, and filled another with fresh coffee from the machine. It had been an upside-down day. Cryer's people had dropped her off at the manor early that morning. They didn't want her to drive. They had said barely a word to her, except that they would deliver her car later in the day. She'd spent the day in a stupor, bone tired after her long night without sleep. She'd read for a while, paced, and after the car was returned, she napped on the sofa, watched some TV, drifted off again.

You're tired, Croft, she told herself. A busy night. Lots of stress and exertion. Zero sleep. You're just tired. You bumbled into the kitchen to make coffee and actually fell asleep standing up.

The wood, the night, the barking fox, the stones, the figures...all of it had been a dream.

But so vivid...

Lara sipped her coffee. She wandered back into the lounge and sat down in front of the muted TV. *I've been more tired than this*, she thought. *Exhausted after stupendous physical effort, brain-dead from days at a time without rest. I've climbed mountains. I've endured and gone through fatigue and out the other side. I've hallucinated from lack of sleep...*

But I've never fallen asleep standing up like that, or dreamt so sharply... After just one late night?

Lara thought about Cryer's account of the nerve agent. Something like that might just be the cause, especially given the tricks it had played on her mind at Candle Lane. She thought about the number Cryer had given her. Maybe she should call it. Maybe the nerve agent had polluted her system more than their tests had shown.

Maybe she needed help.

Lara was startled by a thump, and then realised it was just the distant drum of thunder outside. She put the mug down and closed her eyes.

Once, during an ascent of the Annapurna, the weather had changed abruptly and without warning. Lara's party had been about seven-and-a-half thousand metres up when the ice storm rolled in. They had been forced to dig in for three days straight. The ferocious assault had been so blistering and freezing, they had been able to do nothing except hang on. It had been too cold to sleep. No sleep, no food, no heat. It had been a constant effort to hold on, dig in, and keep from being buried in snow.

Towards the end of that ungodly trial, she'd started to hallucinate. The mountainside had seemed to go calm. The sun had come out, warming her bones. She'd seen her mother and father walking easily up the snow slope towards her, smiling.

They had come to find her. She had felt such extraordinary joy.

It had seemed so real.

But afterwards, recovering in the medical facility at base camp, the reality of it had faded quickly. Lara had been able to see it for what it had been: a trick of the mind—utterly vivid, but brought on by physical and mental extremity.

She had hallucinated, but afterwards she had known that she had hallucinated.

But in the cyst chamber under Candle Lane, and just now in her own kitchen, the things she had seen had been real. In hindsight, now they did not seem less real.

She was unable to recognise them as hallucinations. Her memory of the cyst chamber, and the figures in the wood, remained utterly real. They hadn't faded, the way vivid dreams fade into nonsense. They hadn't lost their quality of actuality.

Lara thought about the phone number again. She didn't want to call it. She really didn't want to have any further dealings with Division Eleven.

A sandwich, maybe. A sandwich, a bath, a glass of wine, an early night might all make her feel differently.

On the muted TV, a quiz show began. It was a show she found diverting and relaxing. Number and letter puzzles. She reached for the remote to turn the sound up.

A fox yapped.

Lara sat bolt upright. She rose slowly. The sound didn't come again. There was just the beat of the rain on the windows and the glass doors. It was definitely a fox, or something that wanted to sound like a fox.

It was exactly the same as the cries she had heard in the misty wood.

There was someone or something in the house, at a distance, upstairs, perhaps, in one of the bedrooms. There was no sound, no footsteps, but Lara felt something, as though there was a weight on the floor above, silently pressing down on her.

With equal silence, Lara moved across the lounge, staring up at the ceiling. Her feet were bare, and she was wearing soft pyjama sweats. Even if she'd been wearing full chain mail, she knew how to move without noise.

She heard a thump, and then the fox yap again, but it seemed further away or muffled.

It was such a wretched sound. It seemed to encompass such pain and discomfort and bitterness. Of all the animal cries she knew of, the fox was the most and least human.

There were foxes in the park sometimes, and other creatures, too. Maybe...

No, it wasn't a fox. Lara became aware of the tightness in her chest, the shallowness of her breathing. The skin on the back of her neck was crawling. Something was generating fear in her, and she didn't scare easily. She didn't scare at all.

Take control, Croft, she told herself. She tried to shake the fear off. She padded through the kitchen to the pantry and quietly opened a cupboard between the cold store and a dresser stacked with cans, jars, and bottles.

Inside the cupboard was the sleek, compact shape of one of the manor's gun safes. She input the PIN code combination and pressed the thumbprint reader. She opened it quickly and took a Sig nine out of the foam liner. Two pre-loaded magazines lay on the lower shelf. She slid one in, checked the gun, and then closed and locked the safe.

Lara edged out of the pantry, holding the gun in a two-handed grip at hip level, muzzle aimed at the floor, her right index finger resting safe against the side of the slide.

She went back into the lounge. The TV was still playing silently. She crossed into the hall. No one there, and the front door was locked and bolted. Inside the security room, Lara turned on the manor's CCTV and checked every monitor, but saw only empty rooms. She checked all the alarm settings, but she was locked in. No windows or doors were open and nothing had been triggered. Methodically, Lara locked down the entire manor, except for the part of the house she was living in. Internal doors wouldn't open, and if a threshold were passed, the alarms would go off. She was ready.

With the weapon held tight, Lara went up the stairs slowly. The landing was empty. She checked her private suite. Her bedroom and bathroom were both empty, too. Lara moved along the landing to her dressing room. She opened the door slowly. The room was dark. Rain pelted the windows. Thunder grumbled outside. There was a feeble flash of lightning, and a shape in the corner of the room resolved briefly. She raised the gun, but even as she did so, she knew it was just her coat stand with jackets and umbrellas hanging on it.

She went back out onto the landing. Thunder rumbled again. The only room left in her private suite was her office at the end of the corridor. Lara edged towards it.

She took a breath and threw open the door, stepping in with the pistol aimed.

Nothing. Her desk, desk chair, the shelves of books and artefacts, the plan chest, the flat-screen monitor, the old threadbare chaise.

More thunder. The dull sheet lightning from outside gleamed off the framed prints and charts that lined the office walls, the glazed doors of her display cases, and the domes of the bell jars she kept her favourite trophies under.

Lara lowered the weapon.

"You're an idiot," she said to herself. The powerful automatic handgun in her grip felt like the most ridiculous overreaction. It was time to go back downstairs, lock the damn thing away, and scale down the manor's security measures. What the hell had she been thinking?

Lara turned. Out of the corner of her eye, she saw something move. Peripheral vision. Something, maybe someone, rushed silently down the stairs away from her...so silently.

A ghost.

Lara didn't get a proper look at it, but she started to move, rushing down the stairs after it, the pistol raised to aim at the ceiling. What the hell had she seen? What the hell could have been up there with her that she hadn't seen in a room-by-room search?

There was nothing in the hall. The front door was still locked and bolted. She stepped towards the kitchen. There was someone in the kitchen. She couldn't see who from her angle, but she knew someone was there. Someone was waiting for her, silently. She could sense steady, calm breathing. She could smell something: lavender or some sweet wild herb. She'd cleaned up the coffee spill with a lemon-scented cleaner. She could still smell that, pungent and chemical.

How could she be smelling the subtle, softer scent of herbs over that? It was as though the lavender smell was stronger, more real. It was wet and slightly musty, a fresh-air, fresh-soil smell—not the stringent odour of an artificial scent.

Lara raised the Sig and stepped quickly into the kitchen.

The grey ghost of the standing stone stood before her, right in the centre of the tiled floor. She could see the lichen patterns on its flanks, the eroded carvings. But it wasn't stone; it was flesh. It was faded tattoos on pale skin, and the shoulders and head of the standing stone were the hooded shoulders and head of a figure and...

There was nothing there at all.

Lara breathed out, long and hard. She lowered the gun and made sure the safety was on.

"So that's what paranoia feels like," she said. "Cryer did warn me."

There was nothing there. In that brief second, a fraction of a second or even less, as she'd stepped into the kitchen, her mind had shown her something so vivid, so clear.

But there was nothing there now. Even the wet bracken smell of lavender had vanished.

Lara put the gun down, rested her hands on the marble counter, and bowed her head. She swore softly under her breath.

"I guess that's what separates the winners from the losers."

Slowly, more composed, Lara straightened up. She shook out her neck. She looked towards the terrace and the parkland beyond.

Rain was still streaming down the glass doors.

Then a burst of red light hit the glass, followed by the blare of the manor's alarm sounding.

CHAPTER SIX: THE VISITOR
London

Lara picked up her gun and ran back to the security room. She closed and locked the door behind her and examined the monitors, selecting her private suite first and then all other areas inside the mansion. When she found nothing, she switched to exteriors.

She watched for several moments, and then reset and zoomed in for a closer look. Then she holstered her gun and ran upstairs for a jacket.

Two or three minutes later, she was at the gates at the end of the drive. She was breathing hard from the run, and heavy rain was blowing into her face.

"What the hell are you doing here?" she asked.

Carter Bell was soaked through. His collar was pulled up against the rain. He looked like the revenant spectre of a drowned mariner who had come back from the ocean to avenge himself.

"Can I come inside?" he asked.

Lara flipped open the cover on the keypad on her side of the gate and keyed in the security code. As the huge gates began to swing open, Lara gestured and Carter Bell scurried through the gap. Then, Lara hit the keypad again to prevent the gates fully opening. They closed silently, and she dropped the cover and stepped towards Bell.

"What the hell were you doing trying to break into my house?" Lara demanded. "You must have known you'd never get past my security."

Bell shrugged.

"I didn't want to draw attention to myself, to being here. I didn't know who might be watching. I tried the perimeter, but..."

"The perimeter wall's really high!" Lara snapped.

Bell stared at her.

"I've fast-roped into chasms under the Great Pyramid," he said. "I thought I could handle a garden wall."

Lara glared at him for a moment more, and then took his arm and began to walk him up the drive to the manor.

"You didn't take account of my extra security measures," she said.

"I realised the gate was my best bet, and then I set off the alarm. All I could do was wait for you," said Carter. "Sorry.

"Where have you been?" she snapped.

"Waiting at the gate, for you," he said.

"Don't get smart with me, Bell. I'm not in the mood, and I've been worried about you. I haven't heard from you since I got back to England, and I only came because you invited me."

Lara let them into the manor and led Carter to the kitchen. She crossed to the range, yanked a clean hand towel off the handle of the oven door, and threw it at him. Bell caught it and began to mop his face.

"I've been calling you for days," she said.

"I had to ditch my phone," he replied.

"Why?"

"Division Eleven was tracking me," he said.

Lara studied him and then took off her jacket, dragged a chair out from the kitchen table, and sat down. Her gaze didn't leave him as she pulled the Sig nine out of her waistband and put it on the table.

"I've had a conversation with them, too," she admitted.

Bell shrugged.

"How did that go?" he asked.

"It was fine," she said.

"Can I sit?" he asked.

"Of course," said Lara. Bell sat down at the table.

"Any chance of a cup of tea?" he asked.

Lara snorted, but got up and put the kettle on.

"What's the gun about, Lara?" he asked, his gaze turning to the Sig.

"No, we're starting with you," she said. "What's going on? Why didn't you call me, and why are you acting like some kind of fugitive?"

"Because of my fugitive status?" he ventured.

He saw her eyes narrow dangerously.

"Okay, okay," he said. "I guess you could say I was in trouble. The M.O.D. closed down the dig. They rounded everybody up. It was...Orwellian, Lara. I managed to give them the slip, and I've been lying low ever since."

Lara took a teapot out of an overhead cupboard and began to spoon tea from the caddy into it.

"There's nothing Orwellian about anything," she said. "There was a security issue with the dig site. The M.O.D. was acting according to procedure. They explained it to me."

"I'm sure they did," he said.

"You're acting paranoid, Bell."

He shook his head.

"Paranoid is when you think they're out to get you but there's no 'they,'" he replied. "Rational is when you think they're out to get you because they are out to get you."

Lara sighed. The kettle was coming to a boil.

"Have you been checked out?" she asked.

"Checked out?"

"Tested. For contamination? I guess not, if you've managed to give Division Eleven the slip."

"What sort of contamination?" he asked.

"From the nerve agent," she said. "It induces paranoia and other nasty complications. Carter, you look exhausted. You look like you've been living rough for a week, and your behaviour is all over the place. I'm worried about you. No one's out to get you. You just may be...sick."

"Oh, God," he said quietly. "They've done a number on you, too."

"The only thing that's happened to me is a certain level of clarification," she replied. "Clarification you'd have got too, if you hadn't gone on the run and—"

"Talk to me about the nerve agent," he said calmly.

Lara filled the teapot.

"The German bomber," she said.

"It's a Dornier," he said.

"You're aware of it, then?"

"Of course," Bell replied. "It was pretty mashed up, but it was a surprise when they found it. No one knew it was there. Annie had it checked, and then roped off for later recovery. It wasn't the primary dig objective."

"It was carrying a nerve agent, Carter."

"It was carrying incendiary flares," he replied. "I checked it myself. It was the marker plane for a bombing raid. Target designation. Most of the flares were still in the bomb bay, but they had long since perished. They were inert and safe."

"It was carrying a nerve agent, Carter."

She handed him a cup of tea.

"This is what Division Eleven told you, is it?" he asked.

"Milk?"

"Thank you. This is their story, is it? Nerve agent?"

Lara opened the fridge and located a carton of milk.

"It's not a story," she said. "The plane was carrying a Nazi terror weapon, and its payload has contaminated the site. Hallucinations, paranoia, a major public health risk. It's—"

"It's a lie," he said.

Lara put the milk carton on the table and sat down again.

"Carter, you've got to get your head straight. If you're contaminated, I have a number to call. I can get you some help and—"

"What about the obelisk?" he asked.

Lara looked at him.

"The obelisk?"

"In the cyst chamber," he said.

"That was a hallucination," she replied. "I saw an obelisk and a cyst chamber, but—"

"So did I," he said. "I didn't just see it. I worked in it for several weeks. Hallucinations are personal, Lara. Individual minds project individual things in relation to personal psychologies. We wouldn't hallucinate the same thing."

"We don't know what we saw," she said. "There could be—"

"We do, actually," Bell interrupted. He stood up. "And I can prove it."

He went to the kitchen doors, slid them open, and disappeared into the garden. Rain pelted in through the open door, making a puddle on the tiles.

"I believe you, Carter. What are you doing?" Lara called after him.

Carter reappeared after a couple of minutes, empty-handed. He closed the garden door and sat down again.

"I stashed my rucksack before hitting your gates," he said. "In case..."

"In case?"

"In case you weren't alone."

"Okay," said Lara, "but you don't need to prove anything to me."

"No," said Carter, "but I think you should see what I've got. I just need to fetch the rucksack."

"I'll go with you," said Lara, picking up the gun.

Carter eyed it for a moment, and then smiled at Lara.

"Okay," he said. "Thanks."

Back in the kitchen, Carter produced a compact DSLR from the soaking-wet rucksack. He switched it on, opened the stored image file, and fast-clicked through images on the LCD screen. He found the image he was looking for and turned the camera to show it to Lara.

It was a high-resolution shot of the cyst chamber and the obelisk, almost exactly as she remembered it.

"Are we still both hallucinating?" he asked.

They sat in her lounge, the curtains closed. While he had showered, she'd run his wet clothes through the tumble dryer.

"So this is why they shut down the site?" Lara asked. She was working through the images stored on Bell's camera, one by one.

"Yes," he said.

"Why? I mean, this...this rewrites British history pretty fundamentally. Indigenous contact in the Bronze Age with New Kingdom Egypt. It rewrites Egyptian history, too. But in this day and age? This is...a fabulous exhibition at the British Museum and the cover story for a *National Geographic* special, not the trigger for a classified cover-up."

"I don't think it's the historical implications they're really worried about," he said.

"Meaning?"

"Annie Hawkes called me in after they found the obelisk," Carter said. "They needed an Egyptologist fast, and at that stage, she wanted to keep everything on the down low. She was worried about the media fuss—the historical implications, ironically—and she knew everything would turn into a circus if it got out. There were so many ways the establishment could fault her discovery. They could claim she faked it, or misinterpreted the find, or botched it, or that she'd been hoaxed."

"She wanted it properly reviewed and inspected before she went live with it," said Lara. "She needed context."

"Exactly. So I started work. It's an amazing thing, Lara. The crypt, the obelisk, and the altar are late Neolithic, or early British Bronze Age. They're on the cusp. The stone is local, quarried in Wales, I think. My assessment of the workmanship is that it's indigenous, too. But there's the design, the inscriptions. It's New Kingdom. It was either made by artisans who had been to Egypt and made a careful study of the monuments there, or by craftsmen supervised and instructed by Egyptian builders. Either way, the cultural contact is startling and revolutionary. It proves a cultural link, or something rather more than that, between two ancient societies that were never thought to have made contact. One is influencing the other. In fact, we hadn't got far, so it's hard to say at this point which is the real influencing party. My guess is that Egyptian visitors—

traders, ambassadors—reached the British Isles and interacted with the local culture. But it's even possible it's the other way around."

"That an indigenous British culture, one we know virtually nothing about, existed in the early Bronze Age and had such significance, on an almost global scale, it influenced the development of the Egyptian civilisation?" Lara asked.

Bell smiled at the look on her face.

"I know. Blows the mind, doesn't it?"

"I think I preferred it when it was a hallucination," Lara said.

"There's very little to go on," he said. "I mean, so very little context. If we could find some other sites to make comparisons, that would be great. But we know a few simple facts. The cartouche on the obelisk, for example. It's very recognisable."

Bell took the camera from Lara and found a close-up of the inscription.

"The name of the pharaoh the obelisk is honouring, or who ordered its construction, or who it was dedicated to."

"Akhenaten," Lara said.

"Yup," he said. "AKA Amenhotep: the rogue, the renegade, the mystery. He's the one pharaoh whose reign no one has ever properly explained. He changed, overnight, an Egyptian society and religion that had existed for centuries and preserved that new belief system throughout his lifetime."

"And then it was violently revised after his death," Lara said. "Everything was put back the way it had been before."

"And no one has ever successfully explained it," Carter said. "There are plenty of theories, of course, some of them pretty far out there. So here's a new one. Amenhotep, a very singular individual, was radically influenced by contact with a powerful pre-existing British culture. Through his contact with them, and his fascination with their worldview, he threw out Egyptian pantheism almost overnight, and revolutionised Egyptian culture into a new, monotheistic system."

Lara's mind was spinning fast.

"There are other inscriptions here," she said. Not hieroglyphs. They look almost Celtic."

"That's as good a word as any for now, but it's not precise enough. Maybe 'Megalithic' is better? I think that script is the writing of the local culture, inscribed in support of the Egyptian text. It shows the cooperation. We hadn't got far translating it. It seems to include a dedication to a local queen, a Bronze Age British leader. Her name is Gwynnever."

"As in...?" said Lara.

"Yes."

"Oh, come on!"

"It says it right there."

"Come on!"

"Look," said Carter, "all this, weirdly enough, is unimportant right now. What's important is that strange things started to happen at the site. They began before I arrived, but they got worse."

"What sort of things?" Lara asked.

Carter shrugged. "Well, haunting. People started to feel uncomfortable, especially when they were left alone at the excavation. People saw things, figures. They heard voices, sounds. It's as if the dig had woken something up that didn't want to be woken. All the aberrant behaviour that Division Eleven blames on Nazi nerve agents...it was some kind of a freaky resonance that disturbed everyone on-site. People left. People quit. People went into therapy. There was some odd behaviour, arguments, even a fist-fight, and there were rumours of a curse."

"Of course."

"Right. That's when I called you. I needed help. The situation needed expert help. It was kicking off. Annie had to let one guy go, a grad student called Strand. He was causing too much trouble. It had all really got to him. I think it was him who went to the authorities and reported what was going on. He broke her blackout, and that brought Division Eleven in."

"And they closed everything down."

"But they didn't get everything," said Carter. "When we found the altar, there were objects placed on it, votive offerings: glass bottles, bowls, small inscribed stones. And a sword."

"A sword?"

"A sword. It was made of obsidian and inscribed. An indigenous Bronze Age design, not Egyptian. We called it the 'Blade of Gwynnever.' It was a royal object. We thought it might be the ceremonial weapon of the warrior queen who ruled the Megalithic culture. It was the most valuable find of all...a massively important object."

"What was its situation?"

"On the altar, the stone plinth in front of the obelisk. It was recessed into that long, shallow groove, which had clearly been cut into the stone to fit it. It was on display, very deliberately and ritually. My working theory is that the cyst chamber is the burial site for Gwynnever, either literally or symbolically, and her sword was placed there as part of the rites."

"A symbol of power?" Lara asked. "A...sword in a stone?"

"Uh-huh."

"I want to hear you say it, Carter."

"A sword in a stone."

"My God," Lara whispered. "So...what happened to it? Where is it? Please tell me it's behind the same rhododendron bushes where you hid your rucksack."

"Sadly, no," Carter said. "Division Eleven marched in one morning without any notice. They just took the place over and bundled everyone away."

"Not you?"

"Would you believe it, I had just stepped out for some air and to grab a coffee? Talk about timing. I came back, saw what was happening, and got the hell out. But staff had been leaving before that, like I said. In the week leading up to the takeover, people had quit or been fired or just stopped showing up for work."

"Because of the...curse, the haunting."

"The morning Division Eleven barged in, we'd got to the site and found that the sword and some of the other votive items were missing. Someone had already taken them. At that point, it had to be an inside job. It was crisis time. There was a lot of arguing, and accusations were flying. The overall paranoia made things worse. Poor Annie was so worked up, she actually accused me of taking the sword. Said I was trying to break the news, steal her thunder, take the credit. She didn't mean it, I know. But that's why I'd stepped out. I was angry. I wanted to walk it off. Thanks to that, thanks to her, I wasn't there when the M.O.D. seized the site."

"And neither was the sword?"

"No," he said.

"And you didn't take it?"

"No," Carter replied more emphatically.

"Okay, okay. But someone did. And Division Eleven doesn't have it."

"No, they don't."

"But they know about it?" Lara asked.

"I would imagine so," he replied. "They took everybody, probably grilled them pretty thoroughly. And the finds were all documented in the site records. I suppose they might have managed to track down all the people who left before they busted in, which might include the person who took it. So they might have recovered it after the raid."

"I sense a 'but'..."

Carter leant forwards on the couch and picked up Lara's laptop. He typed something into the search engine, scrolled through the results, and then opened a site to show her.

Lara studied the page on the screen.

"Wow," she said. "Okay, that's... Wow. This is either an incredibly lucky break, or spectacularly dumb."

"Can't it be both?" he asked.

She nodded.

"Absolutely," she said.

"When you say 'lucky break,'" Carter asked, "are you saying...?"

"That sword," said Lara, "is the key to understanding the whole thing. It's also a priceless artefact that needs to be studied and cared for and evaluated by the major institutions. The precision of that obsidian blade, and the quality of the carving and decoration in the hilt and guard make this one of the most significant objects in world archaeology, even without the possible connections. So we need to get it back. We need to find this idiot and get the sword away from him before he does something even more stupid with it, something we can't undo."

"And when you say 'we'?" he asked.

Lara grinned at him.

"Oh, God, Carter, I'm in this now, all the way."

"So you can find this guy and the sword?" asked Carter.

"You bet your life," said Lara. "Just give me a couple of hours on the computer."

"Good, that's what I was hoping for," said Carter. "I'm not a hundred percent sure, but I think the guy holding the sword is our man Strand."

"That helps," said Lara.

"So, one last question," said Carter. "That Sig you've been carrying around all afternoon? You got another one like it?"

"You know I do," she replied.

The website with the picture wasn't spectacularly dumb; it was specialist and clever. It was, however, the lucky break that Lara needed, and with her specialist tech knowledge, she was soon able to unravel the links and hack a password.

"We're going to Turkey," she finally said, "to an underground antiquities auction run by none other than the infamous Zizek."

"This just got interesting," said Carter.

"*More* interesting," said Lara.

CHAPTER SEVEN: BLACK MARKET
Kurkarob

"I suggest," said the man with the AK47, "that you leave the city."

He helped himself to the bowl of dates on the table beside Lara.

"Or," he added, munching, "we could kill you."

Lara sat back. She wasn't going to be intimidated. There were four keepers in the room with her, and they were blocking the only exit to the stairs. There was the window, of course, but they were two floors up, and she very much doubted the awning shading the street below would stand being used as a trampoline.

"I admire your approach," she replied in conversational Turkish. "Often, threats are so indirect. Plain speaking is good."

The man spat a date stone into his palm and flicked it out of the window into the sunlight. It was clear he didn't know what to make of her.

The keepers were a private army, the city's unregulated security force. They wore shabby, mismatched army fatigues that had been borrowed or looted from several different regional militaries. Their only insignia was an early-Roman coin. The coins had holes punched through them so they could be sewn onto the fronts of their tunics.

"You have an insolent mouth, American," the man said. He leered at her. His teeth were gappy.

"I'm not American," she replied.

"She's not," a voice agreed. The four keepers turned and came to some kind of attention. A man had entered the hotel room. He was short but heavyset, and his bald head and clean chin were the work of a skilled barber. He wore an expensive three-piece suit.

"I am Zizek," he said.

"Master of the keepers," Lara noted. "This is an honour."

"It is," he agreed. "You are Lara Croft. The famous thief of antiquities."

"I am an archaeologist."

Zizek shrugged, as if such a difference was merely pedantry.

"What are you doing in Kurkarob?" he asked.

"I am here for the weekly market," said Lara. "I didn't know there was a law against that."

"There are no laws against anything, madame," said Zizek. "This is just a city. It is not Turkey; it is not Syria. It is a demilitarised zone. No nation holds sway here. No laws..."

He looked at her.

"...except for the ones I make."

"I applied to your office for a permit to attend the market."

"Sadly, that has been denied," he said. "I have a difficult job, you know? Antiquities come from all places to be traded here."

"Looted antiquities," Lara said.

He did not react.

"I do not ask where they come from. Looted goods. Trophies. Spoils of war sold to the highest bidder. Artefacts offered by terror groups to finance their campaigns. I do not ask for provenance."

"Maybe you should."

"I think it would be unwise," Zizek replied. "The market here survives...and my administration survives...through one factor. The keepers maintain peace inside the city walls. With high-value items coming and going, madame, there is a great potential for disruption. Brigandry. Killing. This cannot be allowed. People would not bring their traffic here to sell if it was not a secure place. So I maintain security. Rivals may fight out their differences with money at the auction, then take their goods and leave the city. Nothing else is permitted."

Lara folded her arms and looked at him.

"The market survives because it's the only place in the region where illegal trade of antiquities can take place. Anywhere else would be subject to international law."

"It's not a perfect world," said Zizek, "but it is a system that works here. I will not permit disruption. Since your arrival, you have been asking too many questions. I think you are trouble. I think you will flout my laws if you get the chance. So you will not be granted a permit for the market. And I suggest you leave."

"I didn't think you were choosy about where the money came from as long as it came. Who's applied pressure on you, sir?"

Zizek's face darkened.

"I am my own man," he said. "Pack your things. The climate in this city is not conducive to your health."

He made a gesture. The men filed out after him. Lara listened to their boots going down the stairs.

She picked up her cell phone and dialled.

"Carter? Where are you?"

They met up at a coffeehouse off the busy main square. Trucks full of separatist troops grumbled by outside, honking at livestock and barrow-traders. Across the street, Lara could see a disused church where migrants were gathering in the hope of jobs or Red Cross parcels.

"You sounded pissed," said Carter. He was beaded with sweat. The coffee, dark as tar, was served in small glass bowls with brass handles.

"I met Zizek," she said.

"Really."

"Piece of work. He wants us out of here."

Carter frowned.

"Did he give any reasons?" he asked.

"No, but I can guess," said Lara. "Someone knows we're here, and someone knows what we're after. They don't want to risk us getting hold of it. They certainly don't want to risk us making the winning bid at the auction."

"So what? They've paid Zizek off? Got the authorities to lean on us?"

"Yes, rather than take us out directly. Zizek doesn't want to lose face. He doesn't want violence breaking out and ruining the reputation of his vaunted market. So he's taken a backhander and he's applying the pressure himself."

"That's hardly a level playing field," said Carter.

Lara looked at him, deadpan.

"You really think corruption is an issue anyone in this city cares about?" she asked.

Bell shrugged.

"The item's still up?" she asked.

"Yes," he said.

"And no luck locating Strand?" she asked.

"None at all. The keepers may have him in protective custody. I don't know why they don't just arrange a direct transaction with the someones who are so keen to—"

"Zizek isn't stupid," said Lara. "What Strand's got is worth a lot. So the keepers place a watch on him. But they want his merchandise in the next sale. Open bids. The sky's the limit. Zizek earns his money from the commission he takes on every sale. A private sale limits his profit potential. Open sale, top-dollar return."

"I suppose," said Carter. "I wish we knew who we were up against."

"I wish we knew how we were going to get into the saleroom," she replied. "Zizek's denying us permits."

"I may have a lead on that," said Carter, "but you're not going to like it."

They walked to the northern quarter of the town. In a quiet residential street, Carter knocked on a yellow door, and a housekeeper let them into a shaded inner courtyard.

A man was sitting in a wicker armchair on the far side of the courtyard, reading from a tablet device. He looked up as they entered and rose with a smile.

"Lara Croft," he said.

Lara glared at Carter.

"You're right," she said. "I don't like it. Let's go."

"Ah, Carter," the man said, coming forwards. "You didn't tell her?"

"Just that she wouldn't like it," said Carter. "And I was right."

"We're leaving," said Lara. "Goodbye, Denny."

Denny Sampson grinned his trademark grin at her.

"Come on, Lara. Won't you even stay for a drink? For old time's sake? I have beer. Bottled, imported. More importantly, I have a refrigerator to keep it in."

Denny Sampson, born in Canada but raised in the Midwestern United States, was approaching sixty. He was past his physical prime and going to seed, but his roguish charm had not diminished, and his paunchy, jowly appearance could not entirely hide the fact that he had once been devilishly handsome. He was tanned and well-dressed. He looked to Lara like a once-popular film star whose career peak was behind him, but still turned up for memorable cameos in TV shows.

He was, by trade, an archaeologist, but Lara knew that title was also merely euphemistic. They'd met before. It had never gone well.

"Carter tells me you're trying to get into the auction," said Denny, handing out bottles of a Canadian microbrew.

"Carter's got a big mouth," said Lara.

"I sure have missed you, Croft," Sampson laughed.

"I've missed you too," she replied. "I believe the last time I missed you, it was with a Remington hunting rifle."

"I really had to catch that plane," said Sampson.

"What did you get for the Malifar Jades," she asked, "in the end?"

"Oh, baby, twice what we had hoped."

"Where's my cut?" she asked.

Sampson started laughing again.

"I'm serious, Denny," she said.

"I know you are, Croft," he replied. "I know I owe you plenty. Honey, I should never have cut you out of that deal."

"But you did."

"What can I say? It's a weakness of mine. When it comes down to it, I always want it all for myself. It's a dog-eat-dog world, Croft."

"And you've eaten well."

Lara looked at Carter.

"Let's go," she said. "He's the same bastard he always was. He even admits it now."

"That's progress, Lara," smiled Denny. "My therapist says owning my flaws is part of the process."

"Good luck with that," she said and rose to her feet.

"I owe you," said Denny. "Let me pay you back something."

"For the jades?"

"Well, sure."

"And the Trondheim Crown?"

Denny shrugged.

"I guess."

"How about the Circlets of Athene?"

"Our relationship sure has been rocky, hasn't it?" Denny smiled.

"I wouldn't trust you further than I could spit," said Lara.

"That's fair," said Denny, sitting back in his chair. "But ask yourself this. How many times have I double-crossed you?"

"Four that I can remember."

"Four. Jeez. Well, Croft, there's a saying. Fool me once..."

"So what?" she asked.

"You kept coming back, Lara Croft. You knew who I was, and you kept coming back. You'd think, by the second or third time, you'd have learned I was bad news."

"Do you have a point to make, Sampson?" she asked.

He beamed.

"You like me, Lara Croft. Always have, always will. Even though you know I'm going to leave you in the dust every time, you keep coming back for more. Can't get enough of the old Sampson magic."

"Thanks for the beer," she said, "you insufferable arse."

"Lara, come on. I like you too. Always have. Breaks my heart every time I have to do the dirty on you. So let me make amends. It's long overdue. I want to change my ways, Lara. I want to make it up to you. And I think you want me to make it up to you."

She glared at him.

"I can't," she said. "I can't fall for your crap again."

"We've had some times, Lara, you and me. Great times."

"True. Amazing times. But the endings, Denny. There were never any happy endings."

He stood up.

"Bell tells me you need permits to get into the auction. I have two to spare."

"Zizek doesn't want us in."

"Well, the keepers won't turn down one of their own permits."

"Why do you have spares?" asked Carter.

"Acquired for business associates," said Denny. "But they got delayed in transit, so I'm a free agent at the sale. Come keep me company. It'll be fun."

"What are you after?" Lara asked.

"Nothing, honey. Like I said, my backers were delayed. This job's shot, but now I'm in town, I might as well go to the auction and see what's good. I'm just there as a spectator."

He eyed her.

"What are you after, Croft?"

"Absolutely none of your business," she said.

"Okay."

"Give us the permits."

"Then we're square?" Denny asked.

"Not even slightly, you old goat."

CHAPTER EIGHT: WOLFSHEAD
Kurkarob

"Are you sure you'll pass?"

"I already have," said Lara.

Carter Bell, dressed as Lara's bodyguard, had been relieved of his sidearm at the door, but Lara had walked past the guards without being searched.

"This is a very classy abaya and sheila, Carter," said Lara. "Modest, but very classy, and the sunglasses are Cutler and Gross. I'll go unnoticed."

She cut an understated but elegant figure in the long, plum-coloured gown. The designer shades were a deft character detail that indicated private wealth. At her side, Carter perfectly resembled a professional minder in his grey business suit and black shirt.

Perception was everything. They were playing roles, and playing them well.

"It worries me that Zizek and his goons have seen you before," Carter replied. "You make an impression, Lara."

"They respect women here," she replied. "They won't look at me. They'll honour the mode of dress, and, besides, they don't know you. There are better things to worry about. Does this staircase remind you of anything?"

Bell and Lara had begun walking up a long, curving staircase. The staircase led up out of a vast, double-height atrium, the grand entry of the Vilet Palace. The Vilet was one of the most magnificent old palaces in Kurkarob, and it was the venue for the market.

As they had arrived outside, Carter had looked up at the grand facade and muttered, "'Market''s not the word I'd use for this."

It did indeed feel more like an embassy ball at the end of the nineteenth century than a black-market antiquities bazaar. Crowds of elegant guests circulated, attended by liveried servants, in a hall of marble columns, ornate gilded plasterwork, and vast crystal chandeliers.

Bell eyed the staircase as they ascended it together.

"The photo?" he asked.

"Exactly," Lara replied. "The photo of Strand with the sword on the Internet. It was taken at the bottom of these stairs. The banister? The angle of the steps? The carpet? All the same as in that photo."

"So Strand was here," said Bell.

"He has to be under some kind of house arrest," said Lara, "for his own security. The artefacts would be long gone by now, and Strand with them, if someone weren't protecting him and their own interests."

"And by 'gone,' you mean—"

"Strand would be dead."

"And by protected, you mean Zizek," said Bell.

"Or whoever has Zizek in his pocket," countered Lara.

Lara dropped her head demurely to look at her hands. She was holding up her abaya as she climbed the last of the stairs, dignified and modest.

And all part of the act.

They passed the armed guards who flanked the head of the staircase. Zizek's keepers.

Their permits, which Bell held, had been checked as they entered the Vilet Palace. Another keeper checked them again as they approached the banks of highly decorated, panelled glass double doors that led into the ballroom where the auction was to be held.

The keeper was another Turkish man with the coin sewn to an American army-issue flak jacket. He had an AK47 slung over his shoulder, and, from the look of the wooden grip sticking out from his belt, a Second World War-issue Mauser HSc pistol.

As he reviewed the papers, Lara took the time to assess her surroundings. That included Zizek's keeper, fussing with the permits. Lara noted the doors, the entrances, the exits, the disposition and armament of the guards, the open spaces, the choke points, the availability of bullet-stopping cover.

You could never be too careful when you walked into the hornet's nest.

The keeper gave her no more than a passing glance. He handed the permits back to Carter with a flourish and nod, and ushered them into the ballroom. As they passed him, he was already moving on to the next clients in the queue.

"Careful, but not thorough," Lara muttered to Carter.

"True of so many people I know," Carter replied.

A vast pink Persian rug of exquisite quality adorned the gleaming ballroom floor. It had been chosen to match the swags and tails of the silk velvet drapes at the mirrored alcoves and windows. The floor had been polished to a glassy finish. Above them, the ornate plasterwork was painted and gilded, and additional gold decorated the room's archways and mirror frames. There was a great deal more glittering crystal, too. Hanging from the centre of the ceiling was another immense chandelier, its design echoed in standard lamps spaced around the edges of the room.

A block of seating filled roughly a third of the ballroom's centre space. The rows of ostentatious gilded chairs had high, padded backs to match the seats, and were upholstered in pink brocade the same colour as the velvet drapes.

The Vilet's main salon was very grand and very formal, no doubt hired to impress Zizek's clients and convince them to spend vast amounts of money on the black market merchandise that was on offer. There were, Lara estimated, about sixty well-to-do buyers, mostly men, many with close protection of their own. Some were accompanied by women dressed much as she was.

The sale items were laid out in an array of ebonised wooden cases and cabinets. The displays were of various shapes, with glass fronts or tops, depending on their sizes. Each piece of furniture had at least one armed guard standing beside it, and some were surrounded by them.

Lara watched as a small cabinet was wheeled out of the salon into an anteroom. An elegant man wearing a beautifully cut dark suit and a green keffiyeh followed it. Evidently an important buyer. He was clearly being offered preferential treatment, and a closer look at whatever was in the cabinet.

"See that?" Lara asked quietly.

"Yeah," replied Carter.

"Okay, stay close," she said. "Remember you're supposed to be my bodyguard, but I also need you to do your job."

He nodded and took half a step closer to her.

Lara strolled slowly around the room, feigning interest in various pieces. She pretended to take an interest in jewels and ceremonial blades, simply in order to establish an observable pattern. Lara assumed she was being monitored. She assumed that all the buyers were.

Bell's task was to survey the room. Staying close to Lara, he checked the location of the entrances and exits and fixed in his mind the positions of the furniture, so that he could get them both out fast and efficiently if things got problematic.

Lara observed the keepers and their distribution throughout the room. Zizek's militia, in their mismatched fatigues with the sewn-on coin insignia, appeared to have two roles. Some stood guard at entrances and exits, monitoring the flow of clients, and checking permits. Others stood guard over the objects for sale.

Lara quickly spotted a second tier of armed guards.

They differed from Zizek's men in two important regards. They were formally dressed in dark suits, and they were obviously attempting to blend in with the clients. However, to Lara's trained eye, they were clearly wearing comms equipment and had been allowed to carry concealed weapons into the market. They were also of both genders. The women, like the men, were in smart Western dress.

Bell drew slightly closer to Lara as they approached the main attraction, a large cabinet to the rear of the room. The cabinet was flanked by four militiamen.

"This is it," murmured Bell. "No sign of Zizek."

"He'll make his entrance at the sale," said Lara. "This is only the preview. We're just here to look around. Take a breath, Carter."

"You think the main players are here?"

"Some, not all. Their representatives, perhaps," Lara replied.

"You make the others? The ones in the suits, packing?"

"I did," she replied quietly. "Private contractors, I think. Someone here carries so much weight, Zizek has allowed him to bring armed staff into the saleroom."

"Oh, it just keeps getting better and better," said Carter.

Lara elbowed him discreetly.

"Stop complaining. We're having an adventure."

"Every time I have an adventure with you, Lara," said Carter quietly, "I find I have more and more things to complain about."

Lara drew level with the cabinet.

A glance reassured her that it contained what she was hoping for.

Carter took a longer look at the sword. He'd seen it before and handled it, in situ, deep underground at the Candle Lane site beneath the streets of London. He could verify that it was the original.

"That it?" Lara whispered. One glance, and she knew that the sword was genuine, but she still wanted to check in with Carter; he'd been at the site and had handled the artefact.

"Oh, yeah," Carter replied.

Lara cast her eyes over the flak jackets of the militiamen flanking the cabinet. They matched and were brand-new. She let her gaze pass over the fatigues the men wore. Again, they were pristine, and the boots were, too. They had all come from one supply source and were Eastern European.

Lara looked again at the contents of the cabinet, before flicking her eyes over the chests of the flak jackets, checking for Zizek's coin insignia.

It was missing.

These men, dressed to resemble Zizek's goons, were not keepers. They hadn't been posted there by Zizek to guard the case. They had been placed by somebody else to watch it, and to watch anyone who took an interest.

Too much close scrutiny was definitely a bad thing.

Lara walked away, with Carter still at her shoulder.

One of the guards suddenly blocked her path.

"Madam," he began. "Aren't you Miss Lara—"

"There you are, my dear Miss Hanover! Have you seen the Etruscan votives?" said a voice, sweeping in and offering Lara an arm.

It was Denny Sampson, and he was grinning broadly.

"I thought I'd lost you," Lara replied and took his proffered arm. Carter stifled a sigh of relief, and all three walked around the guard, but not before Lara had seen the pin on his lapel.

It was small, grey enamel on a gold base and depicted the head of a wolf.

"Having fun, Croft?" asked Denny, his arm linked to hers dutifully. "Playing dress-up?"

"I like to dress for an occasion," said Lara.

"And may I say you look positively ravishable," said Denny.

"No, you may not," said Lara. "And you mean 'ravishing.'"

"I know what I mean," Denny replied, with a grin. "Word of warning. As beautiful as you are, this sure is no place to wander around unaccompanied."

"I'm not unaccompanied. I have Carter, and now you," said Lara, flashing a smile at Denny. "Unless you'd prefer not to be seen with me."

"On the contrary," said Denny, "I like nothing more than to have a hotsie-totsie gal on my arm."

"Even a hotsie-totsie girl who is liable to *break* that arm if you use the phrase 'hotsie-totsie' again, Sampson?"

"Oh, come on. If you can't be politically incorrect, where's the fun in anything?"

"You're a pig."

"I'm the pig who just saved your bacon," said Denny, "but no need to thank me. Just make sure Bell's on the ball and doesn't let this sort of thing happen again."

Carter glared at Denny, and then nodded his agreement. Denny grinned at him, bowed to Lara, and walked away.

"Let's go," said Lara. "I've seen enough."

"I'm sorry about that," said Bell as soon they were out of earshot and making their way back down the staircase.

"Don't worry about it," said Lara. "Me being recognised was a long shot, and there wasn't much you could have done about it. If Denny hadn't stepped in, I would've talked my way out of it."

"Of course," said Bell.

"Besides, it was useful," said Lara. "More data. The guard wasn't one of Zizek's keepers. He was wearing a pin, not jewellery, but a signifier, some organisation he belongs to. Now, let's get out of here."

"The sale's this evening. Wouldn't it be better to stay in the building?"

"We have the permits," said Lara, "and I need to look the part. This abaya's classy day wear, but tonight I'll need something special. This was a dummy run, a reconnoitre. Don't worry, Carter, we're in."

If the preview had seemed glamorous, the auction itself was positively extravagant.

The atrium of the Vilet Palace was lined with buffet tables laden with silver dishes that decoratively displayed all manner of canapés and sweetmeats.

Drinks, including a wide variety of colourful virgin cocktails, as well as some very good champagne, were being served from behind a series of bars installed for the purpose.

Lara was glad she had changed her abaya. She had switched from a plain dark silk to a heavy black silk trimmed in gold, with a sash. Although traditional dress for a Muslim woman, the abaya was beautifully cut with elegant sleeves, and a simple neckline that sat high on her collarbone, framing her throat. The floor-length gown with sleeves to the wrists was modest but elegant with a narrow waist, tied with the sash. The gold sheila that circled Lara's face and covered her hair was a simple length of cloth, expertly wound and draped. She was dressed appropriately and matched in style and status the dozen or so other women attending the auction.

She couldn't wear the sunglasses in the evening, but she could wear makeup, and she was virtually unrecognisable. She was also happy that she had insisted on buying Bell a tuxedo, since all of the men were formally dressed, almost exclusively in the Western style, despite them being from all corners of the globe.

Security had more than doubled since the preview, and, again, Bell was relieved of his sidearm at the palace door. Lara noted that the close-protection agents of some of the clients were allowed to carry concealed weapons.

There were clearly tiers of VIP privilege.

All buyers had also been required to register payment details for any purchases before being allowed into the market or being issued a bidding paddle. Lara had the

.

use of a numbered bank account, untraceable, so she used that. It was sufficient. Bell handled the registration on her behalf, using the name Hanover, inspired by Denny's efforts earlier in the day.

No questions were asked.

Zizek dealt with many people of whom it was foolish to ask personal questions.

There was tension in the air.

This was clearly serious business, and while refreshments were available, the food went untouched. The women drank the fruit cocktails. One or two of the men drank whiskey; more took steaming glasses of Turkish coffee. The bodyguards took nothing.

Lara understood the etiquette. She approached a buffet table and gestured to Bell, who picked up a cocktail for her, and then the two climbed the staircase to the ballroom.

Lara made her way directly to the rows of gilded chairs, choosing an end seat halfway back. One or two men were still perusing the cabinets. Others were standing in small groups, doing business or talking quietly. This was not a social event. All of the women were seated.

From her position in the room, Lara had an almost comprehensive view of the gathering.

She'd been careful to sit on the side of the room with no exits, so she couldn't be surprised by people entering from rooms behind her. She was also fortunate that there was little of significant interest in the cabinets that flanked the walls to her left.

Lara made a careful but unobtrusive study of the other clients as they took their seats. In just a few moments, the auction was due to begin. She paid particular attention to the lapels of the men's suit jackets.

She spotted several more of the Wolf-Head pins.

She wondered what they meant. Were these members of some society or fraternity, or were they employees of one of the bidders?

There was no opportunity to speculate, or to have a quiet conversation with Bell as, right on cue, Zizek strode into the ballroom from the staircase, flanked by two of his flunkies.

"Here we go," said Bell, under his breath.

"Denny Sampson didn't show up," said Lara.

"So things are already better than we expected," said Carter.

CHAPTER NINE: BIDDING WAR
Kurkarob

"My lords, ladies and gentlemen, it is my very great pleasure to welcome you all to the palace ballroom for this evening's auction."

"He's in his element," whispered Bell.

"Of course," said Lara. "He's making money."

"Forgive me," said Zizek, beaming out at the audience, "and I hope you'll bear with me while I go through the necessary formalities. As I'm sure you will have noticed, there is no catalogue, but I'm certain you've all made a note of the items you wish to bid on. All items will be described. All bids will be made in the room. No phone bids, and no left bids. My role is as agent of sale—nothing more, nothing less—and my fee is twenty percent of all sales, payable by the purchaser. All contracts are between the buyer and seller. Objects are sold as displayed. Authenticity is not guaranteed by the agent... That's me."

Zizek smiled and allowed a ripple of dry laughter to pass through the audience.

"Caveat emptor. Likewise, caveat venditor... Am I right?"

"He's making jokes," whispered Bell.

"The man certainly has an ego," said Lara.

"It only remains for me to introduce your auctioneer for this evening's event," Zizek told the crowd." Mr. Christian Somersby served as principal auctioneer at Sotheby's London until his retirement two years ago. He honours us with his presence. Mr. Somersby?"

Zizek took a step away from the lectern as a small, dapper man, not nearly retirement age, stepped up from his seat in the front row of chairs and strode to take his position.

Lara did not care to speculate what he might have been paid for the privilege of conducting the auction, but assumed it was a handsome fee.

Somersby was worth the money.

The auction ran very smoothly. Somersby's manner was fluid and mellifluous. His calm voice had a rhythm that kept the momentum going. Paddles rose discreetly, and figures rose with them quickly before the gavel was dropped on one lot at a time.

Lara raised her paddle once or twice on some items of jewellery, but withdrew when the bidding got serious. Mostly, she watched the room. Being careful to keep her interest centred on areas of the room where bidding was most active, she was able to track the guards wearing the Wolf-Head pins. Their attention seemed to centre on one man.

"Our lot's coming up," said Bell.

Two more lots were sold, and then Somersby began to describe the sword.

"The next item, a truly fine object. An obsidian sword, perhaps Celtic European or Near East, estimated at least four thousand years old, in extraordinary condition. Can we—"

Somersby paused.

"One moment, ladies and gentlemen," he said.

There was movement in the room, and Lara could feel the tension rising. Was it because this was the star of the show? Or was something else going on?

Lara put a hand on Bell's arm briefly, still scanning the room. She needed him to be ready.

Zizek had stood up. He'd taken Somersby's seat for the duration of the auction. Two of the Wolf-Heads, who had spent the sale positioned in one of the alcoves opposite Lara, had walked down to the front row of seats on the right-hand side, furthest from Lara's position. They were talking quietly to Zizek.

Some of the buyers had risen to stretch their legs during the pause.

Lara got out of her seat and led Bell to the rear of the ballroom, glancing into the display cabinets as she went, as if she were filling the time and having a last look at some of the objects there.

She turned once or twice and caught a glimpse of Zizek putting a hand over Somersby's mic to say something to the auctioneer without being heard by the room.

When they reached the rear of the room, Zizek had returned to his seat and Somersby was making an announcement.

"I beg your pardon, ladies and gentlemen," said Somersby. "That item has been withdrawn from sale."

"Not just withdrawn, the sword's gone," said Bell, under his breath, as Lara watched the room. "The cabinet's empty."

Bell followed Lara as she walked halfway down the right side of the salon and stopped in front of another display case, as if looking for something else to buy.

One of the Wolf-Heads was leaning in to Zizek, who stood and allowed himself to be escorted to one of the doors to his right. Moments later, a man in a bespoke silk suit left his seat. Lara was damn near certain it was the man in the green keffiyeh whom she'd seen that afternoon, but she couldn't be absolutely sure. Two more Wolf-Heads fell in behind him, and the three of them followed Zizek out of the ballroom.

Somersby moved, seamlessly, on to the next item for sale, but there was more disruption in the room. Several of Zizek's goons had left their posts at the cabinets, and two entered the ballroom through the double doors behind the lectern.

Four more Wolf-Heads left their seats, dotted around the room. A tall, broad-shouldered man with black eyes and a bald head strode up to the lectern. He spoke briefly with the auctioneer.

"I want to get in that side room," said Lara.

"We should leave," said Bell. "Do you know how much firepower there is in here?"

"Almost as much as I've got concealed under this dress," said Lara.

"The sword's gone," said Bell.

"Ladies and gentlemen, that concludes the sale for this evening. Thank you, and good night," said Somersby.

Somersby turned to take a step towards one of Zizek's goons, but the broad-shouldered man with the lapel badge caught his arm. Somersby was startled for a moment, but straightened up and composed himself.

"Whoever's in that room wants the sword," said Bell. "And he's got a small army working for him."

"Then we'd better get ahead of him," said Lara.

The sixty or seventy people in the ballroom, the bidders and their retinues, were preparing to leave the building, filing out through the double doors and down the staircase.

The tension was palpable. Bodyguards were hustling to get their wards out of the building quickly and efficiently.

Lara and Bell joined the rear of the group. Zizek's keepers were guarding the top and bottom of the staircase. The Wolf-Heads had formed a phalanx, cutting off the landing and funnelling people down the stairs through a narrow gap between the double doors to the ballroom and the top of the staircase.

Bell tried to stay close to Lara, but there was only room for two or three people to walk abreast between the rows of guards, and bodyguards were herding their charges out of danger.

When he turned to speak to her, she was gone.

"Dammit," he growled.

Lara felt the firm grasp of a gloved hand around her upper arm. She was being pulled out of the press of bodies by two guards, who closed ranks behind her.

She glanced around for Carter, but there was no sign of him.

"Miss Croft," said a voice close to her ear. "The boss forbade you from attending this event."

Lara glanced at the coin stitched to the lapel of the keeper's fatigues. She flashed her left hand over the piece strapped to her thigh under her gown.

"A girl's got to try," she said.

The two keepers walked her back into the ballroom through another set of double doors, one of several pairs that lined the landing. The room was empty, apart from the guard standing beside the closed door to the room that Zizek had entered with the mystery man.

"Sit here," one of the keepers told her. "There will probably be a fine to pay. Mr. Zizek will deal with you."

Lara didn't wait to be dealt with.

"I think I should discuss it with him immediately," she said and strode across the ballroom to the door of the side room. The two keepers and the guard stationed by the door all hesitated, not knowing quite how to deal with the foreign woman's boldness. Before they could decide on a suitable reaction, Lara had turned the door handle and walked right in.

The man in the beautiful suit and Zizek were both seated. They looked up in surprise. Lara caught the last words that Zizek had spoken, breathless and panicked, as she entered. They included a name.

She stood in the doorway, trying to look confused and embarrassed. By luck, she'd overheard the information she wanted without having to confront anyone or risk a firefight. Perhaps she could simply walk away.

"I'm so sorry, Mr. Zizek," she said. "I didn't mean to interrupt." She turned to leave the room.

Zizek didn't turn to look at her. He kept his eyes firmly on the other man.

The man in the suit gestured minutely to one of his henchmen, who stepped in front of Lara.

"Madam," he said, his soft tone masking a hard note of warning.

"Allow me to introduce myself," said the man in the suit, rising from his chair and turning to Lara. "Dritan Vata, and you are...?"

"Samantha Hanover," said Lara. "And I'm a little lost. I got separated from my man. Oh, dear." Lara placed a hand high on her chest, as if she were about to swoon. She turned to step out of the room, hoping that the chivalry would continue. She had what she needed.

Dritan Vata took Lara by the elbow and steered her to one of the chairs in the ballroom to let her sit down.

"Thank you, Mr. Vata," she said. "I'm quite all right."

"You had business with Mr. Zizek?" asked Vata.

"No," said Lara. "I was outbid."

"Someone will find your man," said Vata, gesturing to the broad-shouldered, bald Wolf-Head.

"Thank you," said Lara, "but if I could just be walked out, I'm sure he's waiting for me."

"Dibra," said Vata.

Lara stood and walked ahead of her nominated Wolf-Head escort towards the main doors out of the ballroom. She kept her hand over the gun strapped to her thigh again, for reassurance.

The crowds had passed by the time Lara appeared once more at the top of the staircase.

Bell was waiting there for her, under the gaze of Zizek's keepers. His eyes widened, slightly, as he saw her escort.

"Madam," he said. "My apologies."

"Just take me home," she said, curtly. Then she turned to the Wolf-Head.

"Thank Mr. Vata, again, for his kindness."

The man nodded.

Bell picked up his sidearm at the entrance, and they left the building to a convoy of armoured limousines exiting the driveway. None of the cars had plates.

"What happened up there?" asked Bell.

"I got a lead," said Lara.

"And you weren't recognised? How is that possible?" asked Bell.

"The clothes and the makeup," said Lara, "and the fact that Zizek is clearly so terrified of Vata that he wouldn't have recognised his own mother if she'd walked into that room. But we need to move fast, before someone makes the connection. We need to find Strand. Right now. He's still in possession of the sword."

CHAPTER TEN: DRITAN VATA
Kurkarob

Zizek knew how to put on a show, and Lara and Carter took advantage of the limousines that were provided to take the guests off-site after the auction.

The back of the car was big and comfortable, and Lara raised the privacy screen so that the driver couldn't see her get out of the abaya and sheila. She was wearing black leggings and a long-sleeved thermal shirt beneath, along with her weapons.

Black patent ankle boots with heels were less practical than her usual footwear, but were a good compromise under the abaya. She was out of the dress clothes before the car had left the long palace drive.

Lara looked up as the car was filled with light.

"Where have I seen that car before?" she asked as a big European saloon swung past them. She banged on the privacy screen, and the limousine came to a stop. The car was followed by a Hummer. Carter turned to look out of the rear windscreen at the car as it drove up to the palace.

"Daimler, I think," he said. "Grey or blue."

Two more Hummers passed their parked limousine.

"Denny Sampson," said Lara. "That's Denny's car. It was parked up when we went to see him. What the hell is he up to?"

She lowered the privacy screen.

"Back to the palace," Lara said. "Fast."

The driver looked at her, nonplussed.

"Just do it," said Carter.

The driver turned the car easily in the wide driveway and drove back up to the palace.

Lara and Carter got out and armed themselves. Zizek's keepers were conspicuous by their absence from the front of the building, and the vast doors to the entrance lobby stood open, spilling light onto the drive.

Lara and Carter walked in. The lobby was just as they'd left it, the food laid out and drinks still on the bars. But service staff were nowhere to be seen, and Zizek's men and the Wolf-Heads were gone.

It was eerily still and quiet, as if the crowds and the staff had just dematerialised.

Then the distant sound of gunfire echoed from above them.

Lara and Carter exchanged glances.

A shot rang out, closer, louder.

A stack of glasses on the bar table beside Carter exploded in a spray of fragments.

Carter threw himself into a forward dive, rolled, and ducked behind the banister to the left of the staircase. A second shot rang out. A chunk of gilded plaster pinged from the wall, an inch from where his head had been.

Lara had slipped behind the banister to the right of the stairs.

She looked up. She could see the barrel of a pistol between the ornate rails of the balustrade.

The more distant gunfire was coming from behind the closed doors of the ballroom beyond.

Lara watched and waited. The barrel of the pistol swung in Carter's direction again, seeking him out. No one seemed to be looking for her. She took aim, waited, breathed, and then fired.

She heard a muffled cry over the sound of gunfire still raging in the ballroom.

"Denny Sampson!" shouted Lara, standing at the bottom of the staircase, gun raised.

Denny stood up behind the balustrade, beaming.

"Lara Croft," he said. "Good shot."

Denny waved at his henchmen to lower their arms, and Lara dropped her aim. She jogged up the staircase.

"What the hell's going on, Denny, you son of a bitch?"

"Slight change of plan," said Denny.

Lara reached the top of the stairs, turned in one fluid movement, and put her gun to the back of a man's head. He was crouching behind the balustrade, pistol raised and aimed at the lobby.

"Put the gun down," she said.

The gunman put his weapon on the floor next to him, and Lara called over the balustrade.

"It's all clear, Carter. You can come up."

"I'm not sure I want to," said Carter, appearing at the bottom of the stairs.

Denny laughed.

"Change of plan, how?" asked Lara, swinging her aim back on Denny.

He put up his hands in a mock gesture of surrender.

"Zizek's been running this racket for far too long," said Denny. "I thought it was time for someone new to step up."

"And that would be you?" asked Lara.

"I might have an interest," said Denny. "I'm tired of the travelling, and the adrenalin. It's time I settled in one place, and I know this business."

"So this is a coup?" asked Lara.

Denny waved at the doors to the ballroom.

"That's a coup, Croft," said Denny. "That's a man who knows what he wants and how to get it, and, along the way, he's going to give me what I want, too."

The gunshots subsided from inside the ballroom.

"Watch and learn, Croft, and come along for the ride. It'll be fun."

With that Denny Sampson signalled for his men to stand. They formed up at the row of double doors to the ballroom, and, on his signal, they entered.

Blood was spattered on the gilding and smeared on the mirrors. The pink velvet and brocade were dappled with gore, and the polished floor was slick with it. Bodies were slumped against walls, behind cabinets, and in alcoves, and there were shards of crystal everywhere.

Lara glanced at the remains of one of the crystal lamps. It looked like a tree hit by lightning, split and shredded by the experience, as if it had died and shed its foliage. It was almost more beautiful than it had been when it was whole.

"Mr. Vata," said Denny Sampson, holding out a broad hand to shake.

"Denny Sampson," said Vata, grasping it, half a smile just reaching his mouth, his eyes remaining cold. "So Zizek was wrong. Strand doesn't have the artefact. I needn't have killed him or his men." He glanced at his phalanx of armed Wolf-Heads and nodded for them to be at their ease.

Denny Sampson signalled for his men to do the same.

"No," said Denny, beaming, "he was right. Strand does have the artefact. I have Strand. One buyer, one seller."

"And you," said Vata.

"I'm a reasonable man," said Denny Sampson. "You've dealt with me before."

Vata looked Lara up and down. He made one of his minute gestures.

"The woman," he said. "I recognise her. Who is she?"

Denny turned, and Lara stepped forwards.

"You looked more beautiful in the abaya," said Vata.

"Croft looks beautiful in anything," said Denny.

"The famous Lara Croft?" asked Vata. "I'm honoured. Had you not given a false name, I would have treated you very differently. Perhaps you can verify my purchase?"

"I'd certainly like to see it," said Lara.

"Sampson?" asked Vata.

"I've written down the details," said Denny, offering a folded piece of paper. Vata minutely gestured once more, and Dibra took the note from Denny's hand as the Wolf-Heads exited the ballroom with Vata safely at their centre.

"So you plan to sell to Vata?" asked Lara. "The ever-reliable Denny Sampson."

They were standing in the lobby of the palace. Denny's men were making short work of the buffet, and Denny had a large glass of whiskey in one big hand.

"Relax, Lara. Have a drink. Have an hors d'oeuvre."

"You set me up, Denny. Did you expect me to get dragged into that firefight? Did you think I'd get gunned down along with Zizek's goons?"

Denny laughed.

"This was nothing, Croft. A means to an end. I'm not selling to Vata. I'm buying time."

"For what?" asked Lara. "A decent meal?" She gestured at the cluttered remains of the buffet Denny's gunmen had left behind them in the lobby.

"Hey," protested Denny, "it's free."

Lara shook her head and turned to Bell.

"Come on, Carter. We're leaving."

Lara strode across the lobby towards the exit, the doors still standing wide open. Carter was hard on her heels.

"Oh, come on, Croft, be a sport," called Denny. "Let me make it up to you."

Lara ignored Denny and kept walking, through the vast doors of the palace and out onto the drive. Vata and his entourage were long gone. The Hummers and Denny's Daimler were parked up facing the palace. There were no other vehicles in sight. The driver of Lara's limousine had clearly panicked and left. She didn't blame him, although she regretted the loss of the clothes she'd left on the backseat.

"What now?" asked Bell.

"We walk," said Lara.

"And the artefact?"

"Denny said it himself," said Lara. "He's playing for time. I've been dealing with Denny Sampson for years, Carter. All we have to do is work out where he's got Strand holed up."

Less than ten minutes later, they heard the roar of engines as the Hummers approached and then passed them. They hadn't even reached the end of the palace drive.

Denny was driving himself. The driver's window lowered silently, and he called Lara's name as he dropped the speed of the car to match her walking pace.

"Let me drive you back," said Denny. "It's the least I can do."

"I wouldn't give you the satisfaction."

"Sure you would," said Denny. "Look at it this way: I got the artefact out of the sale for you, and at the same time, I got Zizek's business for me. All without putting either one of us in the firing line."

"You put me in that auction room tonight," said Lara.

"So, I had a little fun along the way," said Denny. "Come on, Croft. Get in the damn car."

"What about Vata?"

"Vata likes pretty things, but he likes weapons more. He collects what everyone else wants, and tomorrow I'll be able to offer him something new, or, better still, something dangerous. I'm connected...more now than ever."

Lara stood still, and Denny stopped the car.

"Come on, Carter. It looks like Denny's moonlighting as our taxi service tonight," she said, opening the rear car door.

Carter got in the backseat of the car, followed by Lara. She slammed the door closed behind her.

"You're a manipulative son of a bitch, Denny Sampson," she said.

"Ain't that the truth," said Denny, grinning.

CHAPTER ELEVEN: STRAND
The Toros Mountains

"This isn't the route back into Kurkarob," said Lara fifteen minutes into the journey.

"The Toros are so beautiful, and so rich," said Denny. "Don't worry, Croft, it'll just be us. My men have homes to go to, and, you know me, I like to travel light. A man like me doesn't need an entourage."

"The Toros?" asked Lara.

"I've got a little villa in the foothills, about an hour from here. You'll love it."

"And Strand?" asked Bell.

"There's nowhere for him to go, and the villa's comfortable. He'll be waiting for us."

"What about Vata?" asked Lara. "What was in the note?"

"A time and a place, Croft. Don't you worry about Vata."

"Tell me about the sword," said Lara.

"You haven't seen it?" asked Denny.

"Tell me why Vata wants it."

"Why does a rich man ever want anything? Because there is only one of it, and because other men want it," said Denny.

"What other men?" asked Lara, on her guard.

"Other *people*," said Denny. "You're very literal, Croft. You want it. Plenty of other people in that room wanted it. Vata believes that I saved him money, and that's why he's dealing with me. He doesn't have to pay Zizek's commission, and he doesn't have to outbid anyone."

Lara said nothing.

"You deal with me because you can't help liking me, Lara Croft."

When they arrived at the villa, the drive was empty, except for Denny's car. The place was well lit, but they were the only lights that Lara had seen for more than half an hour. The house was very isolated.

That didn't concern her. It took more than that to concern her. There was only one heavy in the place, and he seemed more than a little relaxed. Lara could take him easily enough, if she had to.

Strand was nowhere to be seen.

"Make yourselves at home," said Denny, almost as soon as they walked through the door, which led straight into a large, comfortable sitting room. "Sandler will find you something to eat, and a room. Or perhaps you'd prefer two?"

"We're not staying," said Lara.

"Well, gee, Sandler's not driving you back to Kurkarob tonight. It's late, so be my guests, Croft. Relax."

"Where's Strand?" asked Lara.

"Bed," said the scruffy man in his thirties or early forties who was lounging on a huge leather chesterfield and hadn't bothered to get up yet. Lara assumed the man must be Sandler.

"And the artefact?"

Denny glanced up from where he was pouring himself a whiskey at a console table loaded with decanters. The table stood against an interior stone wall, rough-hewn and clearly very old. There was a cavernous fireplace on the end wall of the room.

"Safe," he said, but she could hear a tension cutting his normally jocular tone.

"Denny," she said, a hint of warning.

"Sit down, Croft. Here, have a drink," he said, walking towards her with a half-full glass.

Bell took the glass out of his hand and sat on one end of the chesterfield.

"It's been a long day, Denny. Just give Lara what she wants," he said, sipping from the glass.

"Thanks, Carter," said Lara. "I want to see the sword, and I want to speak to Strand. And I want to do both tonight."

"Fair enough," said Denny.

They were eating and talking in the big kitchen when Strand appeared, wandering in, still half-asleep and dishevelled. He was a tall, slender young man, but he was also pale and wide-eyed and anxious-looking. It was the same man from the photograph.

Strand stopped in his tracks when he saw Lara, and then his mouth fell open when he saw Carter Bell. He made a move as if to turn and run, but thought better of it. There was nowhere for him to go.

"Ah, Strand," said Denny. "Join us."

"Mr. Bell," said Strand.

"Strand," said Carter.

"You can't take it back," said Strand, petulant. "It's mine now. They would have just locked it away. They were shutting us down."

"Do I look like the police?" asked Carter.

"Who's she?" asked Strand, pointing at Lara.

"She?" said Denny, in disgust. "Lara Croft is not just some *she*. Have some damn respect."

"Lara Croft?" said Strand. "*The* Lara Croft?"

"The very same," said Denny. "So mind your manners."

"So you did take the sword?" asked Lara.

"What's it to you?" asked Strand.

"Manners," said Denny. "Why don't you just answer the question?"

"She's not the police," said Strand.

"Then it shouldn't matter what you tell her," said Denny. "If I'm going to sell this thing for you, you need people like Bell and Miss Croft to authenticate it for me."

"I was selling it through Mr. Zizek," said Strand, still petulant and still standing.

"And look how well that turned out," said Denny. He laughed, a belly laugh, and thumped the table. When he'd composed himself, he looked around at Bell's and Lara's unsmiling faces.

"Oh, come on," he said. "That was funny."

"Sit down, Strand," said Lara. "Tell me where you got the sword."

"And tell us what else you took from the site," said Bell.

Strand stood for a few more moments, under Lara's glare, and, finally, he pulled out a chair and sat.

Jamie Strand, a young graduate, had been part of the team at the Candle Lane dig. When things had got hairy—and Strand himself had clearly been spooked by the atmosphere at the dig—he had made a fast exit.

And he'd taken some items with him with a view to getting some compensation for himself.

Strand seemed a contradiction to Lara: he knew enough about the business to realize that Kurkarob offered him the best market for such high-value loot, and he was evidently smart and well educated.

But he was also naive. He had thought he could just walk into Kurkarob's den of thieves and come out intact, with his pockets full of cash.

"I'm not getting paid, am I?" asked Strand, when he had finally satisfied Lara and Bell. "This has all been for nothing."

"You wanted to be an archaeologist," said Lara. "What happened to your ambition?"

"Student debts," spat Strand, "and government directives, and low-grade jobs with crap pay, and underfunding..."

"So you thought stealing was a good plan?"

"You do it," said Strand.

Denny Sampson laughed again, long and hard, his face reddening and his eyes watering. He dabbed at his face with a napkin, breathed hard, and brought himself under control.

"I do the jokes around here," he said. "But that was the funniest thing I think I've ever heard. Lara Croft, a thief!" He burst into a renewed fit of laughter.

"I leave that to the Denny Sampsons of the world," said Lara.

A mobile phone rang with the theme song to the *Halloween* movie. Denny coughed and pulled himself together.

"That's me," he said and rose from the table.

"Weird ringtone," said Carter.

"Weird to get mobile reception out here," replied Lara.

"You're weird," said Strand. He was sulking.

Sandler sighed and began to clear the kitchen table.

"I can't stand babysitting," he announced. "Especially babysitting *babies*."

"You're going to steal the sword from me," said Strand.

"You heard what Denny said," said Carter. "Lara's no thief."

"She just works with thieves," said Strand, "or is Mr. Sampson an innocent?"

"You can't just take important artefacts away from an active dig," said Lara.

"Yeah, but it's not active, is it?" said Strand. "They were shutting it down. It was messed up."

"It was an important dig," said Lara. "It *is* an important dig."

She turned in her chair and looked at Sandler.

Denny had been gone for what seemed like a long time.

"Sandler, what's Denny doing?" asked Lara.

Sandler shrugged. After another few moments of silence, he said, "He's a businessman. He takes a lot of calls."

Two minutes after that, Denny walked back into the kitchen carrying a packet. The packet was long and narrow and wrapped in layers of lint-free, unbleached cloth. It was wrapped just the way Lara would have wrapped it.

"I think it's time you had a look at the prize. Don't you, Croft?" said Denny, placing the packet on the table in front of her. "I mean, it's the star of the show. It's why we're all here. It's cost a lot of people their lives."

"That was mainly you," Lara pointed out.

"Ah, to-may-to, to-mah-to," replied Denny. He laid the packet on the table.

Lara stood and leant over the parcel. She wiped her hands on the knees of her leggings, and, with her forefingers and thumbs, began to carefully peel away the layers of cloth.

"Gloves?" she asked Denny as the sword was finally revealed.

Denny reached into his pocket and pulled out a pair of cotton gloves. Lara put them on. They were too big, fit for his hands, but she didn't care.

The sword was extraordinary.

It was double-edged, about thirty inches long, with the elegant leaf shape of Bronze Age weapons. It had been formed in one piece, essentially carved from a single, perfect piece of obsidian, including the grip. There was no sign of knapping or tool marks. The sword maker had been incredibly precise and skillful in his shaping of the blade.

There was no sign of wear either. Between the simple disc pommel and the curved crossguard, the hilt had been wrapped in leather that looked as supple and new as the day it had been placed there. There were simple linear carvings on the ricasso and the crossguard that resembled early- or proto-Celtic line and knot work.

The black obsidian seemed deep, like a mirror, with a tinge of oceanic green to it.

It was as Carter had described it, and just as she had imagined it. *Dreamt* it, in fact. Lara realised, though it seemed familiar, she had never properly seen it or examined it before.

Dreamt. That was it. Lara felt a cold shiver. It was as though this sword had been present in one of the dreams that had haunted her before leaving London.

She traced a finger along the full length of the blade of the ancient weapon and then followed the pattern of the hilt. Then she took hold of the grip, lifted it several inches, and bent to cast her eye down the length of the weapon. She carefully turned the weapon over and looked at the other side of the blade.

She lifted the weapon again, in both hands, holding the sword horizontally in front of her, testing its

weight. Then she took a firm hold of the grip and
weighed the sword in one hand. She held it close to
her face and examined the proportions of the pommel
and crossguard. She pressed a finger against the
unsharpened ricasso, feeling the carvings there. Then
she turned the sword, so that her hand was low against
her thigh and the tip of the sword was close to her head.
She looked at where the fuller met the centre ridge and
noted the proportions of the fuller as a fraction of the
blade width.

Lara took her time.

It was a ceremonial weapon. Until the development
of bronze and iron, stone and glass weapons had been
a practical choice, but they were prone to damage and
not at all hard-wearing. They seldom survived intact or
unchipped, unless they had been purely ceremonial.

So why, she wondered, had this sword been made
so perfectly? Its balance, edge, and construction were
practically precise, not decorative. It weighed like well-
balanced steel in her hand. Lara felt she could use it,
not just carry it as a sign of prestige or status.

This sword would cut. It would fight.

Why, in ages of bronze and iron, had a decorative
object been made to such perfect specification? And
if it had been intended for practical use, why was it so
terrifyingly unmarked and perfect?

"Well?" asked Carter.

"It's perfect," she said. "It's utterly right." She laid
it back on the layers of cloth and began to remove
the gloves.

Denny flicked the layers of cloth back over the sword, wrapped it, and picked it up.

"Where are you taking it?" asked Carter.

"Even out here I like to keep things locked up," said Denny. "If you wouldn't mind doing the honours?" He handed the cloth parcel to Sandler, who strode out of the room with it.

"It's not *too* perfect, then?" Denny asked Lara. "It seemed a little pristine to me, for its purported age."

"No, it's definitely right," said Lara. The sword wasn't a fake. She knew that. But she chose not to share her more uncertain reservations about it.

Denny beamed.

"Told you," said Strand. Then he winced, almost cowered at a sound from outside.

An animal had howled.

He turned to Lara, his eyes wide and face pale, all the petulance gone out of him. Lara was reminded of the foxes she'd heard howling in the parkland surrounding the manor, and almost felt sorry for Strand.

"Are you going back to London?" he asked.

"Yes, I think so," said Lara, sitting beside Strand.

"And you won't turn me in to the police?"

"Now that we have the sword, I don't see any reason to," said Lara, "assuming you don't try a stunt like this again."

"In that case, can I come back with you?" asked Strand. "I can't wait to get back to civilisation."

There was another howl outside in the night, a little closer to the villa this time.

Strand visibly quaked.

"Scared of a few wolves?" asked Denny.

"You said it was hyenas, yesterday," said Strand.

Denny laughed.

"Damned city boys," he said. "Can't tell the difference between a hyena and a wolf."

There was another howl, and then several more, as if in answer to the first. An eerie chorus.

Lara tossed a smile in Denny's direction.

"Hanging around you, I'm not surprised he can't tell the difference," she said. "You qualify as both."

Denny burst into one of his belly laughs, and for a moment, the cries of the wolves were drowned out.

"You're hiding something, Denny," said Lara. "I'm a better archaeologist than you are. We both know that. You had doubts about the sword and you needed me to authenticate it. But why? It shouldn't matter to you, if you plan to give it back to me... You're a sneaky bastard, Denny Sampson," she said, standing and drawing her gun, in one graceful movement. "You were going to sell the sword out from under me, and use my reputation to get the best price."

"I wouldn't do that if I were you, Miss," said Sandler, stepping through the kitchen door, gun raised and trained on her. "After you, Mr. Sampson," he said, ushering his boss safely out of the range of Lara's rage.

Denny walked out of the room, digging his ringing phone out of his pocket and calling over his shoulder, "Nice catch, Lara. Pity you couldn't make the touchdown."

When Denny had gone, Sandler kept his gun on Lara for a few seconds longer. It was a standoff. Lara watched the bodyguard's eyes for an opportunity. She knew that where the eyes went, the gun would follow, and she'd get her shot.

Sandler's eyes moved, almost imperceptibly. Then the barrel of his pistol moved down and right in a quick jerk.

Strand had been staring in terrified wonder at the gun pointing at the woman standing next to him. He couldn't take his eyes off it. His head jerked as Sandler adjusted his aim, and suddenly he was staring right down the barrel of the gun.

Strand screamed and flailed. He tried to drop off his chair to take cover, but instead crashed into Lara's legs, just as she was taking her shot. Strand sent them both sprawling to the floor.

Lara's shot went wide.

Sandler fired, reflexively, at the sound of gunfire, but his aim was still on where Strand's head had been a split second before, and the bullet ricocheted off a stone wall, lost its momentum, and fell to the floor.

Carter reached for his gun, and Lara disentangled herself from Strand's flailing limbs and rose to take another shot. It was too late. Sandler had seen his chance to leave, and he'd taken it.

Carter shot a couple of rounds blindly into the corridor between the kitchen and the sitting room, and he and Lara went after Sandler.

Sandler had reached the front door when he heard footsteps following him. He turned and fired across

the sitting room, covering the doorway through which
Carter and Lara would have to enter the room. Still
firing, he opened the front door with one hand and
ducked around it.

Lara timed Sandler's shots. She stepped into the
doorway of the sitting room, gun raised, and shot at
Sandler's receding figure.

The door closed, and he was gone.

Lara gestured to Carter, and they crossed the sitting
room. Lara turned the door handle and pulled, but
nothing happened.

"Let me," said Carter.

The door wouldn't move for him either.

"This one's locked," said Lara. "Let's try the back."

The kitchen door was also locked. Carter covered the
rest of the ground floor, but there were no other exits.
Meanwhile, Lara went back into the sitting room and
looked out onto the drive. Denny's car had gone. It was
too late to fight back, and they'd need a plan to find
their way back to the city without a vehicle. It was dark,
so probably better to stay where they were until they'd
worked something out.

CHAPTER TWELVE: PACK ANIMALS
The Toros Mountains

"I've seen some amazing artefacts in my time, but I think that's the most beautiful thing I've seen come out of Britain," said Lara.

"It's very special," said Carter. "Important. And he took the bloody thing."

He was glaring at Strand.

"How was that even possible?" Lara asked the young man.

"I just wrapped it up and walked out with it," said Strand.

"There was so much crazy going down, and it was just sitting there..."

He paused and looked towards the window.

"I wish those bloody dogs would let up," he said.

Denny and Sandler had been gone for almost an hour, and, after a brief discussion in which Lara had persuaded them they shouldn't move until the morning, they had been left sitting around the kitchen table, talking about the sword. The wolves outside continued their more singsong conversation.

"Maybe it's a full moon," said Carter.

"That's not even funny," said Strand, petulant again. "I can't wait to get out of this place. Why can't we go now?"

"We could leave now," said Lara. "We'd have to break windows to get out of this house, the mountains are full of wolves and hyenas, it's dark, and we don't have any transport. Frankly, none of those things bother me very much, and I'm sure Carter would be fine. You, on the other hand..."

"So," said Strand, "if it doesn't work, if we get lost or something, we just come back here."

"To a house overrun with your favourite wolves and hyenas, who are ransacking the place, having got in through the broken windows," said Carter.

"I just want to get out of here," snapped Strand, getting up from the kitchen table and flouncing off.

"Me, too, and as far away as possible from that little shit. If he hadn't got in the way, this would be over by now," said Lara.

"Nothing we can do about that, now," said Carter.

"Except make the best of it," said Lara, smiling at him.

"It's no wonder Denny had doubts about the sword," said Carter, getting back to the subject. "I might have, too, if I hadn't seen it in situ. It really is in remarkable condition. The environment must have been ideal to have preserved it so perfectly. The humidity, temperature, air circulation... The conditions must have been exceptional."

"Everything about the Candle Lane site was exceptional," said Lara, "and the Egyptians knew how to seal a tomb. Maybe it was one of the technologies that transferred to Britain across the cultures."

"Interesting theory," said Carter.

"I'm trying to come up with another interesting theory," said Lara.

"About the sword?" asked Carter. "Ask me anything. I was there, remember, and with your insight, we might come up with something."

"No, not about the sword," said Lara, "about Denny's buyer."

"He's selling to Vata," said Carter.

Lara thought for a moment.

"I don't think so," she said. "If he were selling to Vata, he wouldn't have needed me to authenticate the piece. Vata would have bought the sword at Zizek's auction. He was committed to the purchase. Denny's got another buyer: someone more demanding, someone with deeper pockets, someone more dangerous."

"Who?"

"I don't know," said Lara, "but I plan to find out. First we need to get out of here."

"But we already decided that wasn't a good idea," said Carter.

"I didn't say it was going to be any fun," Lara replied.

"What's happening?" asked Strand. He looked nervous as he walked back into the kitchen.

"Nothing," said Carter. "Precisely nothing."

"Well, at least the damned dogs have stopped howling," said Strand.

Lara turned her head and listened intently.

The wolves *had* stopped howling.

She slowly made her way to one of the front-facing windows, drawing her gun as she went.

"Well, that confirms it," she said. "Denny definitely wasn't selling to Vata."

Carter craned to listen. Now he heard what she had: the hum of a very expensive car engine and the crackle of tires on the dirt road to the villa.

Two cars pulled up in front of the house.

It was too late to take countermeasures. Too late to turn off lights, to pretend that no one was home.

"This is a setup," said Lara. "That note, the one Denny handed to Dibra. The meet was tonight, and it was *here*."

"Now what do we do?" asked Carter.

"Find somewhere safe for Strand," said Lara. She looked at the young man.

"Unless you know how to use a gun?" she asked him.

He looked petrified. He shook his head.

"Why am I even asking?" she said.

Carter took Strand by the arm.

"Somewhere safe, then," Carter said. "An internal corridor, no windows. Maybe a cupboard?"

"Anything like that," said Lara.

"I'll check exits, see if there's a way out of here."

Carter manhandled the frozen Strand out of the room, and Lara went back to the kitchen.

The first knock sounded on the main door. *Thump thump thump*. An ominous rapping.

They both ignored it. They had a very short window of opportunity to assess their situation.

Denny had seemed casual about the villa, as if it was a domestic dwelling, a home.

But it wasn't. It was a modest fortress.

Every door and window was shut and locked. There was no way out, and there was no way that Lara could let Vata in, even if she wanted to. As a known associate of Denny Sampson, she wasn't sure she could talk Vata around. He had killed Zizek and his keepers because the sword had been withdrawn from sale. It didn't bode well.

There were two cars. There could be as many as ten armed Wolf-Heads against just her and Carter.

They were effectively under siege.

The knocking at the door turned to pounding. Lara continued to ignore it.

Carter came up behind her.

"We're sitting ducks," he said. "I hope you've got a plan."

"We fight our way out, or they fight their way in," said Lara. "It's as simple as that."

"Countermeasures?" asked Carter.

"Confusion," said Lara, "preferably theirs."

"Are you comfortable with the layout of this place?" asked Carter over the thundering noise of several bodies throwing themselves at the door.

Lara glanced around, and then closed her eyes, breathed, and thought for a moment.

"Yes," she said. "There's some ambient light outside: the moon, stars, and the cars, if they've left headlights on. We can go dark inside."

"Okay," said Carter. "So we kill the lights. Then what?"

"Then we make them fight their way in," said Lara.

More pounding sounds came from the rear of the house, as the Wolf-Heads tried another door, but Denny's villa was like Fort Knox.

Lara and Carter took up positions in the darkness and waited. They checked their ammo loads.

Outside, someone got tired of beating on the door and opened fire. A single shot, perhaps from a large-calibre handgun.

The shot hit the front window of the ground-floor drawing room, but did not penetrate. Toughened glass, maybe.

"Wow," said Carter. "Was Denny expecting World War Three?"

"Be happy I didn't choose to fight our way out," said Lara. "I'm guessing my nine millimetres wouldn't have much effect on whatever those windows are made of."

They both ducked instinctively at the sudden hammering of AK47 gunfire. The visitors, now weary of knocking, and finding themselves getting nowhere with shots from a handgun, had switched to automatic fire.

Brutal gunfire raked the house. Lara and Carter heard the hard cracking of the panes in the windows only metres from where they were hunkered down.

"Someone's getting impatient," said Lara. "Check the kitchen. I think they've given up there."

Staying low and dodging furniture, Carter made his way to the rear of the house.

"Can't hear anything back here!" he called to her as loudly as he dared.

Lara held her position, aiming her weapon in the direction of the gunfire. They weren't letting up. They were hosing the house. Lara figured they must have spent several magazines.

She hoped for their sakes the men had brought a trunk full of ammo.

She hoped so for her own sake, too. I might be her best way out of the villa.

Burst after burst. She could see the dancing flicker of muzzle flash out front.

But there was no sound of glass shattering or falling. Just the bullet impacts and the cracking noises.

Carter was back to join her. The noise of pounding started afresh. This time it wasn't thumping on the door. This time, it sounded like a sledgehammer on plate glass.

"It's got to give," whispered Carter. "The sustained gunfire will have weakened the windows. Even armoured glass—"

"Any minute now," said Lara.

The first piece of the shot-frosted windowpane separated along its cracks and fell onto the tiled floor, bouncing with the clatter of hard plastic, rather than glass.

Lara immediately fired into the gap where it had been. She heard the impact of bullet on flesh and fired again, but visibility was poor.

"Hold this position," said Lara. She ducked around Carter and crossed the room.

"Where are you going?" he hissed at her.

Lara jabbed a finger upwards, hoping that he'd be able to see it.

"Okay," he hissed again.

The Wolf-Heads couldn't make a real impact until they could get into the house, and while they were trying to take out the window, it only took one person to pick them off, one at a time. She and Carter had the advantage. It was like Horatio holding the bridge.

The slow and difficult progress of ingress gave Lara the chance to check the windows on the first floor. If they opened, or if they were regular glass, she could go on the attack.

Lara ran down the long corridor, through the centre of the house.

Someone grabbed her from behind before she reached the stairs.

He was screaming like a banshee and clinging to her back, one arm around her neck.

She grasped the top of his arm with both of her hands, swung out her hips, and dropped her head, pulling hard. Her attacker had no choice but to let go of her neck.

She flipped him onto his back on the floor in front of her, winding him. His screaming turned into coughing.

It was Strand.

"Idiot!" she said. "For heaven's sake, Strand, get back to wherever Carter put you and stay there. Get out of my way!"

Strand was still coughing, trying to recover from his fear of an invasion, and from the flip.

"Is that you, Lara? Why is it so dark?"

Lara didn't answer. She booted him in the side to make room to walk past him, and continued on up the stairs.

The master bedroom, at the rear of the house, had floor-to-ceiling windows looking out onto a balcony. Beautiful, but useless, except that Lara could see the Wolf-Heads had abandoned the route into the villa.

The smaller rooms at the front of the house were clearly used by Denny's men. The wall was old stone, and the windows were small, in the traditional Turkish style, to maintain ideal temperatures, year-round: cool in the summer and warm in the winter.

Lara tried a handle but could already tell that the windows had been painted shut, probably inside and out. She put her palm flat on one of the small panes. It was far too small for anyone to escape through. The glass felt cold and smooth, but not quite flat, not quite true. It felt like the kind of glass the Victorians used in sash windows.

The room Lara was in was directly above the main entrance to the villa. She left it and moved along the corridor to the end room, a bathroom. It had the same type of small, old windows. She wished she could remember what was below the bathroom, on the ground floor.

The pounding on the window below became rhythmic once more. Lara held her gun firmly by the slide and punched out the window with the grip in time with the next blow. She barely heard the tinkle of the glass as the pane shattered easily. Lara got rid of the last shards and looked out. There was only just room for her head.

The sky was clear and the moon was high. Visibility was much better outside than inside. That was something to bear in mind when she moved back into the interiors of the house.

Craning her neck, she could make out five figures below.

Three were definitely men, big men. Two of the figures looked as if they could be women. Lara had seen women at the auction, wearing the Wolf-Head badge. From her angle of view, she assumed that she was not able to see whoever was pounding on the window. She also assumed that Vata was in one of the cars—although she could only see their roofs—and that he would have at least one more bodyguard with him.

That made eight, in total.

If she fired her weapon, she would give away her position, but she had a good line of sight and easy targets. She could take out two or three of the eight. Easy kills. How long before they got into the house? Had she hit someone with her first shot, and, if so, how good had that hit been?

Lara heard a shot. She didn't see a muzzle flash, so the shot had to have come from inside the house. It had to be Carter.

She decided not hesitate any longer.

She pulled her head back inside and aimed the gun out.

Her first shot was aimed at the body of one of the men. He was a big target, and he went down hard. The Wolf-Heads responded immediately, taking cover and looking for a target. Her second shot was lucky. She got it off quickly, targeting the second man, but he was ducking, and it hit one of the women instead. She had literally walked into the bullet meant for Lara's target. It glanced the side of her head and probably wasn't fatal, but the scalp bled badly, and the woman wouldn't be in a state to fight for a while.

Her companions rapidly dragged her into cover.

Lara couldn't rule her out of the fight, long-term.

She began taking potshots at moving targets or at people in cover. Then, the opportunity was gone. Three guns were shooting back at her. Bullets smacked into the window surround and sprayed chips of stone. She took a couple more blind shots, and then ran out of the room. She was reloading as she ran down the corridor.

Under the cover of gunfire, Lara broke a window in the bedroom over the main entrance and fired on the Wolf-Heads again, winging another man.

Instantly, she found herself under fire once more.

"Two down, I think, maybe three," she whispered at Carter as she returned to the drawing room.

"They're almost through," said Carter. "How many?"

"Maybe eight."

"Jesus," said Carter.

"Do you want to do this?" asked Lara.

"Do we have a choice?"

There was another almighty crack, louder than the subsiding gunfire, as another piece of the window broke free and fell onto the tiles.

Lara reflex-shot into the gap, but there was no one there.

"They're getting good at this," said Carter. "How do you think they'll do it?"

"Guns blazing!" said Lara.

The gunfire came in low, tracking across the floor in a wide arc. Machine-gun fire. Flagstones cracked and chipped, and carpet fibres billowed into the air.

Lara had no idea how it had missed both of them. Instinctively, they both leapt off the floor, Carter onto the chesterfield, belly down; Lara, crouched, onto a large, low table. More gunfire came in at shoulder height, but the Wolf-Heads were shooting blind.

It was obvious that Vata's men couldn't see into the black depths of the drawing room after the moonlight exterior they had become used to. They were shooting hard, but they were also visible, backlit by the starry sky. They were clambering in through the window, over the prone body of the man giving them covering fire at ground level.

Assault tactics. Polished and effective. Lara couldn't allow them to be successful.

"Take the one coming in," she hissed to Carter.

She'd given him the easier shot. She aimed, carefully, for the prone man supplying covering fire. Lara and Carter began firing in unison.

Lara Croft and the Blade of Gwynnever

She hit squarely. The prone gunman jolted. His trigger finger locked. He was no longer raking the floor at a low angle to clear the room. The misaligned weapon tilted, and one bullet after another emptied into the wall of the drawing room a couple of metres behind Lara.

Carter blasted at the men storming the window. Framed in the moonlight, a standing gunman jerked. His gun dropped from his hands, but still hung from its strap, thumping against his body. He fell clumsily, like a sack of loose rocks, onto the man he'd been stepping over, and the covering gunfire finally stopped.

Silence. Smoke curled in the air. Lara could hear a thick, ugly gurgling coming from the throat of the intruder Carter had taken down.

Then Lara heard a wild cry.

She raised her gun instinctively, ready to aim it at the next Wolf-Head through the window.

No one came.

She heard the cry again. It wasn't human. Was it the wolves? It sounded quite different from the howls that Strand had hated so much.

A single shot spat into the room.

It spanged off the leg of the table that Lara was crouching on, and she stepped off it, ducking into her original cover.

More shots followed. The remaining Wolf-Heads were using their dead colleagues as cover, but the gunfire was erratic and undirected.

Lara counted three dead, for sure, and two injured. Probably more.

She and Carter kept in cover, guns aimed, but there were no clear targets, and they didn't want to give away their positions. Denny's house was keeping the Wolf-Heads at bay.

The siege was on.

Then the crying noises started up again in earnest.

Eerie, almost human cries came out of the darkness all around the house, fast, repeating, overlapping. The shrieks and screams hung in the night air.

Then a howl, a proper howl this time, penetrated the baying, crying voices. It rose and built to a blistering crescendo. It was answered by a second beast, and then a chorus started up, a new wolf taking up the cry as each howl abated.

The shrieks and the howls, like two demented choirs embarking on an atonal music combat, became an unbearable symphony.

"I can't stand it!" yelled Strand, bursting into the drawing room.

A gun went off.

The shot looked good. Someone outside had spotted the open movement, aimed, and hit his target.

Strand dropped hard to the tiled floor, unable to gasp, let alone cry out. Lara assumed that he was dead.

Moments later she heard ferocious growling, then another gunshot. This time, the shot wasn't aimed into the house.

"What the hell?" said Carter.

They listened, guns ready.

They heard a shout, a scream, another gunshot, and all to a background of snarling and growling.

Then, quite clearly, a woman's voice. "Get it off me, Dibra! Kill it!"

Carter looked at Lara, and raised his eyebrows.

"I think our friends have run into trouble with the local wildlife," he said.

"It's a dog-eat-dog world," she replied. "Denny Sampson told me so."

Gun still aimed, Lara stepped out of cover and hurried towards Strand's prone body. She squatted beside him and reached out a hand to take the pulse in his neck. It was strong and steady.

The commotion outside had worsened, taking attention away from her and Carter. Lara holstered her gun and turned her attention to Strand. She located his injury. Not fatal, thank God. A superficial shoulder wound. She didn't care for Strand, but she didn't wish the stupid kid dead.

She used Strand's own shirt to strap up the wound. Then, one hand over his mouth to try to prevent him making too much noise, Lara shook him conscious.

"Shut up, and do as I say," she hissed at him. "You're fine. No harm done. Get on your stomach and be ready to move back to your hiding place when I tell you. Got it?"

She took her hand away from his mouth, and then immediately clamped it back down again when she felt the tension in him.

"You need to calm down right now, Jamie, or I'll put you out again," she snapped. "We've got this under control, Carter and me. Do you get it?"

This time she didn't remove her hand. She waited for Strand's nod. Finally he nodded, and she took her hand away slowly. She waited while he rolled onto his front. Then, she armed herself and took up her old position.

"Okay, Carter, covering fire," said Lara. As Lara and Carter fired into the gap where the window had been, Lara called out over her shoulder, "Move it, Strand! Right now!"

Strand was clear and Carter was reloading when Lara saw the grenade beyond the muzzle flashes of her twin guns.

"Duck!" she yelled, and hit the deck, with Carter a split second behind her. The grenade was thrown hurriedly and landed long, several metres behind Carter and Lara, and against the stone wall that divided the large living room from the corridor beyond. The impact was noisy, but did little damage to the wall and only cratered the tiled floor. The fire was the real problem. The rug was smoking, and flames were beginning to lick over the big couch where Sandler had been slumped when they'd first arrived. In a moment, a wall hanging was ablaze, and then the decanters on the console table began to explode. Lara and Carter were caught between the fire, which now had a momentum all its own, and the Wolf-Heads.

"Time to leave," said Lara.

Outside, the voices were still yelling.

"Help!"

"Do something!"

The howling had not stopped. It was close, very close, and the Wolf-Heads were calling out. The gunfire was sporadic.

But there had been no mistaking the authentic desperation in that cry.

Lara rose to a crouch.

"Okay," said Carter, getting up beside her. "Let's do this."

CHAPTER THIRTEEN: FIGHT OR FLIGHT
The Toros Mountains

Carter saw strings of spittle shining off long, yellow teeth. He saw a flexed, pink tongue and black gums. He saw wide-set, yellow eyes, fringed with black, and he saw acres of tawny fur.

The wolf slammed into him.

He didn't even have time to curse or cry out. He'd been ready, tensed, and still the sheer speed of the thing had taken him by surprise. The moment he'd emerged through the window and dropped onto the ground outside, it had come at him, rearing up, attacking with its full height and weight.

Carter was knocked flat. He landed with a thud on the corpses of the Wolf-Heads blocking the window, and expected his last sensations to be teeth wrenching into his throat and ripping it out.

A shot rang out. He heard a yelp and felt weight slump onto his chest. Warm blood soaked him, spreading.

"Carter?" Lara called from close by.

"I'm okay!" he shouted back.

He heard more shots, and heaved the dead wolf off his body. The wolf's blood was cooling quickly on his shirt, sticky and uncomfortable, but he didn't care. Comfort could wait. Lara needed his help.

Carter got up, gun raised. He hunted for targets. Shapes moved like ghosts in the darkness around him. He opened fire, aiming at the guttural growls, at pelts, at anything with four legs.

He could see the bright, strobing flashes of two gun muzzles to his right.

Lara was holding both of her 9mm handguns at arm's length and was trying to keep the pack at bay. Vata's men hadn't been lying.

One of the big dogs slunk in low and snapped at her ankle. She kicked at it, and it grabbed the toe of her boot, piercing the patent leather with its incisor. The power of its bite was frightening. It clung on. Lara tried kicking free, but the beast was too strong. It wrenched back and whipped her off her feet. She landed flat on her back.

The wolf clamping her foot worried at it hard, shaking her. More animals bounded in, eager to reach prey that had been brought down.

Lara calmly got off two more shots, one from each gun, fending off the predators lunging hungrily at her prone body. Then she aimed at the dog wrestling her foot. That took concentration. The wolf was swinging its jaws savagely from side to side. She matched the movement and fired, blowing a hole between its eyes.

It dropped, its jaws still clamped on her boot. Her focus had given another dog the chance to come in on her left side.

It snagged her braid and began trying to toss her head. Lara brought her right hand around and smashed the wolf in the jaw, the grip of her sidearm adding weight to the blow.

The dog yelped and let go its hold. It glared at Lara, snarled, and was suddenly felled by a bullet. Lara couldn't tell where the shot had come from.

Lara sat, shot at three more of the wolves, and tried to get to her feet. But the dead dog's jaws were still locked around her boot.

One of the dogs let out a wild howl. She looked up and saw it twenty metres away on a rocky rise, silhouetted against the moonlit sky. Its neck was stretched up, its jaw extended. The shrieking and yelping of the other animals ceased for a moment. Then, the remaining wolves returned his call, and they began to pad away.

At the sound of more gunfire, Lara dropped and scanned. She saw a wolf go down, and then a muzzle flash from the window of a car parked several metres away to her right. There was another howl, and the wolf pack stopped, turned on the car, and began to surround it. Suddenly, they were growling and barking, and throwing themselves at its doors, trying to get at the driver and passenger within.

The headlights went on, the engine ignited, and the car turned hard and sped off, ploughing through the remaining wolves, who lunged after it until it accelerated away. Then another howl from their leader sent them padding off in the direction of the ridge.

Lara breathed a sigh of relief.

But it wasn't over.

She heard snuffles and snickers and looked around. Not all of the animals were gone.

Hyenas, drawn by the smell of blood, were gathering. She reloaded and began shooting bursts at the dark forms. Carter fired, too, but it took a lot of rounds to drive the hyenas off.

Several of the hyenas had toppled dead before the rest of the pack was put off its feast. The hyenas cleared the area, skipping and running away into the mountains.

Lara holstered her guns and took a blade out of her ankle sheath. She used it to pry open the dog's jaw and release her foot. Its incisor had pierced the leather of the toe-cap, and its lower teeth had scored deep grooves in the sole. The boots were ruined. She'd chosen the boots to wear with the abaya, and they had very pointed toes, so the last inch, where the wolf had bitten down, was empty. Her feet were intact.

Lara wiped her knife and sheathed it and accepted Carter's offered hand to get back on her feet.

"Are you okay, Lara?" asked Carter.

Lara smiled.

"Denny can add a good pair of dress boots to the long list of things he owes me," she said. "But we should probably see if Strand survived the house fire."

They turned towards the house, as the last of the fire guttered out. All of the soft furnishing had perished, but the house was built of stone. There was nothing left in the room to burn, except for the wooden beams and joists holding up the first floor, and they were huge and ancient. It was safe for now.

"You ever hear of wild animals that didn't bolt at the sound of gunfire?" asked Carter. "Or the presence of humans or fire?"

"Welcome to my world," said Lara.

They walked back into the house and found Strand in a hall closet, his hands clamped firmly over his ears, apparently reciting a prayer. They had to manhandle him out, under protest.

"You hold him, and I'll hit him," said Lara, exasperated. "And I'll put us all out of his misery."

"No...no..." said Strand. "Not again... I'll come quietly, only don't let the wolves get me."

"I should've let them kill you," said Lara.

"Not the wolves!" shrieked Strand.

"The bloody Wolf-Heads," said Lara. "It's a pity they couldn't shoot straight. Now, on your feet, Strand, and let's get out of here."

Strand tried to stand, but couldn't, and when Lara hooked an arm under his armpit, his legs still turned to jelly.

"Let me do the honours," said Carter, bending to pick up Strand in a classic fireman's lift. The kid went limp.

"Right, let's get out of here," said Lara.

"I can't carry him all the way back to the city," said Carter.

"You won't have to," said Lara.

They strode past the mauled bodies of animals and humans. The hyenas had not discriminated between types of carrion. It was dark, with only moonlight to guide her, but Lara had no trouble finding the second vehicle that the Wolf-Heads had arrived in. They wouldn't be needing it now.

Lara opened the rear door, and Carter dropped his shoulder and lowered Strand onto the backseat. Strand didn't resist. He curled up, shaking. Carter closed the door and went around the back of the vehicle to get in the passenger side as Lara had already climbed into the driver's seat.

The keys were in the ignition.

"Fancy car to leave unsecured," said Carter.

"Close protection," said Lara. "In a situation like this, they want to ensure a quick turnaround for pursuit or a fast getaway. They don't want to be fumbling for key fobs."

"Good point," said Carter.

"But Vata's a clever man. He didn't leave until he was sure Denny wasn't in that house. He knows we were here. This car belongs to him, so it's bound to have GPS tracking. We need to be sensible about this."

"So, what's the plan?" asked Carter.

"We'll talk when we get back to the city," said Lara. "This car could be wired for sound, and I have no intention of sharing my plans with Mr. Vata."

"Another good point," said Carter.

"Let's just enjoy the drive," said Lara, putting the car in gear and pulling away hard, making the gravel of Denny's drive kick out in a spray in their wake.

CHAPTER FOURTEEN: THE YELLOW DOOR
Kurkarob

"The house is shut up. Mr. Denny is not here," said the housekeeper, firmly.

Lara had walked to the house with the yellow door, alone. She didn't expect to find Denny at home, and an unaccompanied young woman stood the best chance of getting across the threshold.

"Do you remember me?" asked Lara. "I was here a couple of days ago. Denny and I are old friends."

She smiled at the old woman and took her hand. "I lost an earring in the house. It belonged to my late mother."

She squeezed the old lady's hand.

"Your mother is dead? Poor child, and so young."

"Perhaps you'd make me some of your wonderful coffee while I look for it."

"Come," said the housekeeper. "I have tulumba, homemade. You will love them, so sweet and delicious."

While the housekeeper was busy in the kitchen, making coffee and arranging the syrupy sweets in a dish, Lara searched the house. She riffled through

Denny's desk, checked his mail, and even browsed the newspapers and magazines on his coffee table. She looked through the pile of books by his bed and turned out his laundry basket. She found nothing to suggest where he might have gone.

After ten minutes she wandered into the kitchen.

"You find?" asked the housekeeper.

"No," said Lara. "Perhaps I lost it somewhere else."

"So sad," said the housekeeper, pushing the dish of tulumba closer to her. "Sit. Coffee and tulumba will make you feel better."

"I should go," said Lara.

"Sit," said the housekeeper. "It is too quiet. I like company. Who knows how long Mr. Denny gone to Egypt?"

Lara had the little glass of steaming Turkish coffee in her hand. She was very relieved that she didn't have any of the rich, dark liquid in her mouth. If she had, she might have choked on it. The search had not only been fruitless, it was redundant. All she'd had to do was befriend the housekeeper.

"A holiday?" asked Lara, all innocence.

The housekeeper laughed.

"Business. Is all business with Mr. Denny. He love it. He say soon he will be home for good. I not believe him. He love travel. He love business. He love business travel. Today Egypt, tomorrow who knows?" She laughed again. Lara laughed with her.

"Eat," said the housekeeper.

Lara ate.

"You weren't seen?" asked Carter.

"Only by the housekeeper. Did you drive the car around the city?" asked Lara.

"I took in the sights," said Carter.

"Nothing too obvious, I hope," said Lara.

"I did what you told me. I hit the records office and the library and an Internet café. I left Vata a nice data trail. I hope you're going to tell me that Sampson did, too."

"No such luck," said Lara. "I was stupid to expect it."

"Dammit."

"He is very close to his housekeeper, however, and she has a soft spot for vulnerable young women. She lets her guard down."

"You found something out?" asked Carter.

"I had to eat a lot of tulumba and drink a lot of Turkish coffee, but, apparently, the pyramids are particularly beautiful at this time of year."

"He's in Cairo," said Carter. He considered the information. "Why Cairo?"

"Because that's where his buyer is," said Lara. "Except...I think it's more than that."

"What do you mean?"

"Think about it, Carter. Cast your mind back to the dig. Put yourself back in that place, on that amazing site. We both saw it."

"The obelisk... The needle... An Egyptian site under London."

"Exactly," said Lara. "This thing is starting to look much bigger than just the sword. It's context."

"So, what do we do?"

"We go to Cairo," said Lara. "I'd like to know why Vata is so desperate to get his hands on the sword. And I'd like to know who Sampson's actually selling to. But there are a few loose ends to tie up here, first."

Strand complained nonstop. He complained about his injury, and he complained more when Lara refused to take him to a hospital, despite her explanations about having to answer for a gunshot wound. She extracted the bullet herself, and he complained about the injections of local anesthetic. Despite a large dose of sedatives, he continued to complain as she worked. He moaned when she cleaned and dressed his injury, and he whined when she reminded him to take his painkillers. He complained when he had to share a hotel room with Carter, and he bitched when Carter left him alone in it to put some data on the car's GPS.

Strand complained about the room service and protested his safety when they ate out in public. He whined about the length of the journey to Adnan Menderes Airport and bitched about his economy ticket. When he found out that the tickets Lara had bought for herself and Carter weren't going to be used, he was almost apoplectic.

Lara was past caring.

"Shut up, Strand. You got lucky," said Lara. "You survived Zizek, Sampson, and Vata, the greedy, bloodthirsty bastards. And you were damned lucky *I* didn't put you out of your misery. Keep your mouth shut, and the authorities might never know you started this whole damned mess. Just get on the plane."

With that, she turned and walked off.

Carter and Strand watched her walk away for a few moments, and then they looked at each other.

"Is that it?" asked Strand, like a lost child.

"I guess so, buddy," said Carter, feeling a little sorry for him. He stuck out his hand for the other man to shake. Strand swallowed hard.

"Oh," he said.

"Just do as she says, and you'll be fine."

"Right," said Strand. "Screw her, then."

Carter's patience ran out. He sighed, turned, and jogged after Lara.

"We leave the car here," said Lara. "The GPS data and the plane tickets should put Vata off our scent, for a while at least."

"Where to next?"

"How do you feel about trains?" asked Lara. "The metro takes us to Izmir, and then it's a comfortable sleeper to Istanbul, where we can pick up a flight to Cairo. We pay cash, we're untraceable, at least until we fly."

"What are we waiting for?" asked Carter.

"Who knew Turkey had such a great train service?" asked Carter, sitting in the restaurant car, eating the last forkful of his chicken dinner.

"You can thank the English, French, and Germans," said Lara.

"What?" asked Carter, surprised.

"A history lesson for another time," said Lara. She pushed her own plate aside and opened her laptop. She logged in, and a screen appeared offering her free Wi-Fi.

"And we're connected," she said.

"How do we track down Denny? Finding one man in a city of seven million people is like finding a needle in a haystack."

"Closer to eight million," said Lara. "But that isn't our problem. I know most of Denny's haunts, and if he's not in any of them, I know the kinds of places he likes to stay. He shouldn't be hard to find."

"So what are we looking for?"

"Links," said Lara. "What do we know about the Egyptian civilisation, the culture? How does it translate to other cultures across the globe?"

"How did it come to Britain, and when?"

"Exactly," said Lara. "And, if there is a connection back to Egypt, who in modern Cairo wants this sword back in the country?"

"Who is rich enough to buy it?"

"And ruthless enough to deal with Denny Sampson?"

"And connected enough to know how to find Denny?"

"Let's get back to our couchette," said Lara, closing the laptop and gathering her things together.

"I'm too excited to sleep," said Carter.

"Not to sleep, to work. Privacy."

"The list of clients Denny has dealt with in the past is too long," said Lara. "And none of them feel like an obvious fit. They're industrialists, collectors. Some of them not entirely honest, most with agendas. Mafia connections in America, Europe, Russia, China, even the Middle East, but not specifically Egypt."

"What about Vata?"

"We don't work for Vata."

"But maybe his interest is the same as the buyer's."

"Okay," said Lara, typing Vata's name into the laptop keyboard. She'd bypassed Google to use more specialist search engines, but it still took her several attempts to track down the man she was looking for. She was glad she'd met him. The only photograph on record was in the Deep Web, and was at least twenty years old.

"Dritan Vata, the youngest son of a woman widowed in 1970 when her husband died in one of Tito's prisons. He's listed because his father was the famous Kosovan separatist, Veton Vata, who died three months before his son was born. The picture was taken when our Mr. Vata was an early member of the KLA, around 1993."

"KLA?"

"Kosovan Liberation Army. After Tito, when Yugoslavia fell apart, and then—"

"It's fine, Lara. I don't need the modern-history lesson. The short version is, he followed in his father's footsteps."

"It looks that way," said Lara. "But it doesn't appear to connect to our site."

"He's paramilitary. Perhaps that's as far as his interest goes. Maybe it's personal."

"Back to the drawing board," said Lara. "Let's start with the key features of the site."

"You saw it yourself, Lara."

"Okay. The sword. One very special sword, a double-edged sword—obsidian, not metal—made for one warrior. Why obsidian? A mystical material. And the proportions. It fit my hand, and my reach. It was small. Small for a man."

"Men were smaller then. Everyone was smaller then."

"That's not necessarily true. Well-nourished individuals in sparsely populated areas tended to be as big at any time in history as they are now, allowing for genetic differences. People got shorter when they crowded into smaller areas and ate less well. The industrial revolution literally stunted the population's growth, in urban areas at least."

"So the sword was made for a small man."

"Or a woman," said Lara. "A warrior woman. What cultures, what legends relate to warrior women?"

"Boudica in Britain."

"Cleopatra in Egypt. That's a start. Nefertiti?"

"The Minoan Egyptian."

"And the famous Cleopatra was Hellenic. Are we widening the net, or are we confusing the issue?"

"We can't be sure this is about a woman," said Carter.

"What can we be sure of?" asked Lara. "We can be sure that the sword exists and that it's right. And, we both saw the site. The obelisk. It was classic Egyptian, eighteenth, maybe nineteenth dynasty. How much do you remember of the iconography?"

"The hieroglyphics hadn't been deciphered, just some of the basic imagery."

"And?"

"It fits neatly with the obelisk, as you describe it, but early indications were that it was specific to one period. Strange really."

"Explain."

"It was single-deity stuff," said Carter, "monotheistic."

"It's the right period for Amenhotep, the pharaoh who renamed himself Akhenaten. 'Of great use to the God Aten.' The follower of one god."

"Yes, but there was no cartouche for Akhenaten, just the imagery."

"But you're happy to date it to eighteenth dynasty?"

"Yes."

"Good," said Lara. "It's not a connection yet, but maybe we have an Egyptian-style or Egyptian-influenced culture in Britain around the time of the eighteenth dynasty. At the same time, we have a heretic pharaoh in Egypt worshipping one god, and we have the most revered consort in the history of Egyptology. Nefertiti, the most beautiful woman in the world, and Minoan."

"She couldn't have been in Britain," said Carter.

"No," said Lara. "But what if she was a model, a paragon? Boudica's dates are first-century Common Era. Britain's legendary warrior queen, and we don't have dates for the sword."

"The sword fit the niche in the stone. You saw the stone, Lara. I saw the sword in situ. It was a perfect fit."

"And the sword was in perfect condition. It might have lain in that niche for three-and-a-half thousand years. But how long has the site been buried? When did the last hands before ours handle the sword?"

"We can't know that, Lara."

"You brought up the possibility of Boudica. You must have known the dates were completely wrong."

"It was a reflex, a response to the romance of the warrior-queen idea. How many women have been written out of history over the millennia, Lara?"

Lara laughed.

"For women to have been written out of history, Carter, they would've had to have been written into history in the first place. Imagine how extraordinary a woman had to be to be written about."

"I take your point, Lara, but where does it get us?"

"Not far, right now," said Lara, "but we'll work it out. Let's get some sleep. We've got a plane to catch in the morning."

CHAPTER FIFTEEN: BEASTS
The Couchette

Lara heard the long, rising howl in her hindbrain.

It subsided, and then swelled again, beginning low, rising, breaking, and then rising once more. She could see, in her mind's eye, the stretched neck of the wolf, the toss of its head, the shape of its jaw silhouetted against the cloudless, moonlit sky.

Lara jostled and tossed. She needed to sleep. She breathed long as the sound receded. Then she relaxed.

There it was again. A perfectly pitched howl. A call, a song, bestial but sonorous, before it ascended through a scale until it was high and clear, breaking, dropping, and then rising once again.

Lara rolled over, opened her eyes, blinked, and brushed her hand over the surface she was lying on. She was surprised to find herself on a blanket of mulch and moss, a scattering of newly fallen dry autumn leaves that shielded her from the cool night air.

She stood and blinked again, her eyes adjusting to the twilight and the woodland canopy of trees, still half-clothed in their autumn leaves, red and gold.

Lara swung hard at the waist as she heard the low rumble, the start of another howl. The wolf was close.

Bcforc it had sung half its scale, a second dog had picked up the call and was answering, not far away. The pack was forming.

Lara stared hard into the shadows between the trees.

There!

Eyes of palest grey stared back at her. Head low, between and beneath slinking shoulders. Howls rang out all over the woods. This wolf was silent. It peeled back its lips, bared its teeth, its gums. Then it grinned, a wide-mouthed threat.

Lara reached for her weapon. She did not think; she acted. When the wolf struck, the blade was already in the air, anticipating the attack.

Lara took a long step forwards and swept the sword across her body in one killing blow. The swing of her arm cut the wolf through the throat, diagonally from left to right.

A rustle of leaves behind her alerted Lara to the second beast. She turned and lunged, blade held firmly out in front of her, the point disappearing into the right eye of the second wolf before it had a chance to pounce.

It was almost as if the weapon had a life of its own, as if it needed only for her hand to be curled around the grip for it to do its work. Lara did not need to exert herself, only to allow the sword to do its work. It felt weightless, magical.

A third wolf lunged and took a blow to its back that severed its spinal column. Lara skewered the fourth through the chest.

Dying, the fourth wolf screamed. The answering howl was a stuttering cry, unlike the clear, confident song, the call and return that had been the pack's pattern.

Then the howls subsided.

Lara stood for a moment, caught her breath. The sun was filtering down through the canopy, spotting the woodland floor with dappled light. It was morning twilight. Time to catch the flight to Cairo.

Lara looked down at her weapon. Why hadn't she just shot the wolves? It would have been quicker and easier. She didn't use a sword. Why was she holding the obsidian sword? The obsidian sword was in Cairo with Denny. Then she heard a guttural sound and instinctively sheathed the blade.

It wasn't the sonorous beginnings of a howl, but something new. Lara heard a gruff snort and shuffling footfalls in the mulch. She heard a tree creak, as if some heavy weight was leaning against it.

On her guard, Lara crept around the clearing, keeping among the trees, looking for signs of company. The grunting and snuffling continued.

Suddenly, she was looking into small, close-set, dark brown eyes. Sad eyes set on either side of a broad, brown, furred nose.

The eyes looked back into hers. The beast tilted its head a little and made a noise, a snuffle, a breath. It tilted its head again, blinked, and almost nodded.

Lara wanted to reach out and touch the bear. She should have been afraid, but somehow she wasn't.

She remembered that it was almost morning and that she needed to catch a plane to Cairo. She remembered that she was tired. She had a while yet. She chose a tree a little way away from the bear and sat down with her back to its trunk. She'd keep him company for a little while.

She leant back and closed her eyes.

"Lara, are you awake?"

"Careful, Carter."

"What? What's the matter, Lara?"

"Bear. Don't disturb the bear."

"Lara. Lara. Wake up. You're just dreaming, Lara."

Lara sat up and then lay back down, clutching her head.

"Damned bunks!" she said.

"You just brushed your head. There's almost clearance," said Carter. "You're fine, just startled. What were you dreaming about?"

"I haven't slept properly in days," said Lara. "I guess I was just reliving the stuff with the wolves, and there was some wish-fulfillment mixed in, wanting to get the sword back. I was killing wolves with it. It was exhilarating, actually."

"Funny," said Carter. "You were talking about bears."

"That is funny," said Lara, getting off her bunk and starting to tidy herself up. "Come to think of it, there was a bear. A beautiful brown bear."

"Do they have bears in Turkey?"

"I wasn't in Turkey. I was in, I don't know... It felt like old English woodland."

"There haven't been bears in Britain for a thousand years."

Lara laughed.

"It was a dream, Carter. Just a crazy dream."

CHAPTER SIXTEEN: THE BUYER
Cairo

Le Riad in Old Cairo was only the second hotel that Lara and Carter visited.

"Can I leave a message for Mr. Denny Sampson, please?" Lara asked the desk clerk.

"Mr. Sampson is in his room," said the clerk. "He has another visitor, but I can telephone, if you'd care to wait."

Lara and Carter exchanged glances.

"No, thank you," said Lara. "I don't want to disturb him. May we wait? If you could let us know when his visitor has left."

"Of course, Madam," said the clerk. "Can I offer you some refreshment? Some tea, perhaps?"

"Thank you," said Lara. "That would be most welcome."

Lara and Carter found a cool, quiet corner, out of the way, under some shuttered windows. Lara could see the entrance to the hotel, so could catch a glimpse of people entering or leaving, but unless visitors had a very good look around, she was unlikely to be spotted. Carter sat opposite her, his back to the door.

"Nice place," said Carter as they sipped strong, aromatic tea from tiny, coloured glass bowls.

"You can say a lot of terrible things about Denny, and I do, but the man knows history, and he has great taste."

"I've never been to Cairo old town."

Lara looked shocked.

"That shouldn't surprise you," said Carter. "I've worked out here—everybody has—but when it comes to hotels, it's the pick of the cheap and cheerful, the crowded, the modern, and the dull." He laughed.

"Remind me to show you around, if we get the chance."

Carter laughed again.

"What are the chances of that happening?"

"Speaking of chances," said Lara. "What are the chances of one of us recognising Denny's buyer if he happens to walk through that door?"

She raised her half-full glass of tea towards the entrance, and Carter looked over his shoulder. "Come and sit beside me. I want your eyes on this."

"Do you think we'll recognise him?" asked Carter, switching seats.

"If we do, it could give us a clue as to why the sword is such an important artefact," said Lara. "Why men are willing to kill for it."

"The sale could be happening right now," said Carter.

"Then we'll have a new lead to follow," said Lara. "More tea?"

"Thanks."

"Shh," said Lara, ten minutes later.

Carter stopped speculating on the subject of women warriors, mid-sentence, and listened. He heard what Lara had heard.

The sound of Denny's distinctive laughter filled the atrium as he jogged down the last few steps from the rooms above and walked towards the hotel entrance.

Then they heard a woman's voice, and Lara flinched.

"So, you'll meet me tomorrow, Mr. Sampson. You know where and when. If you can get me that footage of Lara Croft at Zizek's auction, I'll trust your authentication of the piece, and we can complete the transaction."

"Miss Croft is a fine woman," said Denny.

"She's arrogant and obnoxious," said the woman. "In short, she's a delight."

They both laughed.

Denny's back came into view as the two figures embraced lightly, and then the woman was gone before Carter had got a good look at her.

Denny stood for a moment longer, his back still to Lara and Carter, and then turned back into the hotel.

"I don't believe it," murmured Lara.

"What? Who was he with? You know her?" asked Carter.

"Florence Race," said Lara. "Manipulative, conniving, hateful Florence Race."

"You want to follow her?"

"I want to punch her in the face," said Lara. "Or worse."

She saw the way Carter was looking at her.

"Long story," she said. "Old story. Bad story."

"You want to talk about it?"

"No need for details," Lara replied, shaking her head. "Last time we met, she went out of her way to double-cross me and try to kill me as many times as possible. She's absolutely irredeemable, and the last person I wanted to find mixed up in this."

"Does this change things?" Carter asked. "Do we need to rethink?"

"No need," said Lara. "This is what it is, and we're in it now. We can deal with Denny."

Lara got up from her seat, and stepped behind a pillar from where she got a view of the very friendly, very efficient desk clerk. She waited until the clerk had turned her back to attend to something, and gestured for Carter to follow her. They crossed the atrium and started up the stairs without being seen.

"We don't know what room he's in," said Carter.

"He only ever takes two rooms here," said Lara. "He'll be in one of them."

Lara stood in front of the door with her right hand casually resting on the grip of the Sig nine in its thigh holster. Carter was standing where she had placed him, to one side of the door, against the wall, out of sight of anyone opening the door.

She knocked. Two light raps. Carter waited with bated breath. When there was no answer for ten seconds, he let the breath go. As they made their way to the next room, Carter said, "Are you sure you want to do this?"

"I don't think I've ever been more sure that I wanted to do something," said Lara.

"Okay, then," said Carter as they stopped in front of a second door. He took up his position. Lara rested her right hand on the grip of her gun, and knocked on the door with her left.

They heard noises from inside, and then the door was opened.

"Lara," said Denny.

Before he could say anything else, Lara had drawn her gun and its barrel was pressed to Denny's forehead. He raised his hands in a gesture of surrender.

"That's me," said Lara. "The proverbial bad penny."

Carter stepped into the doorway beside her.

"Back up, Denny," said Lara.

Denny made a move to turn around.

"There's nothing behind you, Denny," said Lara, "and I want to see your face. Now, back up."

Denny stumbled backwards into the room, Lara's gun pressed against his forehead the entire time. Carter stepped into the room behind them and closed the door. He moved past Lara, and she tossed him a cable tie. He took hold of Denny's hands, and secured them behind his back. Then he sat him down on the bed.

Lara handed Carter her other gun, and he trained it on Denny. She lowered her own weapon, but didn't holster it.

"You seem upset, Lara," said Denny, trying a half-smile on her.

"Upset doesn't begin to cover it," said Lara.

"That's a pity," said Denny, "because you were just the person I wanted to see."

"This must have something to do with your dealings with the despicable Miss Race," said Lara.

"Oh," said Denny. "You found out about that, huh?"

"You left us in that bloody fortress in the middle of nowhere to die," said Lara. "If Vata hadn't killed us, the wolves would have."

"And the hyenas would have devoured the evidence," said Denny. He laughed. "There isn't a scrape on earth you couldn't wriggle your way out of, Croft."

"You double-crossed me," said Lara.

"That's what I do," said Denny.

"With Florence Race."

"You make it sound like a delicious love triangle," said Denny.

"You're a pig," said Lara.

"So you said," said Denny. "But this little piggy can take you to market."

"What the hell's that supposed to mean?" asked Lara.

"It means that I'll scratch your back if you scratch mine," said Denny. "Okay, so I set you up. If you do me one small favour, I'll do you a big favour in return."

It was Lara's turn to laugh.

"You're bound and I've got a gun trained on you, Denny, and you still think you stand a chance," she said. "What do I have to do to convince you that you've screwed with me for the last time?"

"Okay, Lara. You win this round. I like you. What do you want?"

"You can start by telling me what you've got planned," said Lara, pulling up a chair and sitting in front of Denny.

"Just free my hands, and we'll have a nice long chat about it," said Denny.

"Not a chance," said Lara, "and keep that gun on him, Carter."

"Okay, okay," said Denny, "but don't expect me to cut you any slack in the future."

"Assuming you have a future," said Lara. "Now talk."

Denny sighed.

"I'm going to sell the artefact to Florence Race," he said. "She has deep pockets, but she wants assurances."

"That's why she was asking for footage of me at the auction," said Lara.

"I told her that you'd seen the artefact and authenticated it. That you would have bid for it at Zizek's market, if I hadn't taken Strand and made him pull it from the sale."

"And she believed you?" asked Lara.

"I'm a convincing storyteller," said Denny. "Mostly because I stay close to the truth. But she wanted proof. She trusts your judgment. She talked about you so much, I wonder if she has an obsession with you, Croft. Perhaps there's a touch of the Sapphic about Miss Race." Denny laughed.

"Well, good for her," said Lara. "But if you have the footage, you don't need me."

"I don't have the footage," said Denny. "There is no footage. Zizek's clients are not public people. The first hint of surveillance cameras and no one would show up for his little spectaculars. I was bluffing."

"Great," said Lara.

"Great that you're here," said Denny. "You can come with me to the meeting tomorrow and tell her yourself that the sword's the real deal."

"Like I said, not a chance," said Lara.

"Hear me out," said Denny. "Here's my half of the bargain. I tell you everything you need to know so that when the transaction's complete—when the money's safely in my pocketbook and the sword's in Miss Race's possession—you get the chance to take it back."

"By force?" asked Lara.

"Didn't you just take out a pack of wolves?" asked Denny, "Oh...and a pack of Wolves!" He broke into his belly laugh, coughed twice, and composed himself, with Lara and Carter looking on in disbelief. "See, Croft, anything can be funny."

"I could just take the sword off you now, by force," said Lara.

"You could if it was here," said Denny. He tried to shrug, but the gesture was limited by the cable tie securing his wrists. Lara raised her gun and pressed it once more into Denny's forehead.

"Search the room, Carter," she said, "thoroughly."

Carter searched the room. He emptied drawers and cupboards, checked Denny's luggage, and then went into the bathroom to search there. He returned empty-handed.

"And the bed," said Lara.

Carter took Denny by the arm and helped him to his feet. Lara stood, too, keeping the barrel of her gun in contact with Denny's forehead at all times.

Carter stripped the bed and checked the pillows, the mattress, and the divan. Then he checked under the bed.

"It's not here, Lara," he said.

Carter sat Denny on the stripped bed, and trained his gun on him once more. Lara lowered her gun and took the seat opposite Denny.

"Where's the sword, Denny?" she asked.

Denny laughed again.

"I'd have to be really incredibly stupid to tell you that," said Denny. "The sword's the ace up my sleeve. If I told you where it was, that would be the end of this delicious game. This is the most fun I've had in years."

"I'm not leaving here without that sword, Denny," said Lara.

"Come on, Croft. It's an adventure. I've heard stories about you and Florence Race. Some of them must be true. Take the sword off her. Be a team player."

"I'm not on your team, Denny. What's Race's agenda with the sword?"

"I sell things; people buy them. What they do with them once they've handed over the money is their business."

"So, maybe Florence knows something about the sword that we don't," said Carter.

"Listen to Bell," said Denny. "You know he makes sense."

Lara leant closer to Denny, until their noses were almost touching.

"Okay, Denny, just tell me where and when you arranged to meet Florence Race."

"Tomorrow, twilight, KV62."

"The Valley of the Kings," said Carter.

"Where else?" said Lara. "Tomorrow, then. Carter?"

"You won't join me at Le Riad?" asked Denny.

"I have my own haunts, Denny," said Lara. "And right now I think it's best for you if there's a little distance between us. Thanks for the information. It had damn well better be more reliable than the company you keep."

Denny pretended to look hurt.

"Oh, come now, Croft," he said. "You're part of the company I keep."

"Not anymore," Lara replied, "and never again."

CHAPTER SEVENTEEN: CONNECTIONS
Old Cairo

"KV62," said Carter as they took the desert road out of Cairo to the Valley of the Kings.

"You know what that is, right?" asked Lara.

"The tomb of Tutankhamen. You're disappointed."

"On the contrary," said Lara. "It tells me more about the buyer, and it helps to cement our theory. You've been concentrating far too hard on the London dig, Carter. You should get out more."

"What did I miss?" asked Carter.

"Florence Race obviously knows about the latest findings at KV62 and has a keen, possibly obsessive, interest in Nefertiti. Women like her are often man-haters. They look for strong female role models and find them in figures like Boudica, Helen, Gwynnever, Joan of Arc, Elizabeth the First, Wu Zetian, Aoife MacMurrough..."

"Well, it's going to take a while to drive out to the pyramids, so you've got plenty of time to fill me in," said Carter.

Their rented Land Cruiser, a battered veteran of tourist transportation, thundered down the dusty highway. Lara was driving, her sunglasses pushed up onto the top of her head.

"I don't know if archaeologists will ever be finished with the Valley of the Kings," said Lara. "It's one of the most extraordinary burial sites on the planet. KV62 is one of the most mysterious tombs."

"One of the most complete and richest finds in the history of archaeology."

"And we're still learning about it," said Lara. "We're still processing the anomalies and finding new areas of interest. Grave goods and paraphernalia found in Tut's tomb might have belonged to a different pharaoh. There are also inconsistencies in the murals, suggesting that his burial chamber was actually intended for someone else. It's all borne out by the fact that Tutankhamen died young and suddenly."

"I've heard some of this speculation before," said Carter. "So, what's new?"

"The latest infrared scans on the tomb show new cavities in the structure that suggest more burial chambers," said Lara, slowing the truck down as they came up behind a convoy of slow-moving sightseer buses. "Archaeologists have been looking for Nefertiti's tomb for decades, hundreds of years, maybe since she was interred."

"And somebody now thinks she was buried in KV62?"

"That's the latest speculation."

"How realistic is it, Lara, in your opinion?"

"From what I've read, it's got to be possible. The relationship to Tutankhamen is close. Some claim that Nefertiti was, in fact, Tutankhamen's mother."

"I thought there was DNA that proved otherwise," said Carter.

"Reading DNA sequences is an art as much as it's a science," said Lara. "And relationships within dynasties in Egypt were complex. There is a theory that generations of cousins procreating produce similar patterns of DNA in third- and fourth-generation offspring as siblings produce in their progeny."

The road ahead was clear. Lara changed down and accelerated to overtake the trundling buses.

"Okay, explain that," said Carter. "Third and fourth...?"

"If Akhenaten and Nefertiti were cousins who produced offspring, and they were the result of parents and grandparents who were also cousins, they could produce a child who appeared to be the genetic product of Akhenaten and his sister."

"You're kidding!"

"DNA is complicated, and it's never been clear who Tutankhamen's mother was. It's an anomaly. Dynastic records for all the major civilisations in the world are incredibly complete, so why don't we know King Tut's parentage? Nefertiti was Akhenaten's favoured queen and most powerful consort. Why wouldn't it be her?"

"You make a convincing argument."

"Not one I'm entirely convinced by yet," said Lara, "but it's fun to speculate. And it can only be a matter of time before we know."

"And the sword?"

"It's the right era, and it was found on a site consistent with the monotheistic beliefs and iconography of Akhenaten's rule in Egypt," said Lara.

"But the site was not in Egypt, and we're speculating that the sword was made for a woman. This weapon didn't belong to Akhenaten."

"What do you know about Neferneferuaten?"

"The rumoured female pharaoh?" asked Carter. "That sounds like something Florence Race would love."

"There are several theories that Neferneferuaten was Nefertiti. She falls in the correct regnal order, between Akhenaten and Tutankhamen. And she's associated both with Akhenaten as possible co-regent, and, obliquely, at least, with a monotheistic religious base. There are also legends of Nefertiti as a warrior with military evidence associated with Karnak."

"Then our sword is her sword," said Carter.

"I think we have to rule that out because of location," said Lara. "But we're archaeologists. We don't always deal in absolutes. Sometimes we deal in ideas. Nefertiti, the great queen, is a wonderful idea, and so is the sword."

"So Florence Race wants the sword as much for what it represents as for what it is?" asked Carter.

"Who knows?" said Lara. "We've been talking for hours. I would draw your attention to another wonderful Egyptian artefact in London, though. We call it 'Cleopatra's Needle.'"

"So?" said Carter. "We know what it is, we know where it came from, and we know it didn't arrive at its current location until, what, about 1820?"

"We also know that there are three of them," said Lara, "and that the other two are in Paris and New York."

"What are you saying, Lara? That there are more swords? More sites? More what?"

"I don't know what I'm saying," said Lara. "We're just speculating, right?"

"I guess so," said Carter.

Off the highway, they lurched along a rough track, kicking ochre dust up in a cloud behind them.

"This is it," said Lara, "and it looks like someone's already here." She rolled the grubby Land Cruiser to a halt and switched off the engine. With the air-con off, the heat became oppressive very quickly.

They got out into the sunlight. Lara flipped down her shades.

There was one other vehicle parked up twenty metres away.

"That's got to be Denny's car," she said. "Let's take a look around, but let's try not to get noticed."

Carter looked around, but there was nowhere to stash the Land Cruiser. The landscape was flat and open. There were no buildings to hide it behind and no other cars to hide it among.

"It's going to be tough to go unnoticed around here," he said.

"But if they can see us, we can see them," said Lara. "We'll be fine. No talking, and move as quietly as you can."

Lara and Carter walked out to KV62, surprised by the lack of any security. Florence had obviously found a way to clear the site, either by force or, more likely, by persuasion. Lara suspected bribery or some other form of coercion or corruption.

They approached the tomb at an angle, avoiding a line of sight to the entrance. Then they turned at the last moment, to get a side view of the entrance. The angle was tight. They could see across the entrance, but not into it. They were less than twenty metres away. Lara lay flat on her belly on the sand, and Carter followed suit.

Three figures were milling around the entrance, stepping back and forth, into and out of view.

"It's Denny," whispered Lara. "I'd recognise that gait anywhere."

"What do we do?"

"We wait," whispered Lara. "We need eyes on Florence Race before we can be confident that Denny brought the sword and plans to go ahead with the deal."

They lay in silence for a few minutes as Denny and his entourage paced. Lara kept her eyes on Denny, but Denny was gazing at the tomb.

There appeared to be no one else anywhere close by.

Twilight did not last long in Egypt. The sky was streaked with flashes of orange light as the vast red ball sank fast below the horizon.

"She's late," whispered Lara.

Bright, yellow light suddenly flooded out of the tomb entrance, illuminating Denny and his party.

"Gentlemen," said Florence Race. Her voice travelled easily through the clear night air. It was as sonorous and insistent as usual.

She had made a grand entrance, emerging from Tutankhamen's tomb, as if into a spotlight, right in front of Denny. She was dressed for the part: the stylish, elegant tourist, understated, but with a few touches of practicality that only a seasoned explorer would know. She was effortlessly chic. Lara wouldn't have been surprised if a team of international fashion photographers had emerged with her, shooting images for some designer perfume campaign. *Nefertiti, pour femme.*

The smell of treachery, more like. Nevertheless, Florence's vanity was a godsend to Lara, who could see every detail of the exchange in the bright, yellow light emanating from the tomb.

"And it's a pleasure to see you, Miss Race," said Denny, offering his hand. Florence ignored it.

"Have you brought the merchandise?" asked Florence.

"That's what we're here for," said Denny. "To do business. Have you got the money?"

"How could you doubt it?" said Florence.

Lara thought that Denny's laugh could probably be heard for miles around.

"Then let's go into my office, shall we?" said Florence, gesturing towards the entrance to KV62.

"After you," said Denny. "Ladies first."

"I'll keep you where I can see you, thank you, Mr. Sampson," said Florence. "Your reputation precedes you."

Denny chuckled and waved his entourage ahead of him. They'd barely taken a step when Florence stopped them.

"You can leave your lackeys out here to enjoy the cool of the evening air. They can stretch their legs before the long drive back to Cairo."

Denny hesitated for just a moment.

"Okay," he said. "He stays here, but Sandler is coming with me."

Race shrugged.

Denny signalled to Sandler to hand him the duffel bag the bodyguard had carried from the car. Denny shouldered it and then took the lead into KV62.

"Now what?" whispered Carter.

"Just wait. Listen," Lara whispered back.

They watched as the third man, with nothing else to do, kicked up some dust for a minute or two, and then decided to walk back to the car. The sun had set, so once he was out of Florence's spotlight, it was hard to see him. After another minute or two, Lara heard a car door open and then close.

"Now, we go in after them," said Lara.

"Into the hornet's nest?" asked Carter.

"I'm not afraid of Denny Sampson or Florence Race," said Lara, "and I've got a pretty impressive sting of my own. Just follow my lead."

"You're the boss, Lara."

"Yes, I bloody well am."

Lara strode through the entrance to KV62, Carter following behind her. Whatever guards Florence had chosen to employ, she was keeping them close, and hadn't left a sentry or any kind of defence at the entrance to the tomb. That was her first mistake. Lara simply walked in, holding a gun in each outstretched hand.

Approaching the end of dimly lit passages, Lara could see the doorway to a better-lit antechamber. The air was dry, and smelt faintly of talcum and centuries.

A few metres back, Lara slowed to a stop, her back to the wall, and Carter followed suit.

"Are you ready for this?" asked Lara.

"For what?" asked Carter, concern in his voice.

"We're going to have a lot of enemies in that room," said Lara. "Florence Race and her lackeys, and Denny Sampson and Sandler. I expect a standoff. So, are you ready?"

"You're just going to walk in?" said Carter.

"It's Florence Race," said Lara. "Brazen confrontation seems like the best plan."

Carter drew his gun.

"If you say so."

"Florence," said Lara, standing in the doorway, guns raised. Heads turned, and the local guards that Florence had employed looked startled. Lara took the opportunity to disable two of them with shots to the shoulders before the others were able to get their weapons up. Two fewer shooters to deal with if...when the time came.

"I'm delighted to see you, Lara," said Florence. "I didn't expect it."

"Denny suggested I should come along for the ride," said Lara, stepping into the room, followed by Carter, wielding his weapon in a two-handed grip. "And I'm a big fan of the Valley, so I couldn't resist."

Florence smiled, and studied Lara's face hard.

"Not a mention," she said, smiling, "not even a mention. Not even a hint."

"Of?" asked Lara sweetly.

Race laughed.

"Our last tête-à-tête, of course, sweetie," she said. "Or do the guns give you away?"

Lara shrugged.

"I'm a professional, Flo," she replied. "Just like you. We win some, we lose some, and sometimes the work gets messy. You put that behind you, write it off, and carry on. Or you spend your life nursing butt-hurt and achieving nothing."

"So, we're good?" asked Race.

"I'm great," said Lara, "but, like you said, I'm the one holding the guns."

Race laughed again.

"Look around you," she said, gesturing at her guards, who now had Carter and Lara in their gun sights. "You must realise this is me winning for the second time in a row. After all, you're here, Lara!"

Lara smiled.

"Law of probability, Flo," she replied. "Winning streaks don't last forever. And you haven't got this one in the bag yet. Didn't your mother teach you not to count your chickens until they were hatched?"

"Is it me, or is this entire conversation loaded with hot, suggestive meaning?" rumbled Denny, giving Carter a knowing look.

"Just you, Denny," said Carter.

"You've seen the sword?" Florence asked Lara.

"It's magnificent," said Lara.

"Is it as beautiful as the photographs?"

"You can see for yourself," said Lara, holstering one of her guns to remove her shades.

Florence turned to her guards.

"Leave us," she said, "and some of you guard the entrance, so we're not disturbed." Three of the guards retreated into the passage. Several others moved into the adjacent room, the infamous burial chamber that had once contained the grave goods and sarcophagus of Tutankhamen.

"You, stay," said Florence to the guard nearest to her.

"Put your gun away, Lara. You're very welcome here," said Florence, gesturing for the one remaining guard to shoulder his weapon. Lara and Carter holstered their weapons. "Now, show me the goods, Denny," said Florence, without further preamble. "The sword last."

Denny dropped the duffel bag onto a large table that was partly covered in old books and maps, research documents, and dozens of pages of handwritten notes.

The first object out of the bag was a fat cylinder, about thirty centimetres long and with one rounded end. It looked like some kind of primitive missile. It was clearly old, and military. The colour and letter/number markings suggested to Lara that it was probably Second World War, and German.

Florence tutted.

Lara turned sharply to Carter.

"You said Strand stole other artefacts from the site...but this?" she said, gesturing at the object.

"I had no idea he'd taken it," said Carter. "I don't know if anyone did."

Then, Denny removed some smaller items from the duffel bag, wrapped in unbleached cloth and sealed in specimen bags. Florence began to unlock the bags and peel back layers of cloth to reveal shards of exquisite pottery and a small, gold brooch, but she soon became impatient. She dropped the finds back in their bags, and pocketed them.

"Now," said Denny, "la pièce de résistance!" Denny withdrew a long plastic tube from the duffel bag with a theatrical flourish and placed it carefully on the table. Florence looked at it for a moment, and then set to work.

Florence unclicked the covers from both ends of the tube and put them on one side. She reached into one end of the tube, and then the other. Holding the tube steady on the table, she carefully withdrew about half of the wrapped object from within. When it was halfway out, she placed her other hand under it, and using both hands, removed the sword entirely from its packaging.

"Move that," she said, nodding at the tube, and Denny lifted it off the table, making room for Florence to put the sword down. Then she began carefully removing the several layers of packing material until the sword was exposed.

It was exactly as Lara remembered it, exactly as it had been when she had wielded it in her dream. She stared so intently at it for so long that she had to blink hard.

In that blink she saw the woods again. She was sitting, watching her bear with its soft brown eyes. When she opened her eyes, the soft brown eyes didn't belong to a bear, but to a man, and she was not sitting in the woods, but standing in a great hall, the space dominated by a vast circular table. The brown-eyed man smiled at her, and left her side to join other men milling around the space, greeting one another, their breastplates clanging together as they embraced like brothers.

She let her hand rest on the hilt of her own sword, hanging at her waist, and blinked again.

"Are you all right, Lara? You look pale."

Lara turned to look at Carter, and then back down at the sword that Florence was now holding in her hands.

"This terrible lighting's enough to make anyone look pale," Lara said. She swallowed hard.

"It looks like it was made yesterday," said Florence.

"It wasn't," said Lara.

"I'm so glad you're here," said Florence. "If I trust anyone, it's you, Lara."

"The feeling isn't mutual," said Lara.

Florence made a mocking "meow" sound.

"Now, now, ladies," said Denny. "Let's not have any pit-fighting...not that I wouldn't enjoy watching you two brawling." He laughed one of his belly laughs, and it echoed around the chamber, bringing one of Florence's lackeys scurrying in from the passage.

Florence turned her right hand around the grip of the sword, dropped her left hand from supporting the weight of the blade, and lunged, throwing her left arm out for balance. The lackey did not see the attack coming. The blade pierced his torso just below his sternum. It entered his body without resistance, and he seemed to crumple around it. There was no sound, and almost no blood, and then the body simply slid off the blade and onto the floor of the chamber.

Lara had her gun drawn and pointed at Florence as the sword entered the guard's body.

"It's perfect," said Florence, straightening up. "No effort. It found its own target. Look," she said, holding the blade up for them all to see, "not a drop of blood on the blade."

Everyone but Lara simply stared.

"That's how you test the merchandise?" asked Denny. For once, his voice had lost its weight.

"You're utterly detestable, aren't you?" said Lara. She didn't holster her gun again, not while Florence was armed with the sword.

"It's as if it was made for me," said Florence.

"I think you underestimate your skill with weapons," said Lara. "How long have you been training for, Florence?"

"I will be the next great warrior queen," said Florence. "It is my fate."

"So you were right, Lara," said Carter.

"You predicted this?" asked Florence.

"You're too filled with a sense of your own importance, Florence," said Lara. "I merely suggested that you might look for female role models. I recognised your pathology. I knew you'd identify with legendary women."

"Not just women," said Florence. "Warrior queens, great leaders. A golden civilisation that outlived every patriarchy, a global culture of Matriarchs. You've heard about them, Lara. You just haven't seen the connections."

"Nefertiti, Boudicca, Elizabeth," said Lara.

"And Guinevere," said Florence. Lara could hear from the way Race said the name that she favoured the Victorian modernisation.

Denny coughed.

"I'm all for the sisterhood, but I can't stand around here listening to girl talk, and we haven't completed our transaction, Miss Race."

Florence transferred the sword to her left hand, and took her smartphone out of her breast pocket. She keyed into it for a few seconds.

"There," she said. "The transaction is complete. I'll have to—"

Denny's phone sounded with the first four notes of Beethoven's Fifth Symphony, and he checked his messages.

"Indeed it is," he said. "Thank you, Miss Race. It's been a pleasure doing business with you."

He looked at the corpse of the lackey curled up on the chamber floor.

"For me, at least," he added.

Dan Abnett & Nik Vincent

CHAPTER EIGHTEEN: THE SWORD
Nefertiti's Tomb

"You can go, Mr. Sampson," said Florence, "you and your sidekick. And you, too."

Florence nodded at Carter, then looked at Lara.

"But you, Lara, you're special, you're one of us. Stay with me, Lara. I have a place for you."

"A place with you?" asked Lara. "I'm my own boss. I don't work for anyone, and I still have you at the end of my gun."

"This isn't work, Lara. This is life, a purpose."

"You're not making a lot of sense, Florence."

"Go," said Florence, waving a hand at Denny and Carter, as if shooing them away. "I want to talk to Lara. This is none of your concern."

"I'll go when Lara tells me to," said Carter.

Florence flexed her grip on the sword, and the blade twitched in response.

"Oh, for goodness' sake, Florence, put that down," said Lara, "and stop being so melodramatic. It doesn't suit you. Carter and Denny, stay. It's a long drive back to Cairo across the desert in the dark, and a convoy's the safest way to do it. Nobody's going anywhere."

Florence hesitated for a moment. She gazed into Lara's eyes, and Lara gazed back, her expression unflinching. Florence adjusted her belt and then fed the sword through it. She was not going to let it go. Then she quickly sorted through the notes on the table, collecting some of them together in her arms, along with a couple of the books.

"Right now, I plan to take a tour of the tomb, and you and the sword are coming with me," said Lara. "I don't trust you, Flo, and I'm not letting you out of my sight."

"Then we go alone," said Florence. "I want you to see something. Guards!" she called. Two guards appeared from the adjacent room, and three more from the passage. "Hold these men."

"Carter, you're in charge," said Lara. Carter drew his gun in a standoff with the guards.

Florence tutted.

"Because this isn't uncomfortable, at all," said Denny.

Lara shrugged at Denny.

"After you, Florence," she said, and the two women walked into the burial chamber. The air was cool, almost clammy, though Lara knew there was no moisture in it. The echoes of their footsteps and movement seemed soft, as if they had been swaddled.

The chamber was exactly as Lara remembered it, apart from a tarpaulin that covered the north wall. Lara could see, in her mind's eye, the famous murals covering the wall, of Tutankhamen journeying into the afterlife and being greeted by Osiris. The wall was divided into three story sections, which were remarkably complete and extraordinarily beautiful.

As Florence drew back the tarpaulin, Lara braced herself to see the murals. The sight always took your breath away.

There was nothing there. The wall had gone.

"What have you done?" gasped Lara. "This is desecration!"

"You're wrong, Lara!" Florence bit back. She threw a switch on a cable hanging from the ceiling, and the black hole where the mural had once been was lit up to show a cavity. Another room. A new room.

"Oh my God..." Lara murmured, staring.

"Tut was nothing, a no one," said Florence. "Men have worshipped a useless, sickly boy for a hundred years, and all the time there were women who knew more, women who knew better. There have been women who knew better for three thousand years, Lara. Women like us."

Lara had taken two steps forwards, but hesitated at the opening.

"Go in," said Florence.

"After you," said Lara. "I like to know where you are."

Florence smiled at Lara and stepped through the hole in the wall.

"Come into my parlour," she said.

Lara could not believe her eyes.

The room was bigger than Tutankhamen's burial chamber. It was larger, squarer, and twice as high. Every surface was richly, ornately painted, much more crisply and precisely than Tut's burial chamber. Nefertiti's image was repeated over and over again, and every time her likeness appeared, she was wearing the pharaoh's headpiece.

The pharaoh's headpiece, Lara thought.

Lara checked to make sure she was right, scanning the walls, top to bottom and side to side. In every image, Nefertiti was not wearing the flattened, black headgear of the consort, but the vast, blue-domed crown of the pharaoh. She was depicted bathed in the rays of the Sun God and even ascended into its great golden orb.

There were hieroglyphics, too, and cartouches dotted around the room. Lara couldn't read them, as they would need a great deal of scholarly study to decipher accurately, but they, too, were clean and complete, and clearly told the stories of Nefertiti's life's work.

Lara noted the guards stationed around the room, but knew they were no threat to her while she had her gun trained on their mistress. Her attention turned to the grave goods and burial paraphernalia that lined the walls and covered much of the floor. Everything from the grandest statues to the smallest jars were gilded and painted. They were absolutely staggering and, unlike Tutankhamen's chamber, where everything had been famously found piled up and haphazard, as if stacked in a hurry at the last moment, this material was perfectly arranged.

It was a recreation of a royal chamber, laid out with ritual precision, exactly as it would have been in a palace in life. This was how pharaonic burial ceremonies were supposed to work. Like stage sets, like necropolis echoes of real life. The queen's home, perfectly recreated in the tomb for her use in the afterlife, containing everything she could possibly need.

Lara crouched down in wonder to study an ornate gold casket. She suddenly stood up again.

"Beautiful," she said. "But this is just the anteroom. Where's the burial chamber? I want to see the sarcophagus."

"Yes, Lara," said Florence, "this is only the beginning. You're in for a real treat. Even you won't believe how magnificent it is!" Florence laughed, an odd, tinkling sound. "Follow me."

Lara had not seen the opening in the far wall, beyond the piles of grave goods.

Nefertiti's sarcophagus stood in a dedicated burial chamber. The walls of the room were covered in gold, lined with blue the colour of the pharaoh's crown, and inscribed with the Aten's sun-ray symbol. It was beautiful, simple, elegant. The shrine, too, was blue and gold. It stood at the foot of the sarcophagus and was bigger and more ornate than King Tut's shrine.

There was an eternal silence that was almost penetrating.

The shrine was decorated with more symbols of the Aten, and with the likeness of Nefertiti, but there were none of the usual pantheon of gods of protection.

"This is monotheistic," whispered Lara.

"Always," said Florence. "The Matriarchy, one god, one universal culture, always and everywhere."

The blue canopic jars that sat on top of the shrine within an ornate gilded gallery had lids carved in the shape of Nefertiti's bust, complete with the pharaoh's crown.

"So she *was* pharaoh," said Lara.

"She was more than that," said Florence.

"Who knows about this?" asked Lara.

"Those whose right it is to know," said Florence. "Those who need to know. I know, and you know."

"And your lackeys know," said Lara, gesturing at the men guarding the room.

"They can be silenced," said Florence. "There's more, Lara. Let me show you the rest."

Lara wanted to touch the sarcophagus as she walked its length. She hadn't even had a chance to examine it, but she'd come for Florence and the sword.

The treasury chamber, situated at one end of the burial chamber, came as the biggest shock to Lara. She stood absolutely still, rooted to the spot as soon as she was through the portal. It was the first time she and Florence had been alone since entering the chambers. There were no guards stationed in the room.

"Yes, let's stop for a moment," said Florence. "I want you to look at some of this." She stood close to Lara and started to riffle through the notes that she had brought with her.

"It's the same," said Lara, half her attention constantly on Florence Race. "It's almost exactly the same." She gathered herself, and walked around the room, the duplicate of the cyst chamber under Candle Lane. The dimensions of the room were the same. The obelisk stood in the same position, with the altar in front of it. The inscriptions on the vast stone pieces looked almost identical to those on the obelisk and altar in the sister chamber, although this was local Egyptian stone, not British. It was also gilded.

Lara ran a finger along the groove in the altar stone. The sword was missing. Everything was so complete, so perfect, so pristine, but the sword now hanging from Florence's belt had been nestled in the altar under Candle Lane. This altar should have its own sword, surely. There was nothing.

"What did you do with the sword, Florence?"

Florence looked up at Lara, and then at her hand resting in the groove on the altar.

"There is but one sword remaining," said Florence. "I need only one. There is only one culture, one Matriarchy, one warrior queen who flourishes in different eras, in different civilisations across the world. With one great cause."

"Your cause?" asked Lara.

"Our cause," said Florence.

Lara laughed.

"You and I have nothing in common."

"They sought *you* out, and they found *me*," said Florence. "I saw who they were. I saw women in need of a new queen. It is time, you see? At first, they employed me to find the artefact, to acquire it for them. I thought there might be a shortcut."

She got up and walked to a finds crate nearby. She opened the lid and took something out.

"Look at this," she said. "I thought I could make a copy and use that."

She was unwrapping another sword. It was a fine piece, the sort of thing an expert craftsman would make if he'd only been given a description and had never actually seen the original.

Florence held it up. The modern copy glinted under the harsh light of industrial bulbs.

"I used every detail I could gather," she said. "Measurements, dimensions of the altar groove, every scrap of knowledge about the original sword. I used a local craftsman and sourced obsidian from the right part of the world. I thought I could make an accurate surrogate, then charge it by performing the same rituals."

"Add a vital modern component to an ancient intricate mechanism?" said Lara.

Florence nodded.

"Exactly. Like replacing the broken mainspring in an otherwise intact antique timepiece. But it was hard work, and there were no guarantees the replica would suffice. Then I learned what Strand had brought out of the London site."

She tossed the sword copy back into its crate disdainfully.

"I didn't need the surrogate anymore. I could use the real thing."

Race paused and looked at Lara for a moment.

"I started out doing what they wanted, doing their research and acquisition for them, until I saw the beauty and sense of it. They are not worthy. They are soft and weak. They are liberal. They think they can rule the world with love and compassion and understanding. They will be my velvet glove, but they need me. I am the iron fist at their centre."

"You're kidding me," said Lara.

"I want you at my side, Lara. You're one of the strongest women I know. You're clever and ruthless and independent. You know how to get what you want. We need women like you. You will be my lieutenant."

"Like I said, I don't work for anyone," said Lara. "And this site is too important, not just the tomb of the Pharaoh Nefertiti, but the connection to the second site under London."

"Seven sites," said Florence. "There are seven sites, seven great ages of the Matriarchy. Seven is the number of perfection, completeness, effectiveness. There are seven obelisks, seven altars. This is the number of women, the number of the continents, the number of life."

Lara gazed at Florence in amazement.

"Where are you getting this stuff from?" she asked.

Florence waved her sheaf of notes at Lara.

"It's all here."

Lara bent, took the notes from Florence's hands, and began to skim them.

"Gwynnever's sword is the last in existence," said Florence. This time, Lara could hear her form the name in its old, true form. There was no one around except Lara to hear her, no glib show to put on. "I had to bring it here, to the home of the first, the greatest queen. I have to perform the ritual... I have to perform it with you."

CHAPTER NINETEEN: THE RITUAL
The Treasury Cyst

All seven sites were there, listed in the notes that Florence had given her: the Andean coast of Peru, the Okanagan Desert in Canada, the Nullarbor Plain in Australia, London, the Valley of the Kings, Lizhou in China...

"There's a site in Antarctica!" exclaimed Lara.

"This culture goes back into prehistory," said Florence. "To before recorded time, thousands of years into our past."

"To a time when Antartica was far enough north to sustain any kind of population?" asked Lara.

"You should not doubt," said Florence. "I know you have seen things."

Lara sighed. It was true. She had seen things. The long drive, the extraordinary sites, and Florence's demanding company were beginning to get to her. She closed her eyes and rubbed them with the heel of her left hand.

Her palms felt strange, like chamois leather, and there was a sudden draught on her cheeks. She dropped her hands from her face and opened her eyes. She was sitting in a circle of women, and the women were looking at her. They all had coppery-brown skin and black eyes, and they were all smiling gently at her. The women wore soft, pale skins, drank from bone beakers, and laughed together. There was a plan. They looked to Lara for guidance.

She was about to say something.

She blinked again, and the sword was in front of her face.

"All we have to do is say the words and place the sword in the groove on the altar," said Florence, "and it is done."

"We...?" said Lara.

"The words are for a group," said Florence, "in the form of a call and response. I don't want to do it alone."

"And you expect me to do it with you?" asked Lara. She snorted.

"I *want* you to do it with me, Lara."

"And the last time we met, you wanted to kill me," said Lara.

"That was business," said Florence.

"As far as I'm concerned, so is this," said Lara.

"This is sisterhood," said Florence.

Lara snorted again.

"You mock me," said Florence. "You should not mock, Lara."

"What's taking them so long?" Carter asked Denny.

"Girls do like to talk," said Denny.

"We're talking about Lara Croft and Florence Race," said Carter. "Not exactly bosom buddies."

"In my experience women can always find something to talk about. I've never understood it."

"Lara's right. You really are a sexist pig, Denny Sampson."

Carter noticed a small smile on Sandler's lips. The bodyguard was pretending not to listen.

The three men were sitting on high stools at the long table in the anteroom.

Carter reached for one of the books that Florence had left there.

One of the guards banged the barrel of his submachine gun on the table, hard.

"No touch," he said.

"You're not the only one with a gun," said Carter.

"You're outnumbered," said Denny. "You could try making it easy on us."

"So much for trying to find out why Race wanted the sword," said Carter.

"Does it matter why she wants it if Croft wants it too?"

"It matters to Lara," said Carter.

"What's that noise?" asked Sandler after a few moments of silence.

"I don't hear anything," said Denny.

Then one of the guards looked up and shared eye contact with one of his colleagues.

There were sounds of a scuffle somewhere, outside or in the passage to the tomb, and a pop.

"The locals are getting restless," said Denny.

"So we can add racism to your misogyny, can we, Denny?" said Carter.

"Quiet!" spat one of the guards. All five of them were armed and facing the exit.

There was a sudden, loud bang. They all felt the pressure of it in the tight confines of the chamber. One of the guards hurried into the passageway.

"What the hell is going on?" asked Carter.

The second flash bang went off in the entrance to the antechamber, its light and shock amplified by the room. Everyone reeled, deafened and blinded. One of the guards began shooting wildly into the passage.

"Crap!" said Denny, dropping to the floor and covering his head with his hands. Another flash bang bounced into the room and went off under the table, scattering the books and loose notes, sending them floating down through the choking smoke and haze.

Lara and Florence turned at the sound of the explosions.

"Are you coming?" asked Lara, drawing her second weapon.

Florence hesitated for a split second and then turned back to the altar.

A gun in each hand, Lara began to make a move in the direction of the explosions. She could deal with Florence later, but right now, she wasn't going to allow the site to be destroyed.

"You can't leave!" Florence called after her. "Not now!"

"Don't worry," said Lara. "I plan to finish up here. First things first."

Agitated, Florence glanced once in Lara's direction as Croft jogged away. Then, she breathed out long and hard, and took the sword in both of her hands.

She raised it above her head and began the incantation that she had learned by heart from the hieroglyphics that had been transcribed for her, at great cost, by a local expert.

She began the rite alone.

Florence Race's local guards did not respond well to the invasion. With guns to their heads, they were on their knees with their hands in the air before they could properly see or hear anything.

"Mr. Sampson," said Dritan Vata, an armed, black-clad bodyguard standing on either side of him. "I implore you not to shoot."

"This looks like another standoff," said Carter.

"But we're on the same side, now," said Denny. "A man can't stay neutral forever. I never did like Switzerland."

Denny, Carter, and Sandler all had weapons aimed at Vata, despite his entourage of half-a-dozen Wolf-Heads.

"Nobody is going to shoot," said Vata. "I have come to give you a second chance to fulfill our contract, Mr. Sampson. I'm sure you won't let me down again."

"The sword is sold," said Sampson.

Vata shook his head.

"Who said anything about a sword?" asked Vata.

"The artefact that you were bidding on at the market. The deal that Denny struck with you...the double cross. You wanted to buy the sword," said Carter.

Vata's lip curled in what might pass for a smile.

"I have no interest in trinkets," he said.

"Then what did you want to buy?" asked Lara.

She was standing on Vata's right, in the doorway of King Tut's burial chamber. She had both guns raised, one covering Vata and his goons, the other on Denny.

"What *else* was in that consignment, Mr. Vata?" she asked.

"Ah, Miss Croft," said Vata.

"I asked you a question," said Lara.

Vata did not answer. His face puckered slightly, and he raised the back of his hand to cover his nostrils against a rancid smell that had begun to fill the room. Denny coughed. Sandler's eyes drifted away from his gun sight, up towards the ceiling from where a white mist seemed to be descending.

There was a low rumble, and the ancient room trembled. One of Florence's guards fell from his knees onto his belly and moaned.

"What the heck..." began Denny.

Then the low rumbling sound was joined by a high-pitched scratching. Then a screech.

Something moved in Carter's peripheral vision.

"Jesus!" he exclaimed.

One of the local guards turned his head and screamed. He scrambled to his feet and fled from the room, down the passage, apparently not caring whether he was shot or not.

But no one was shooting. Everyone was looking around in bewilderment and fear.

The walls were crawling with bugs. Scarabs, locusts, and grasshoppers were climbing over each other, clicking and squealing, the clatter of wing cases forming an unlikely chorus with the sawing of legs. The black, seething, fricative mass of them covered every inch of the chamber walls like heavy tapestries.

One of the Wolf-Heads began to gag at the stench. He shifted his aim from Carter to the wall and began to fire into the mist.

"Don't shoot!" spat Vata. "Cease fire!"

The mist evaporated, for a moment. The gunfire had blown patches of bugs away from the walls, leaving gaps, but those gaps quickly filled and vanished as the bugs moved. There were so many of them. They shifted and drew new patterns. Iridescent, they changed colour, and coalesced.

They became a mass of shimmering blue-black, like an oil slick on the wall. Then the pattern changed again, and everyone watched, mesmerised, as a recognisable shape emerged. The shape moved, flexing. It began to stretch out, three-dimensional and solid, from the crawling black mass of the wall.

It was a falcon. A falcon formed from thousands of cooperating insects.

Its neck stretched and its head rose, black eyes blinking out at them. The falcon opened its beak, shrieked, flapped its wings, and launched itself into the room. A strong smell of incense followed in its wake.

Everyone ducked, and Vata's right-hand man, Dibra, took a potshot at the vast bird.

"Fire again, and I'll have you killed," yelled Vata. His men ducked and shouted as the falcon swooped around their heads. The mist was growing thick again, filling the chamber air.

"Let's get out of here!" said Lara. She holstered her guns and quickly dragged Carter through into the next room. Sandler followed them.

Neither Dritan Vata nor his men tried to stop them.

"We're leaving, right?" said Carter, unable to hide the fear in his voice. "Now seems like a good time."

"No," said Lara. "We've got to find Race. Find her and stop her."

The mist around them grew thicker.

Two of the Wolf-Heads tried to drive off the strafing falcon, swinging the butts of their rifles. Dibra gathered together everything that had been on the table and shoved it into the duffel bag. He worked fast, his hands shaking. He held the German gas canister up for Vata to see it. It was dusty and dented, but appeared to be intact.

"Good," said Vata. "Now we leave."

Dibra could see the panic in his boss's eyes.

More of the bugs on the walls had coalesced, and a new pattern was forming in the writhing mass adjacent to the exit. Another falcon. Its head protruded first from the wall, then its wings, and then it was flying into the room, joining its companion.

They flew low over Vata as he ducked, reaching down and plucking at his shoulders. One of them banked hard and swooped at one of Vata's men.

There was a sound, an impact like a cabbage being split by a cleaver.

Its talons took off the man's face.

"Holy God!" Dibra cried.

He got off a shot, and one of the falcons hissed. It swung around and dived at Dibra. Another Wolf-Head threw a flash bang across the room. The light and sound disabled everyone for the next four or five seconds but appeared not to deter the beasts.

It seemed to anger them. Another falcon emerged, then another, then another, until the air was full of beating black wings and hissing beaks. The bird-shapes spiralled around, mobbing them, pecking and rasping.

Dibra was the first to recover his vision. Frantic, he looked for a safe exit. Then he looked for his boss. Vata was doubled over the table, facedown, his hands over his head. The exit to the passage was crawling with insects. The air was full of flickering, rushing wings. The conjured falcons were attacking Florence's local guards, the weakest of them. The falcons were swarming the length of the passage, diving back and forth, picking off the dead and injured. One impact followed another. Talons sliced. Men screamed. Blood spattered up the ancient walls.

"No way out," said Dibra grimly.

"Then we go in. We follow Sampson," said Vata, rising from the table, his hands still protecting his head. "For now, we have no choice."

The walls were not moving in the antechamber to Nefertiti's tomb, but the grave goods were.

As they hurried in, Lara and Carter could see the dense white mist fogging the light of the halogen bulbs dotted around the space. But where the fog was most dense, visibility was low. Race had left men stationed in the chamber, but there was no sign of them.

Sandler and Denny blundered in after them.

"What is this?" Denny murmured.

Around them, the grave goods stirred. Caskets shuddered; boxes and flasks rattled. It was as though they were being vibrated by a train going past outside.

It wasn't that, Lara realised. The lids of the jars and boxes were rattling as if the contents were trying to get out.

The room was changing, and it wasn't just the heavy scent of incense or the mist. It wasn't just the movement of the air, or the faint trembling.

There was something in the room with them. Something was manifesting.

Lara heard a growl.

The growl reminded Lara of the howling dogs in the Toros Mountains. She turned, guns held at arm's length in front of her. She had almost rotated full circle when she detected movement to her left. She jerked sharply in that direction.

There was something in the ghostly mist.

She saw the hands first and then looked up to see the head. The figure loomed at her: two-and-a-half metres tall, slender, androgynous, and black, with almond eyes and gold jewellery.

"Idiot!" Lara said, and relaxed. It was a statue.

"Lara!" Carter yelled.

The statue was moving.

Lara gritted her teeth and fired reflexively, two shots into the torso of the figure and one into its forehead. The statue took another step towards her. She sidestepped, and three more shots entered the chest of the figure. Lara saw dust fly out of the wounds on impact. Dust, not blood.

The thing lunged and grabbed for Lara. It had her tight by the arm, its grip like an iron band. Its mouth opened wide in a scream so high-pitched that it was barely audible. The inside of its mouth was gold, and its tongue was blue.

Lara recoiled. She flexed her knees, bent her back, and tossed the tall figure over her body and onto the floor beside her.

It landed hard. She holstered the guns and reached for a weapon, anything to break the statue. Guns were no good. The statue moved like flesh and bone, but when it was shot, it acted like wood.

Lara pulled her knife out of her boot and thrust the tip into the figure's left eye. The statue threw up its hands and convulsed.

She straddled its chest. It clawed at her legs. Snarling, she took out its other eye, and then thrust the blade into its mouth and shoved hard.

The thing convulsed again, and then lay still.

She turned and saw Sandler. He was wide-eyed and scared.

"What's going on?" he asked her, his tone desperate. "What the hell is this—"

He never finished the question.

Something under the mist that surrounded him grabbed him and dragged him down violently.

She heard him scream and heard a wet crunch. She thought it was over. Then a figure rose through the mist where Sandler had fallen. Like some ancient warrior, it wore a horned helmet and various pieces of ancient armour over its rags. The creature's flesh was all but desiccated off its bones. Its bright eyes locked on Lara's. She felt a moment of recognition and then of abhorrence.

Whatever had taken Sandler down had turned him into this ravening undead monster in an instant.

Lara fired, reflexively. The thing's eyes dulled, and it crashed back into the mist from whence it had come.

Lara backed off fast. There were things moving under the white mist, cruising like sharks beneath the surface of the sea.

The knife in one hand and a gun in the other, Lara looked for a way out. There was no sign of Denny, but she could see Carter, wading around in waist-deep mist, like a man stuck in a swamp. He was swearing, pistol raised in one hand, trying to flap the white smoke of the rising mist away from him with the other.

Suddenly, he uttered a brief squeak and vanished, dropping out of sight. Something had grabbed him and pulled him down into the mist. The same fate as Sandler.

Lara started forwards, dreading Carter reappearing as some altered, inhuman wretch. He must not die.

Then, she heard a dog snarling through gritted teeth as it set to rending something. It sounded wet, fleshy.

She heard Carter scream... So, he was still Carter.

Lara threw herself in the direction of the cry. The wet, snarling sound was hideous. She scrambled through the choking mist and almost collided with the flanks of a sleek black jackal.

The beast had Carter by the leg.

Lara lunged, desperately, grabbing the jackal around the throat, her arm locking like a noose. She tried to drag it back. It was strong as hell. She attacked its eyes with her blade, as she had the statue. It loosened its grasp on Carter's bloody calf, yelped, and tried to turn its jaws on her. It snapped and bit. Holding it tight, Lara rammed her blade into its gullet.

Lara heaved the creature's dead weight off her and tossed it aside. She scrutinised Carter for a moment and then offered him her hand.

"Thanks, Lara," he said. His face was pale. His leg was a mess, blood soaking his torn pant leg, but he was still Carter. She hoisted him to his feet.

"Use a blade, Carter," Lara said. "Eyes and mouths. Bullets are useless. And fight like your life depends on it. Sandler came back, undead, after being attacked by one of these *things*."

Carter gasped, possibly turning even paler. Then he nodded, put away his gun, and drew his utility knife.

"Blades, got it," he replied.

They heard gunfire from the anteroom.

"Should we tell *them*?" asked Carter.

Vata's henchmen and the local muscle Florence Race had hired were squaring off.

Florence was a hard taskmaster, but she paid fairly when her men did their jobs. They had no hesitation opening fire on the Wolf-Heads as they entered Tutankhamen's tomb.

It was a nightmarish environment. The pall of mist had settled low around their feet, and the air was full of swarming locusts. The Wolf-Heads were better combatants, but Florence's men were local, and they were less bothered by the insects.

The replica sarcophagus and shrine offered cover, and visibility was poor.

Dibra gave the word and, under cover of fire, got Vata clear into the next chamber. There was no turning back.

"We have to get the canister and its contents safely out of here," said Vata. "That is all. Nothing else matters."

The treasury room was remarkably still and silent. A soft yellow glow permeated the chamber. It was ethereal and quite unlike the harsh blue-white light thrown by the halogen bulbs that threaded the rest of the tomb complex.

Florence Race, tall and elegant, stood serene, almost radiant, in the flattering light.

She held the sword horizontally before her in both hands and spoke the last words of the ritual invocation. All that remained was the utterance of the ceremony itself. She had made all the preparations. It was time to slip the sword into the groove and deliver the final prayer of investiture.

She would be a queen. *The* queen. The world matriarch.

Florence adjusted her position at the end of the altar, took hold of the sword's grip in her right hand, and closed her left hand around it. She raised the sword vertically in front of her face. Then she lowered the tip and began to slide it into the groove that stretched out in front of her.

The tip danced and juddered in the "V"of the groove, as if it wanted to jump free. Florence tightened her grasp and steadied the blade, stopping for a moment and breathing slowly to calm herself. She looked down the length of the sword. It had appeared to be true, and so did the groove, but she could not line them up.

She slid the tip of the sword back into the groove more firmly, dropping the angle as she went. The sword jerked and slipped, and the tip jumped out of the stone slot. It jumped as if it was alive, as if it had been electrified, and the jolt unbalanced Florence, throwing her against the altar. A flurry of sparks flew from the blade's edge as it knocked against the altar's lip.

The yellow light dimmed slightly, and grey smoke rose from the altar.

Florence murmured a curse of frustration. She straightened up and took the sword in both hands. She moved to the side of the altar so that the groove lay horizontally in front of her. She held the sword out parallel to the groove, fifteen centimetres above the altar. It cast a shadow.

She lowered the sword towards the altar to make a closer comparison. More grey smoke rose from the altar, turning blue-black as the shadow began to smoulder. A strong smell of incense drifted up.

Pain flared into her fingers.

Florence dropped the sword. It bounced off the altar and onto the floor. When she picked it up, she did so gingerly and found that it was still hot. Hot, as if it had come fresh from the forge. She left it on the floor to cool and retrieved the copy that she'd had made.

Florence slid the copy sword into the groove on the altar. She did it without ceremony, without thought. It fit neatly. It had been made to fit.

But it was utterly inert.

Then Florence laid the copy sword over the scorch mark on the altar, the shadow made by Gwynnever's sword.

The two swords were not the same.

The differences were slight, but there were differences nonetheless. The length of the point differed by a millimetre or so, the angle of the blade's taper by a degree or two.

Florence picked up Gwynnever's sword and ran the blade against the altar, as if against a whetstone. She made two passes and cried out. She dropped the sword and put her scorched fingers in her mouth. The sword glowed purple at its edge, and more blue-black smoke curled from the altar.

Florence swore for several seconds. Then she took up the copy sword and ground it against the altar. There was no smoke, no scorching heat. It would take some energy, but she would make a tool from the sword.

She would rework it. She would not be thwarted. She would *make* the sacred weapon fit Nefertiti's altar.

Lara and Carter almost ran into Denny outside the entrance of the treasury chamber.

Denny looked anxious and tense.

"I was looking for you," Lara said.

"It's been kinda busy in here," said Denny, "in lots of nasty ways." Gunfire and yelling echoed through the chambers around them.

"You can say that again," said Carter.

Lara raised her weapons and led the way into the treasury. Denny and Carter glanced at each other, then followed her.

"There," Carter whispered.

Florence was sitting on the floor of the treasury, Gwynnever's sword braced between her knees. With agitated effort, she was using the copy sword to try to taper a new edge, and form a new point.

"It's over, Florence," said Lara, her guns aimed. "Give me the sword."

"She did pay for it, Croft," said Denny.

Lara turned her head and glared at Denny.

"Because that's what really matters!" said Carter, his sarcastic tone mirroring the expression on Lara's face.

"You'll have to take it out of my cold, dead hands," said Florence, dropping the copy sword and standing.

"That can be arranged," said Lara, panning her aim around to follow Florence's movement.

Florence looked down at the altar and uttered a sigh of frustration and determination.

"Florence—" Lara warned.

One-handed, and in one swift motion, Florence Race shoved Gwynnever's sword into the groove in Nerfertiti's altar.

There was a burst of bright, golden light.

Florence was thrown backwards off her feet as though she had grabbed a live cable.

Blue-black smoke rose into the air, acrid and hot. Lara winced at the sound of flesh and bone hitting stone as Florence's body landed hard against the chamber wall.

"Oopsie," said Denny.

Lara holstered her guns. She strode up to the altar, reached into the cloud of smoke, and drew out the sword by its grip.

"Lara!" yelled Carter.

Lara turned as Florence lunged at her. She had not expected the attack. She had assumed Florence was out cold after being thrown across the room by whatever mystical energy had blasted out of the altar.

Florence seemed almost feral. Her face was a snarl of hatred. Lara met her clawing attack and punched her away. Florence staggered, then scooped up the copy sword from the floor. She uttered a fierce shriek and swung it at Lara.

Gwynnever's sword came up to parry the attack and then to counter.

Obsidian flashed against obsidian as the two blades met. The women circled each other, passing, trading blows fast and ruthlessly. The striking blades made a ringing noise like bells chiming. Lara swung and parried, and the swords locked. Lara threw out an elbow to drive Florence back and break the clinch.

They circled again, exchanging brutal blows. Each ferocious flurry ended with them locked, and each lock broke when one of them hooked a knee or punched a kidney. The fighting was fierce, uncompromising. Florence Race was good, and she was driven by rage.

Another flurry of blows and they locked together again. Lara blinked and breathed, trying to clear her head.

What was wrong with her? She couldn't think clearly. Her mind was—

The pelts were bound to her body with tendon twine, like a second skin, allowing her ample freedom of movement. She strode across the tundra, through the hair grass and acid-yellow pearlwort, and followed the flight of the albatross. The beast was close. They could smell it. She looked left and right along the phalanx of women warriors spread to either side. She was the spear tip.

She saw the lumbering shape in the distance, drew her sword, lifted it to the heavens, and raised her voice to rally the battle cry. Throats yodelled in response.

The beast rose to its full height, dense grey fur cascading from its broad shoulders. It turned to face them, its heavy brow creased, its square jaw and simian features tensed. The beast beat its chest and then dislocated its lantern jaw in an inhuman howl.

It would not kill more of them. She would not allow it. She raised her voice, and the chorused, ululating battle cry of the women drowned out the monster's threat.

Denny and Carter watched, mesmerised, as the two women clashed in battle. Florence was like a woman possessed. Lara was poised, economical in her movements, precise, brutal.

The chamber's yellow light waxed and waned, and then turned from yellow to green, and then to an incandescent blue. The floor trembled, but Lara did not seem to notice.

Florence lost her footing and fell out of the reach of Lara's precise thrust. The fall saved her life.

Carter set a wide stance and aimed a gun. Denny leant heavily against the nearest wall, and then bounced off it as he felt the wall move against his back. He landed on his hands and knees on the floor.

"It's happening again," said Carter.

"Whatever *it* is," said Denny.

Lara wasn't listening. She was turning wide circles, thrusting, parrying, lunging, swinging, almost as if she was going through a set of exercises, except that she never repeated a move, and her head was tilted, as if she was looking up at something or someone.

Lara had to look up into the eyes of her opponent. Past the cheek guards of his helmet, she could see the swarthy skin of his hairless face and his dark eyes. The red cloth of his garment was already dull with dirt and blood where it was not covered by his mail tunic. His legs were unclad, revealing more of his swarthy skin, and he had lost his shield.

There was surprise on his face, too, hesitation. She was a woman. She struck first, fiercely, and low, ducking and swinging hard into his thigh. Her reach was shorter than his, but her shield work was good, and he was taken by surprise. She fought hard and fast, getting in a second strike before he could react. His first and second blows were defensive. He was exhausted, bewildered, and losing blood before he counterattacked. She would have this Roman; the first of many who would die by her hand on Iceni soil.

Denny tried to stand, but he couldn't, and Carter had to brace himself against a wall as the floor began to writhe beneath him. The texture was changing. The stone was breaking, cracking, and remoulding. It shifted and throbbed. Then it began to cohere at the centre of the room.

Carter got his footing. He grabbed Denny by the back of his jacket and dragged him to his feet. They were both armed, and they watched the floor.

Florence had been jostled by the floor as it rumbled and undulated, shoved against a wall, crumpled in a heap. As the floor began to stabilise, from the walls inwards, she lay still, lifeless.

Only Lara seemed comfortable on the floor as it swelled and moved beneath her, sending up a green mist. It was almost as if she were surfing or moguling. Her knees bent and flexed to the rhythm of the floor, and her hips swung and her body weight adjusted to the movement as if instinctively. And all the time, her upper body was doing battle with some imagined adversary, her sword arm swinging, her free arm balancing, or coming in to throw an elbow or a punch.

Lara stood on the prow of her ship. They were under attack; the boarding party was clambering up the keel, being beaten down by her loyal crew. Her lieutenant was at the helm.

Then the enemy was upon her. She did not hesitate as he plunged across the swaying deck. She struck first. He snarled, expelling his breath as he parried. She crossed, defended, lunged, ducked. The ship yawed, throwing her attacker off balance, and her blade pierced his right shoulder. He cried out and tried to swing, but his arm was partially disabled. He switched his sword to his other hand, but it was too late. Lara brought her blade hard across his belly, eviscerating him.

Carter and Denny watched as mist rose to shroud Lara, and a shape began to emerge from the floor, green and brown, rough and scaly. The curved back ended in a long, thrashing tail, the thick neck in a long, flat, tapering jaw filled with a mass of protruding teeth. Lara rose into the air, standing astride the emerging back.

"The Sobek!" gasped Carter.

He drew his gun and began to fire on the beast. Shots spanged and pinged off the dense, petrified skin of the creature, ricocheting into the walls and altar.

Denny reached out and batted the barrel of the gun down.

"For God's sake, Bell! You'll get us all killed," he said. "You'll get Croft killed!"

"How?" Carter asked. "How the hell do we get close to that thing?"

The great crocodilian tossed its head and snapped its jaws as it began to surge forwards, its tail swinging back and forth. Lara continued on its back, riding it, carving a path through the mist.

The beast's passage was relentless. It surged through the tombs and chambers, tossing its head and snapping its jaws. All other beasts cleared a path for it, turning their backs or casting down their eyes. Obstacles were crushed or swept aside by its swinging head or clamped between its jaws before being discarded.

"Oh, the waste," said Carter, as he and Denny followed in its wake, walking at a distance behind its lethal tail, single file, staying in the creature's blind spot. "The history being lost."

"Never mind the history," said Denny. "I could make a fortune out of this stuff."

The Sobek entered Tutankhamen's tomb in a low veil of green mist. The locusts, which had been swarming, dissipated at once, vanishing into the shadows. Dibra suddenly had a clear shot at Florence's guards. The sight of the monstrous apparition did not faze him. He had good cover and honed skills. He relied on his training, training that would help him avoid panic, get them out alive, and protect his principal. He picked off two of Florence's men before any of them got a shot off. The others were all terrified by the appearance of the ancient Egyptian reptilian god. One fainted clean away; another was a gibbering wreck.

"Time to leave, sir," said Dibra. He sounded ridiculously calm. He pushed Vata out of cover in front of him and then followed.

The Sobek saw the movement. It rushed them.

"Dammit," said Dibra. He aimed at the charging creature.

"Run," he told his boss.

The beast's jaws opened wide. The Sobek launched its full weight, turning its huge head sideways to strike.

The massive jaws clamped around Dibra's torso. The bottom jaw pierced his thigh, hip, and abdomen. The top jaw went through his shoulder and arm, and pierced an artery in his neck.

When the Sobek's jaws shut entirely, Dibra's head was sliced from his body, and his legs severed above the knees. Everything else, including the duffel bag with its precious cargo, disappeared into its insatiable maw.

Denny and Carter stopped dead. They watched Lara launch herself off the ascending back of the crocodilian as it flew forwards. She landed on its shoulders, feet wide, knees soft, dipping her hips low and then rising upright as much of Dibra's body disappeared between the Sobek's jaws.

Mist bellowed from its nostrils, and from the pall rose another ancient, long-dead warrior. What was left of Dibra raised its single hand, now armed with a chain mace, fixed its hollow glowing eyes on Lara, and swung the weapon.

Lara sidestepped the mace, and brought her sword down to put Dibra out of his misery.

The Sobek swallowed the parts of Dibra that it had torn away, and, satisfied with its snack, continued its plodding passage through the tombs. The falcons formed an honour guard high above its giant form, as if drifting on invisible thermals in a great, black archway. They did not strafe Lara, or pluck or pick at her.

She looked left and right, and as far as Lara could see was a great Arab force riding into battle. She was at its head. She thundered across the desert to meet her adversary, her blade flashing in the sunlight. She split a head, carved an arm from its body, pierced a femoral artery. Every cut, every thrust took down an enemy.

Then her horse was gone from under her and she was standing on the shifting sands. Even at a height disadvantage, she wielded the sword around her shoulders and above her head like a whirling dervish, carving at the enemy mounts, thrusting at legs and groins, unseating her adversaries, and making her kills.

Carter and Denny watched as Lara made easy prey of the falcons. She swung her sword around her shoulders and over her head, ripping through their oily feathers, slicing through wings and necks, reducing the birds to scattered, crackling black insects that rained to the chamber floor.

"I don't know how she's doing it," whispered Carter.

"Is she even conscious?" asked Denny. "Doesn't matter. It looks like we're going to get out of this godforsaken place."

"That is a god!" said Carter, pointing at the Sobek.

"Don't remind it," said Denny.

The Sobek cut a path through every chamber back to the passage and out of the tomb. All the while, Denny Sampson and Carter Bell followed in its wake. The other creatures in the tomb bowed to it, hailed it, formed honour guards. It was their superior. It cut a swath through the humans, too, turning any and all who crossed its path into undead warriors, only for Lara to kill them anew.

Florence's men knew the legends. They hid, played dead, or kowtowed. The Wolf-Heads were more pugnacious. Any who were roused to attack were cut down; any who underestimated the Sobek died twice. Dibra had been the first, but several others followed.

Then they were in the desert, out in the darkness, in the cold, under the night sky.

There was no sun.

Carter and Denny followed the Sobek for a hundred metres, but it began slowing. Another hundred metres and it was crawling on its belly, its skin turning a sickly grey. Its joints were creaking.

It was petrifying.

Its jaws stopped snapping, and its tail stopped curling and swinging freely.

Then it stopped entirely.

Lara had slowed, too. Her feet were still braced apart, but her hands had dropped to her sides. She had stopped striking with the sword. Her face was expressionless. She was no longer surfing the Sobek. She was almost entirely still.

Gradually, the crocodilian began to slump into the sand. Its skin became less firm, less scaled. Its jaw and limbs were less defined. Its tail began to disappear. It was almost as if it was sinking into quicksand. Wind rose, blowing the sand up off the ground in little zephyrs of dust. Some of the billowing clouds were the structure of the Sobek, reducing to fine sand, vanishing into haze like a turning dune.

Carter and Denny moved a little closer. Then they saw Lara's chin drop.

"Oh my God!" said Denny. They both moved, but Carter was closer. He caught Lara in his arms before she hit the ground. By the time she collapsed, there was no sign that the Sobek had ever been there at all.

CHAPTER TWENTY: DELIRIOUS
London

"Crap!" said Lara, reaching a hand up to cradle her throbbing head.

"You're awake," said Carter.

"What are you talking like that for?" asked Lara.

"Like what?"

"Like I'm dying or something. I've got the mother and father of all headaches, but really, Carter, the pity whisper?"

Lara tried to sit up in bed, and then lay back down and closed her eyes.

"Lie down, Lara."

"I think you'll find I am lying down. Speak normally, for heaven's sake. I'm not an invalid. Did I hit my head or something?"

"What's the last thing you remember, Lara?"

"What?"

"Maybe you should get some rest."

"Didn't I just wake up?"

"Ye-es," said Carter, hesitating.

"So, how long have I been asleep?" asked Lara.

"On and off, three days," said Carter.

Lara sat up, groaned, and held her forehead in her hands.

"Three days! How the hell have I been asleep for three days?" she asked.

"I don't know if you'd really call it asleep," said Carter. "I think you've been delirious. What's the last thing you remember?"

"I remember...I remember...a lot of dreams. I was dreaming, Carter. I was leading Arabs in a battle against the Romans. I did battle twice against the Romans, once with the Arabs and once with... I dreamt I was Boudica. That's..."

"Okay, Lara, you're fine now. What do you remember about Egypt?"

"That's where we are," said Lara, relieved. "We're in Egypt to find Denny. No...we went out to the Valley of the Kings to confront bloody Florence Race." She looked around to reassure herself.

"Lara—"

Carter began to speak, but Lara cut him off.

"How did I get home, Carter? Why are you in the manor?"

"Calm down, Lara. Everything's fine."

"Oh, no! The sword! Carter, where's the sword?" yelled Lara.

"It's fine. We've got it," said Carter. "It's right here." He reached under the duvet and retrieved the sword from where it had been lying next to Lara. "You wouldn't let go of it, and when we were able to get it out of your hand, you wouldn't let it out of your sight."

"Okay," said Lara, breathing with relief, and lying back down, letting her eyes close. "Okay."

"Rest, Lara. You need to recover."

Lara sat up again, eyes wide.

"Three days," she said. "It's been three days! There isn't time to rest. Just get me some water and find me some painkillers. We need to work."

"You're not going anywhere. At least not until you've eaten something," said Carter.

"There are takeout menus in the drawer next to the fridge," said Lara. "Order whatever you want, as long as you get something with vegetables. But first, water and something for this damned headache."

Lara had showered and dressed by the time the takeout arrived. The painkillers had taken the edge off her headache, and she was beginning to remember.

"Do we know what happened to Florence or Vata after we left them in the tomb?" asked Lara.

"We thought it was best to get out of there," said Carter. "Denny had his money, so he just wanted to get out and lie low for a while. I couldn't do much without you."

"I was unconscious the whole time?" asked Lara.

"Unconscious or delirious," said Carter. "I still have no idea how we kept you conscious enough for long enough to get you on the plane without raising any suspicions."

"Okay," said Lara, "so Florence could still be out there. She could still be after the sword."

"That's possible," said Carter. "Vata might be a problem, too."

"Okay," said Lara. "Explain that to me."

"We think, Denny and I, that he was after the payload in the German bomber that was also found at the Candle Lane site. Whatever was in the duffel bag was destroyed when Vata's man Dibra was killed."

"The canister," said Lara. "I remember the canister in the consignment that Florence bought. Do we know what it contained?"

"We have no idea," said Carter. "It could have been anything. Speculation suggests some kind of nerve gas, which is why so many of the archaeological team at the dig ended up being affected."

"So we're back to Division Eleven, the Ministry of Defence, and Theresa Johnson," said Lara. "You told me that was all a lie. You said there was no nerve agent on the Dornier. What was it you said you found?"

"I said it was carrying incendiary flares," said Carter. "I said it checked out."

"So, who's right?" asked Lara. "Because Division Eleven was damned keen to get me out of the Candle Lane site, and keep me out."

"I can't explain it, Lara. I wish I could," said Carter.

"All we know about Vata is that he was associated with a Balkans paramilitary group as a young man, and that he's bloody dangerous," said Lara.

"He's also willing to go to great lengths to get his hands on this payload," said Carter.

"Great," said Lara. "So you think the visual disturbances, hallucinations...the mayhem might have been caused by some kind of nerve agent in that canister," said Lara. "At Candle Lane, and in the tomb."

"It seems possible," said Carter.

"And I had the highest susceptibility," said Lara.

"Smallest body mass," said Carter. "There were some very big men in that tomb, including me and Denny, and Florence Race was out cold for most of the time."

"What about your theory of shared hallucinations, Carter?" asked Lara.

"It's true. We did all see the same things, shared the same experiences," said Carter. "I don't understand it, but what other explanation could there possibly be?"

"Sometimes there are no explanations, Carter. Right now the best we can hope for is that Vata didn't survive the Valley of the Kings," said Lara. "My main interest is the sword. It belongs on the altar at Candle Lane, and I plan to return it."

"It'll be lost forever," said Carter.

"Sometimes it's better that way," said Lara. "Some artefacts don't belong in Perspex cases to be ogled by the general public, who don't know any better. Some things have a rightful resting place. They belong to everyone, not just to the few who can afford to look at them. The sword belongs in that groove on that altar. I'm taking it home."

Lara pushed her plate away and got up to get her jacket.

"Now?" asked Carter.

"Why not?" said Lara. "There's no time like the present."

Candle Lane was awash with lights. The city was never dark, but there were more lights in Candle Lane than anywhere else in London. There were also security guards everywhere. Lara recognised them as Division Eleven. They all had the buttoned-up, too-young, too-alert appearance of highly trained military personnel.

Lara and Carter passed the end of the street but didn't enter it. They passed again.

"That's enough for now," said Lara. "If we pass again, someone's going to get suspicious. Let's find somewhere close by for a drink, and see how far I can get with surveillance in half an hour."

It was late afternoon. Offices were closing for the day, and there were a lot of people around. They wouldn't attract much attention. They walked into a pub a couple of hundred metres away, bought drinks at the bar, found a table for two, and sat down.

Lara took out her laptop and found some Wi-Fi signals. She quickly hacked a password to one of the corporate local offices and started work.

"What do I do?" asked Carter.

"Just chat to me," said Lara. "We're friends, and I can multitask. Just don't draw attention to what I'm doing. Anyone even thinks about looking over my shoulder and you start talking about the weather."

"How does that help?" asked Carter.

"It's a signal, so I can switch to a dummy screen that should put anyone off if they happen to glance at it."

"Fine," said Carter, taking a sip of his Coke. He fidgeted for several moments, moving the glass from one spot to another on the table between them.

"Are you okay?" asked Lara, looking up from what she was doing.

"I just can't think of anything to say," said Carter, sheepishly.

Lara smiled.

"Just tell me about the last dig you were on, the one before Candle Lane, obviously."

Carter started talking, and soon got into his stride. Lara asked a simple question once or twice, in case they were being observed, but she was only half-listening to him. Most of her attention was on her work.

Lara cycled through a couple of search engines, and then went deeper. She found out where the CCTV cameras in Candle Lane had originated. Division Eleven was using them, but they belonged to the Council. Lara worked fast, finding a back door into the Council's computer system, and hacking a password for the security department. She soon found the codes for all the CCTV cameras in the Candle Lane area.

She looked up at Carter and beamed.

"Can I ask how it's going?" said Carter.

"You can ask," said Lara, "and I can tell you that it's going very well. Now tell me more about the trench with the multiple human burials in it."

Carter continued to talk, and Lara continued to probe the Council's computer system. In another minute, she was able to ascertain that the Council still had active feeds to the cameras on Candle Lane that Division Eleven had taken over.

"Well, that saves me a lot of time and effort," said Lara, under her breath.

"What's that?" asked Carter.

"Nothing," said Lara, "just someone not doing his job properly." She turned back to her computer, hit a key, and the screen blacked out for a second before coming back to life. It was divided into four moving, black-and-white images from four of the cameras on Candle Lane.

Lara zoomed in on the first screen and watched. Every so often, she hit a key. After two minutes she switched to the second screen and continued the process. Then she switched to the third screen.

Thirty seconds into watching the feed, Lara's eyes widened, and she began to hit a key on the keypad over and over again. She stayed on the screen for twice as long as she had on the first two screens, and hit the key dozens of times. Finally, she switched to the fourth screen.

In a little over ten minutes, Lara had everything she needed. She'd watched the live footage, and she'd taken screen grabs of anything and everything that might be useful, particularly from the third camera. What's more, Division Eleven had made it easy for her, or someone at the Council had. The Council's CCTV live feed should have been cut when Division Eleven took over security at Candle Lane. Someone had made a very bad mistake, but it meant that Lara hadn't had to spend hours trying to hack Division Eleven.

CHAPTER TWENTY-ONE: BREAKING AND ENTERING
Candle Lane

Back at the manor, Lara collated the screen-grab photos from the CCTV footage and began to manipulate them. First, she concentrated on buildings close to the site. Then she turned to the photos from screen three. As she'd been watching, several security guards had come into view, surrounding two or three men. They'd spent the next couple of minutes talking together very seriously. There was no sound on the live feed, but it had been clear that the group of people was being detained.

"What can we see?" asked Carter, peering over her shoulder at the screen as she made adjustments in Photoshop.

"Look there," said Lara, circling an area on the screen.

"Is that what I think it is?" asked Carter.

Lara isolated the area, resized and reset to amplify and sharpen the image. It resolved into a circle with the outline of a wolf on it.

"It's their badge," said Carter.

"Vata's still in the game," said Lara.

"This time they didn't get in," said Carter.

"So," said Lara, "we need to move fast. Vata's determined, resourceful, and ruthless. Division Eleven won't be able to keep him out indefinitely. I managed to hook up to their CCTV surveillance, and even if it were a mistake by the Council, it still shows weaknesses at Division Eleven. Their security isn't as impenetrable as they think it is."

"So, how do we get in?" asked Carter.

Lara switched to the images of the buildings closest to the site.

"We start here," she said, pointing at the screen. "And if that fails, we look for another way in."

Lara identified the buildings adjacent to the site and set Carter to work on the architecture, to find out whether they had exits onto adjoining streets, and, if so, whether there was any possible access via them onto the site. He drew a blank.

"No fire exits?" asked Lara. "No windows? No adjoining roof spaces or basements where we might break through?"

"Nothing," said Carter.

"They're Victorian buildings," said Lara.

"All renovated," said Carter. "All business premises. All passed by buildings inspectors."

"Crap," said Lara. "I've got to get into that site."

"If it's any consolation," said Carter, "if you can't get in, Vata and his Wolf-Heads don't stand a chance."

"It isn't," said Lara. "What else is there? What do we know about the area? What can we find out?"

"What about the Underground?" asked Carter.

"The M.O.D. will have that covered," said Lara. "You know London better than anyone I know. You know the city's history. There must be something."

Carter thought for a moment.

"Okay," he said. "It's a long shot, but there's just a possibility I might have an idea. Hand me your computer. I need access to my Dropbox."

"There's a good chance someone out there is monitoring our computer traffic," said Lara. "I've been able to mask a lot of what I'm doing here, but if you access your own Dropbox, it could be a giveaway. If Vata is monitoring us, somehow, and we find a way in, it'll be a race."

"I don't know of another way to get this information. It's not in the public domain," said Carter. "Do we risk it?"

"We'll have to be ready to move fast," said Lara. "Let's prep first. What do we need?"

"Sensible clothes and boots, mostly," said Carter.

Lara looked down at herself and gestured, as if to say, "When aren't I dressed for action?" and Carter grinned.

"Right," he said. "Some basic climbing equipment might be useful, too."

Lara stepped out to the utility closet in the hall, and came back opening a knapsack. She started showing Carter the contents: rope, carabiners, slings, head torches.

"That's more than we'll need," said Carter. "I think we're good to go. You've got ink in your printer, right? I'll need hard copies of my maps, just in case. If Vata is tech-savvy and has access to my Dropbox, then using it now will flag up my smartphone, too. Let's not give him the chance to lock into any signals."

"Sounds like a plan," said Lara. She ducked out again and came back with the sword and several of her own blade weapons. She sorted them until she found a sheath that fit the sword pretty well. While Carter was accessing and printing the data he needed, she put on a snug jacket, strapped the sword to her back, and fit the knapsack on top.

Less than half an hour later, Lara Croft and Carter Bell were in Clerkenwell.

"We're not even close to Candle Lane," said Lara.

"Closer than you'd think," said Carter. "In a straight line."

"This is London," said Lara. "There are no straight lines."

They were sitting in the Horseshoe pub on the corner of Clerkenwell Close, and it was about ten o'clock.

"We weren't followed?" asked Carter.

"No," said Lara. "We're good." Carter drank the last of his Coke and stood.

"Let's make a move, then," he said.

They walked directly to the entrance marked "School Keeper," which stood on the street, in a long expanse of brick wall. Nobody stopped them. They walked across an unlit courtyard, through a gate, and began to descend a flight of steps.

It was only at the bottom that Lara allowed Carter to shine a light.

"Everyone knows about the House of Detention catacombs," said Carter. Lara glanced at him. "Well, maybe not everyone. There are things about them that people don't know, though."

"So, enlighten me," said Lara.

Carter led Lara through the main part of the catacombs, with its brick structures and its various cells and anterooms.

"This was a holding area for as many as three hundred detainees. It's pretty grim. The original building was here from about 1600. It became a school in the nineteenth century, but the catacombs retained their original purpose until the whole lot burnt down."

"And what was their original purpose?" asked Lara.

"Aboveground was a pretty conventional prison," said Carter.

"And down here?" asked Lara as Carter led her to the mouth of a long, narrow corridor, more like a tunnel.

"This is a bit of a clue," said Carter. "We'll need those head torches down here." They fixed the torches and entered the tunnel. The floor of the corridor curved into the walls, as did the ceiling, and the tunnel was so narrow that only one person could walk along it at a time, and two people couldn't pass. "I hope you're not claustrophobic."

"It's a tunnel," said Lara, matter-of-fact.

"As opposed to a corridor," said Carter.

"So there is some secret site at the end of this tunnel?" said Lara. "Prisoners were coming in from a second, undisclosed location?"

"Exactly," said Carter.

"What does that have to do with Candle Lane?" asked Lara.

"Proximity and social change," said Carter. They continued along the tunnel until Carter stopped to look at his map. It was a hand-drawn schematic with the tunnel marked with a series of dotted and hashed secondary tunnels and shafts running off it.

When they had walked for about five minutes, Carter broke through a rotten wooden cover in the wall of the tunnel to reveal an aperture. They climbed through and dropped down into another, similar tunnel that ran at an angle to the first. Carter had to stoop to walk along it, and Lara could hear the rustle of his jacket as his shoulders brushed the walls as he advanced.

Three or four minutes' walking brought the tunnel to an abrupt end. Carter took a step back, almost knocking Lara onto her ass.

"Sorry, Lara, I just need to..." he said, trying to crouch. There wasn't room for his bulk with his knees bent, so he straightened up and bent at the waist instead, flexing at the knees until he was able to release the trapdoor in the stone floor at his feet.

They descended seven or eight metres to another level. This tunnel was wider and squarer, but still Victorian, or even earlier, made of stone and brick, and vaulted.

"You know this secret location?" asked Lara.

"My work on the British military led me to some interesting discoveries," said Carter. "Some crazy shit went down with your monarchy in the seventeenth and eighteenth centuries."

"You said your research wasn't in the public domain," said Lara. "Most of what ailed the monarchy was aired in public long ago."

"The connections to the military and to Clerkenwell aren't public knowledge," said Carter. "You people look after your own."

"You still haven't explained how this relates to Candle Lane or anything else," said Lara.

"You've heard of Pindar?" asked Carter.

"The fortress under the M.O.D.?" asked Lara. "Yes, I've heard of it."

"It's not the first time the military has built underground in London. There has been underground connective tissue between Parliament, the royal palaces in London, and various safe houses for centuries. The catacombs were prepared under Buckingham Palace before it was built. The House of Detention was a safe house and part of the complex. The military ensured the safety of royalty and the nobility. Criminals, the insane, and even the exhausted or persecuted had military protection and safe havens."

"I still don't see how this relates to Candle Lane," said Lara.

"Things changed," said Carter. "Queen Victoria's reign changed things. She was a different kind of monarch, and it was a different kind of family. The industrial revolution altered things. People became more mobile. She hated the secrecy, she hated relying on the military, and she hated the idea of hiding her failures in a prison... That's how the stories go, anyway, and this is all anecdotal, of course."

"So, she shut it down?" asked Lara.

"That's more or less it," said Carter.

Lara stopped. She stopped for a moment, looking around, despite the fact that she could see nothing but brick walls, and listened.

"Trains," she said.

"It's hard to be anywhere underground in London and not hear trains," said Carter. He looked at his schematic. "It's this way."

They walked along a brick walkway flanking what appeared to be a service tunnel, and then ducked through a door into yet another shaft.

"At about the same time that Victoria shut down the royal bolt-holes, the Underground was being expanded. The infrastructure was in place, and the engineers took advantage of it. Candle Lane was built close to one of the tunnels leading from Buckingham Palace to Clerkenwell Close. A maintenance tunnel that used to service Candle Lane Tube is part of the original complex."

"And you think you can find it?" asked Lara.

Carter stopped at a patch of wall.

"Hand me a flashlight," he said. "I need more light." Lara handed him a torch from the knapsack. He played it over the brickwork, moving slowly along the wall a couple of feet at a time. Finally, he stopped. "Here," he said. "It's just the other side, where these bricks have been infilled. See how the mortar's different?"

"Let's get to work, then," said Lara.

The bricks were only one skin deep. When they had dislodged one, dim light shone through from the other side. Lara hand-signalled to Carter. They killed the lights on their head torches and worked in silence. They scraped away more of the old mortar and more of the bricks, which were easy enough to pull free, until Carter and Lara had made a gap big enough to climb through.

They stepped onto the track only twenty metres from Candle Lane Station. The light was coming from the site.

They stopped, hunkered down, and listened.

"All clear," said Lara. "Let's move."

They dropped onto the tracks and began to jog in the direction of the site. They hadn't gone more than ten metres when Lara shoved Carter hard into the platform and ducked in beside him, fingers to her lips. Carter crouched, and they both listened. There was a faint sound of footsteps, then voices, and then nothing for several seconds.

Lara and Carter armed themselves, and, staying low, in the lee of the platform, moved towards the site.

Her previous surveillance of the site told Lara that it was just a Division Eleven guard. She'd have no problem silencing him without being noticed. Most of the station was wide open and well lit. Carter covered Lara as she sped across it, keeping low, her gun raised. Once safe, Lara did the same for Carter. He was bigger, heavier than Lara, and he was three metres from cover when the guard appeared.

Carter launched himself from his position at the same time Lara instinctively threw herself at the guard's back. The man went down hard. Lara had taken him by surprise and got a good solid blow in fast. He was unconscious before he'd hit the ground. Carter clung around his waist, but let go when he realised that the man wasn't fighting.

"Division Eleven?" whispered Carter, patting the man down, and going through the pockets of his jacket before finding some ID. He held it up for Lara to look at.

The guard had not made a sound as he'd gone down. The only noises were the sounds of the attack, of his body falling. They should have gone unnoticed.

"Checks out," Lara whispered back. She took a length of nylon cord from the knapsack and secured the unconscious guard. She gagged him for good measure. Silence was golden.

Carter and Lara proceeded with caution, but Lara didn't expect any further encounters. Her surveillance had only ever shown one Division Eleven agent belowground at any given time.

"Show me everything," said Lara as they entered the site proper. "If Vata is still in play, I want to get a good look at the canisters he wanted from Denny."

"Shouldn't we leave that to the M.O.D.?" asked Carter.

"Do you think Theresa Johnson and her minions can stop Vata getting his hands on anything he wants, if he wants it badly enough?" asked Lara. "If Strand can walk out of here with a canister, not to mention the sword... If I can hook up to their CCTV for long enough to get a couple of dozen good shots of Candle Lane..."

"Good point," said Carter.

Then he did a double-take, his face draining of colour, his eyes wide.

"What?" asked Lara.

"Shit," said Carter. "The canisters. The nerve gas. We should have HAZMAT gear. What the heck are we doing here?"

"So much for preparedness," said Lara. "But with the possibility that Vata could be close on our heels, the faster we work, the better. This should just give us the incentive we need to get the job done quickly."

CHAPTER TWENTY-TWO:
UNINVITED COMPANY
Candle Lane

Lara took off the knapsack and opened the large pocket on the front. Whatever else she carried, she always had nylon knapsacks, specimen bags, dust masks, and gloves. She handed some to Carter and began to put gloves on.

"Will the mask help?" asked Carter.

"It can't hurt," said Lara, "and it's the best I can do."

She stowed the knapsack with the climbing gear, and Carter led the way through the scaffold and over duckboards to the area of the site where the Dornier had been discovered. It protruded from one wall of a narrow cavity, a little above head height. The fuselage was shredded and concertinaed, and had penetrated at a steep angle. Most of the nose had been compacted, and the cockpit was crumpled and distorted. The damage to the front of the plane was extensive and certainly not survivable.

"There," said Carter, pointing up and to Lara's right.

"I can't see much," said Lara. "Let's get up there."

They climbed the ladder onto a platform that was one scaffold plank wide. There was no room for manoeuvre, and no way into the body of the plane. Close up, however, Lara could see where the canisters were packed into the rear of the payload space.

"Is that usual?" she asked, pointing at the reinforced areas that had helped to keep the compartment more or less intact.

"I know very little about Second World War aircraft," said Carter, "but, from a simple engineering point of view, it looks like they wanted to keep this stuff from getting crushed."

Lara reached in and touched one of the canisters. It moved freely in its cradle. She touched another and another. It would be simple enough to lift them out and bag them.

"Okay," said Lara. "Let's do this."

Lara lifted the canisters out of their cradles one at a time and handed them to Carter. He bagged and sealed them individually and then put them into the two nylon knapsacks, keeping the weight distribution even.

They worked quickly, but cautiously.

"That's four in each knapsack, Lara," said Carter. "How many do you plan to take?"

"Oh, I think that's quite enough, don't you?" said a voice from below.

"Shit!" said Carter.

"That's one way to put it," said Florence Race. "Now why don't you just turn around so I can get a good look at you?"

Carter and Lara stood and turned on the narrow scaffold plank. Below them, Florence Race was standing in the chamber with three of Vata's Wolf-Heads, all pointing guns at them.

"Brava!" said Lara. "You got here faster than I anticipated. I guess with Mr. Vata on board, two heads are better than one. Or, in this case, two heads are almost as good as one, since I got here first."

"As pretty as your head is, Lara, I've beaten you to the prize more than once before."

"So, why don't you just shoot us now, Florence, and be done with it?" asked Lara.

"I wouldn't dream of it," said Florence. "You and I still have work to do, Lara. I would have preferred Nefertiti's tomb, but you rather ruined that. Perhaps Gwynnever's tomb is better. You can make it up to me on your home soil."

"What's the trade, Florence?"

"Trade, Lara?"

"With Dritan Vata?" asked Lara. "He helped you get in here, and you're surrounded by his goons. Are you doing his dirty work now? Shame on you for letting a man use you."

Florence laughed.

"Is he using me, Lara, or am I using him?" she asked. "If we both get what we want, does it matter?"

"Neither one of you has got what you want, yet, Florence, and you're the one in the firing line."

Florence laughed.

"You see which way the guns are pointing," she said.

"But they're never going to fire," said Lara. "I saw Vata in the tomb. He won't risk gunfire anywhere near these canisters."

"So come down, and let's talk," said Florence, signalling the Wolf-Heads to lower their weapons.

Lara pulled off her mask and gloves and made her way down the ladder. Carter followed, carrying the knapsacks, one over each shoulder. He preferred to keep the gloves on and mask in place.

"Perhaps you could lead us to the chamber, Mr. Bell," said Florence. "After all, you're such a useful guide. Without you, we would never have found our way here through the catacombs."

Carter stood his ground.

"Come on, Carter. Let's get this over with," said Lara.

Carter glared at her but did not speak. He turned and left the chamber with the Dornier, through a narrow portal, down some crude steps carved into the earth, and along a passage with a duckboard floor and props holding up the earth above. He had to tear hazard tape from every opening, and there were lamps clipped to various pieces of equipment.

This was not the way that Lara had come into the chamber on her first visit to Candle Lane.

Carter tore down the last piece of hazard tape, and Lara followed him into the wide-open space. It was just as she remembered it. It felt almost more dramatic than Nefertiti's treasure chamber, perhaps because it was not surrounded by rooms of great majesty and ceremony, but by mud and filth, by modern London above, and by the tube station.

Lara couldn't help walking up to the altar and laying a hand on it, briefly, her back to Florence.

"I see you brought the sword," said Florence. "Good."

Lara turned to face the other woman. She reached over her shoulder for the sword grip, but Florence had already given the signal to one of the Wolf-Heads.

Reaching for the sword, Lara was not in a good position to defend herself. She took the punch to the solar plexus as her hand took hold of the grip. She was drawing the weapon, but the Wolf-Head's blow took all the air out of her lungs. Her hand opened reflexively, and the sword slipped back into the sheath. Winded, Lara folded. The punch to the chest was followed by another under her chin. Her neck was extended, her head thrown back, and she was toppled onto her back, unconscious.

Carter tried to come to her aid, but he was too aware of the danger of the canisters and their contents, and he didn't put up much of a fight. All the time that Lara was alive, he wasn't going to put either of them in greater jeopardy.

He watched Florence kick Lara's prone body onto its side and reach down and retrieve the sword from the sheath on her back. She held it in both of her hands and grinned.

"It's perfect," she said.

"It doesn't belong to you," said Carter. He felt he had to make some kind of protest.

"On the contrary," said Florence, "I paid Denny Sampson a lot of money for this sword. It is mine now. I am the next great warrior queen."

"The sword was stolen," said Carter. "It belongs to the nation."

"You're right," said Florence. "It does belong to a nation...to a nation of women, and I am its queen."

Florence stood in front of the altar, the long groove stretched out before her. She held the sword out in both of her hands and began the incantation, still fresh in her memory. She had been speaking for no more than thirty seconds when Carter spoke.

"Wait," he said. "What's that sound?"

Lara groaned beside him.

"Keep her quiet," said Florence.

The Wolf-Heads aimed their weapons at Carter and Lara.

Carter helped Lara to sit up. She rotated her neck on her shoulders to ease the pain and breathed deeply to clear her head. She sat closer to Carter and took one of the knapsacks filled with canisters from him and held it in her lap.

Florence began the incantation for a second time.

Lara and Carter both heard distant movement. They looked at each other, and Lara made a sign to stay quiet. She discreetly held two fingers up. Carter wondered what it meant, for a moment, and then realised that Lara was signalling "11." If Division Eleven was checking the site, then all this would be over soon. Lara and Carter would be detained with Florence Race and the Wolf-Heads, but at least the canisters and the sword would be saved.

Moments later, the Wolf-Heads heard sounds, too, of footfalls. Several people were moving towards the site, apparently underground. There seemed to be no sounds from above. They turned, guns raised, and covered the entrance to the chamber.

Florence didn't waver as she came close to completing the first part of the ritual.

"So you accessed the site," said Vata, stepping into the chamber between the Wolf-Heads guarding the entrance. Several more of his bodyguards stood behind him, clearly visible to Lara.

"Miss Croft, I did not expect to have the pleasure of your company yet again."

Florence paused. She had her back to Vata. She stood perfectly still for several moments, the sword still raised in her hands. She spoke a few more words of the incantation, and then appeared to stumble over a phrase.

"My consignment," said Vata. "Have you secured it?"

Florence sighed. She took hold of the grip of the sword in her right hand, held her left arm out for balance, and swung. She cut hard into the waist of one of the Wolf-Heads who had accompanied her onto the site. He dropped his weapon and clutched at his side, but the wound was too deep, and he was suddenly on his knees. Blood spilled from the wound, and he fell, pale-face-first onto the stone floor of the chamber.

Florence turned to Vata.

"You interrupted me," she said. "My work."

"We had an agreement," said Vata, stony-faced. "My consignment."

"Ask them," said Florence, waving the sword in Lara and Carter's direction. "Those hideous orange knapsacks."

Vata made one of his micro-gestures, and one of the men behind him stepped around his boss and crossed the floor to where Lara and Carter were sitting.

Lara pulled her gun and held it against the bag of canisters.

"What do you want, Miss Croft?" asked Vata.

Lara's neck and chest ached, and she was tired. Wasn't it obvious what she wanted? She turned to Carter, searching for inspiration, for the right words and the right tone in which to deliver them. She looked him in the eyes. Those deep, dark, brown eyes. Lara blinked, and when she opened her eyes, she saw something else: the eyes were a softer brown, closer together, deeper set, and they were separated by a broad bridge of soft, dark fur.

Lara blinked again and turned back to Vata.

"The sword," she said. "I want the sword."

"How many canisters?" asked Vata.

Lara didn't answer.

Carter looked at her. She seemed pale and hazy, and he was worried for her. She hadn't fully recovered from her ordeal in Egypt, and she'd taken a serious blow. She'd been unconscious for at least a couple of minutes.

"Eight in the bags," said Carter. "More still in the payload bay."

Lara didn't hear Carter. She was watching Florence. She was watching the altar, the obelisk. She shook her head and blinked when the altar appeared to bulge and shimmer. When she opened her eyes, the light was too bright, and the script carved onto the faces of the obelisk seemed to be writhing and dancing.

Lara blinked again and turned her attention to Florence's face. It seemed to be changing. The hair had gone, and a great domed headdress seemed to have replaced it. Florence's features were refining: a long, elegant nose; a perfectly proportioned chin; high cheekbones; and wide, almond-shaped eyes. She looked more youthful, and more beautiful than any woman had a right to be.

Then Lara realised that she could hear words. At first she could not make out their meaning, but then they came into focus.

It was a warding, a summoning, an investiture. It was a prayer and a constitution. It was all things to all women. It was a declaration of nationhood, of sorority, of reign. The words filled the chamber like a great aria.

Then Lara heard another sound: a low rumble, the snarling bass notes of the beginning of a howl. She turned her head slowly, not wanting to take her eyes off Florence but knowing that she must.

No one was speaking except for Florence, lost in her incantation.

There were new figures in the chamber. They were all looking at Lara. Half-a-dozen pairs of eyes were on her, palest grey and golden yellow, framed in black and brown.

Wolves.

Wolves, spectral and eerie, had entered the room like shadows.

Lara blinked and turned to Carter for reassurance. But it was no longer Carter. Soft brown eyes looked back at her, on either side of the broad bridge of fur. The ghost bear's snarl rumbled and rose and grew into a howl. The wolves joined in.

Lara blinked hard. Her neck hurt. She rotated it on her shoulders and looked around the room again. She closed her right hand firmly around the grip of her gun.

Then something moved fast, from left to right in front of her—sleek grey fur, back arched, flying through the air. She had aimed and fired before she knew what she was doing.

The wolf fell to the ground, but not before it had bowled over one of Vata's men, taking the boss down with him.

Lara stood. She looked down at the beast she had killed. There was no blood on its pelt where she had shot through its spine. There was no blood anywhere. She watched the wolf roll left and right. It was two beasts now, back on their feet, low to the ground, a stalking pair.

The ghosts were multiplying.

She felt something brush past her legs and turned to see another wolf, tawny, its yellow eyes flashing up at her as she looked down on it. It did not attack her. It yawned slightly and smacked its chops before walking around her. It tensed, snarled, and charged another of Vata's men.

Lara fired again, and the guard was saved.

She hated herself.

The second wolf, like the first, lay still for a few moments, then rolled onto two new bellies and walked away as twins, leaving no trace of its former self.

Dritan Vata tried to back out of the chamber, allowing the three Wolf-Heads behind him to enter and protect him.

Carter had worked his back up the wall he was sitting against until he was standing. He dared not draw his gun, and he pressed his back against the wall in the hope of feeling more secure.

The light in the room turned grey, as if overcast, and Carter felt movement behind him. Something was moving, pressing against his back.

Lara cast her eyes around the room as the light changed, growing darker and greyer, like a stormy sky.

The hieroglyphics on the obelisk had stopped dancing, and the marks had become deeper and bolder—but more random, and less like pictograms. The stone was changing form and colour. Lara watched as cracks and splits began to appear in it and then wave and curl away in organic shapes. Then nodes and tumours began to appear on its surface, as if growing out of it. The surface looked moist to the touch, brown, organic.

Lara felt the stone floor begin to crease and crack under her feet, as the texture broke down and began to flake.

Carter had to take a step away from the wall as something nudged him in the back. Another tumour appeared under his arm, growing out and curling around as if to clutch at him, trap him.

Then he heard snuffling at his feet.

Lara pulled her knife and was on the beast. The wolves were stalking Vata's men, and she didn't care— not while Carter was under threat.

Something was moving at him. Not a wolf. Something heavy and hunched. A wild boar.

Lara dropped onto the beast's humped back, put an arm around its throat, and thrust her blade deep into the thick wad of flesh between its front legs.

The wild boar squealed once, a hard, grunting shriek, and then died, slumping into the mulchy undergrowth.

Carter looked at Lara with a nod of gratitude, but she had to blink hard. Carter's face kept becoming the head of a bear: pathos in its eyes, its broad snout tapering, its cheeks furred.

She turned her attention back to Florence.

It was not Florence; neither was it the beautiful woman who seemed to be emerging in her place.

Where Florence had been now stood a hideous wraith creature. The skull was naked, Florence's hair burnt and frazzled away from her shrinking skin. Her lips were pulled back tight, her cheeks sunken, her eyelids pulled down tight over shrunken, desiccated eyeballs.

Florence's incantation, once a song, was now the rasping whisper of an ancient crone. Lara could hardly make out the words that had resonated through the space only minutes before. They were overwhelmed now by the sounds of ancient forest.

A great tree creaked and moaned, its branches moving with the wind that had caught the rhythm of the incantation and was lifting and swaying the canopy, moving the light in speckles and spatters on the forest floor. There was a strong smell of fresh rot, of sap and damp and of the creatures, of warm wolf pelts, and the musk of bear.

Lara looked at the altar. The great stone was now shaded by the tree. She stood mesmerised. She watched.

Florence moved her right hand to the grip of the sword and took its weight, freeing her left hand to wrap around her right. She held the sword upright in front of her ruined face.

The tone of the incantation had changed. The cadence and the rhythm were new.

Lara drew her guns, one in each hand, aimed at arm's length, and fired them into what had once been Florence's body, but the shots had no effect.

Florence plunged the tip of the sword into the stone. It was, as it had always been, the perfect fit.

The sword had found its home.

For a moment, the sword sat in the stone, the blade buried almost to its hilt, Florence's hands still holding tightly to the grip.

Then the stone began to change colour around the hilt of the sword, white-hot at the epicentre, growing black as the blade's energy travelled through the stone. The stone seemed to creak and moan, and then there was an explosive cracking sound, like nothing Lara had ever heard.

Florence's body flew backwards across the chamber, crashed hard against the thick trunk of a well-grown tree where once the wall had been, and crumpled to a heap among its roots.

The sword flew out of the stone after her and landed point first in the tree a metre above her head. It glowed red-hot.

The atmosphere darkened instantly to a rich grey-blue, and the wind thrashed through the trees. The wood groaned and screamed; the bark swirled and the branches wove.

The wolves that had stalked and surrounded the Wolf-Heads craned their necks and lifted their heads, raising their voices over the thunderous storm that was brewing. As their howls filled the air, their shoulders rose, their manes thickened, their teeth extended, and their eyes flashed. They were bigger, fiercer than they had been moments before.

There was more snuffling, and several wild boar staggered out from between the densely packed trees, their heads broad and strong, their tusks pointing fiercely skywards, their humps dense with muscle.

Lara did not hesitate. She strode across the forest floor and pulled the blade free from the tree trunk that was quickly growing around it.

She did not feel the extreme heat of the grip, still glowing dark red.

CHAPTER TWENTY-THREE: THE SWORD IN THE STONE
Candle Lane

Lara sheathed the sword.

The battle was won. She knew that Florence Race was dead. It was over.

She was exhausted. More than that, she was overwhelmed with a sense of enormous relief, but also with huge responsibility. She felt momentarily feverish, light-headed, faint. The forest world around her turned black; the sounds of the ghost beasts faded. She did not feel anything after that. Lara did not crumple to the ground in a dainty faint. She crashed headlong, like a felled tree.

Lara awoke, facedown on a cold stone floor. She rolled over and opened her eyes, shielding them from the harsh light of the halogen lamps that seared the atmosphere.

The walls of the chamber, like the floor she was lying on, were solid stone, and the obelisk and altar with their hieroglyphics were exactly as they had been for more than three thousand years. Wild boar no longer snuffled and roamed, and the only sounds were of the Wolf-Heads, pulling blades, ready to attack.

The canisters! thought Lara.

She had secured the sword, but in good conscience she could not allow a man like Dritan Vata to escape the site with the Dornier's payload. Besides, they were ready to kill her and anyone else who got in their way.

Lara got to her feet, drawing her own blades. The Wolf-Heads came at her from all angles, but could only fight her one at a time, and she was faster and smaller than they were. She could also deploy two blades at once, as effective with a knife in either hand.

She got in under her first assailant's guard, flicking a blade across his left wrist before cutting down across his cheek and then plunging in hard under his collarbone. All the time Lara was fending off his knife hand with the blade in her left hand.

The Wolf-Head bled profusely from his left wrist, but the strike to his chest made him retreat. Clutching his left wrist with his right hand, the Wolf-Head took a step back and dropped to the floor, allowing one of his colleagues to take his place.

Lara had no choice but to thrust at her new opponent's groin, while ducking under his attempts to jab at her neck. He managed to slice a chunk off her ponytail and cut into the sheath on her back. Metal sang against obsidian.

The Wolf-Head fell backwards into one of his comrades, opening up an angle for Lara to slice into his thigh. He was out of the fight.

Before his colleagues could clear him out of the way, Lara dropkicked the Wolf-Head who was charging in on her right. She'd seen him in her peripheral vision. He

Lara Croft and the Blade of Gwynnever

was too big to take down with a single blade. Her stance was off-kilter, so the kick was the best she could do.

The Wolf-Head landed hard, and Lara recovered faster. She straddled his chest, trapping his knife hand with her left knee. He freed his left hand and brought it up to throttle her, but Lara was quick to respond. His reach was longer than hers, so she struck at the soft inside of his elbow, carving through the veins and connective tissue. His arm collapsed, and she was free to deal with the next assault.

A strong arm was around Lara's throat, a Wolf-Head attacking from behind before she was able to rise from her seated position on the corpse's chest. She was dragged up, choking, still holding her blade. But once her feet were off the ground, she struggled to defend herself.

Lara felt the hot breath of the attacker on her neck. Then she heard his scream. His hold loosened, and she braced her legs, knowing that he would drop her. She landed soft in her knees and turned, staying low.

Her assailant was on fire. His jacket was ablaze, and he was trying to rip it off.

How had it happened? Her back had been pressed against his chest. Where had the extreme heat come from? Why had she felt nothing?

Instinctively, Lara reached over her shoulder. Her hand closed around the grip of Gwynnever's sword, and she drew it in one swift, effortless movement. But there was no need to attack; the Wolf-Head was engulfed in fire and would not survive.

The chamber did not grow back into a forest. It simply became one in the blink of an eye...except that Lara wasn't even sure that she'd had time to blink.

The ground beneath her feet was springy and yielding, giving her the perfect base. Light shone through the canopy. The trees gave her perfect cover, and the sounds of the animals were like a symphony— no, like the perfect soundtrack to the movie of her battle.

Lara glanced over her shoulder at a roar to her left, and the next instant the bear was beside her. High on its hind legs, it reared, shook its head, and bellowed another great roar.

Lara smiled, satisfied.

The bear was huge, standing head and shoulders above her, but not over her. It would be her ally, not her nemesis.

Several of the Wolf-Heads at the rear of the group turned at the sight of the beast and ran from the fight. One fired a shot, but it only angered the beautiful creature. The bear's jaws opened wider, and it tossed its head as it lunged towards the nearest foe on its great paws. It felled its first victim, clawing out his throat, and moved on to a second.

Lara cut and thrust and swung her blade. It was weightless in her grip, responding to her every move, her every thought.

She could hear throaty rumbles that she knew would turn to howls and the snuffle of the wild boar that frequented the old English woodlands, but she did not fear these primordial beasts.

This was her time, her place, and the bear was her companion, her champion, and the king of the woodland.

They would cause her no harm while he stood beside her.

Dritan Vata had remained calm, cool, detached in all his dealings with Denny Sampson, with Florence Race, and with Lara Croft. His only concern was securing the payload of the Dornier, his only fear that the canisters would be destroyed.

Vata dreaded gunfire. His first, last, and most crucial order was that there must be no gunfire. He wanted the canisters intact so that he could deploy them for his own ends, in his own war.

Since he knew that the contents of the canisters could be lethal, Carter Bell wanted to avoid gunfire, too. He knew the canisters must be kept intact, but he was far more concerned about not being shot by Vata's men. He did not particularly want to die. He kept possession of the canisters, knowing they wouldn't dare shoot at him while he carried them. Everything else was an insane blur.

When there was nothing else to be done, Dritan Vata retreated to the rear of his phalanx with a bodyguard. The Wolf-Heads were well trained and well paid, and they were schooled in his cause. They were his countrymen; they all shared an ideology. They looked up to their leader and would do anything for him. They had lived through wars.

None of them had seen or lived through anything like this.

Faced with a bear attack...faced with a madwoman and a bear, one of them had drawn his sidearm and fired. Faced with the impossible, the Wolf-Heads had wanted to run.

Dritan Vata slipped his right hand under his jacket and pulled the Glock 42 from the holster under his arm.

He gave no warning. He shot the Wolf-Head squarely in the chest at a range of about a metre. Nobody walked away from Vata. Nobody walked away from the fight, not one of his men. Not a Wolf-Head. His bodyguard looked at him.

"Fear is of no use to me," said Vata, slipping the gun back inside his jacket. "Men who are afraid are of no use to me."

Carter could not let Lara fight alone. Doing battle with Florence Race for the sword was one thing, but now she was waging a war against a regiment of soldiers. He would not stand by and watch her die. Besides, he had an advantage. He had the one thing that Vata wanted.

He had the canisters.

Carter Bell pulled the straps of the knapsacks up over his arms and secured them at his shoulders, one on his back and one on his chest. He wore them like body armour. The Wolf-Heads could not attack him without destroying the payload.

Then he armed himself. He stood, his guns aimed at the Wolf-Heads.

But Lara was fighting so hard, swinging, attacking, reacting with such force and energy that Carter could not get a clean shot. He stepped from one side to the other, trying to lock on to a target.

Finally, Bell began to move forwards, knees bent, weaving. He moved to Lara's right, away from the great tree where the altar had once stood, and took a shot. Then another. He winged one Wolf-Head, shooting him in the left shoulder. The man drew his gun, but somebody barked at him not to shoot.

Carter smiled. He hadn't liked their chances: just one man and one woman against more than a dozen hardened paramilitary types, but they had two distinct advantages. Lara Croft was a force of nature, and Carter Bell was the only person in the fight who could legitimately fire a gun.

CHAPTER TWENTY-FOUR:
DIVISION ELEVEN
Candle Lane

"What happened to Sweeney?" asked Franks.

"Nothing, sir," said Beecham.

"Well, you see, that's my problem."

"What do you mean, sir?"

"No sitrep from Sweeney?"

"No, sir."

"I'm calling command," said Franks. "After the fiasco with that art student earlier, and the thing with those men walking onto the site, we'll be cautioned for vigilance at the next debrief. I don't like this."

The two black-clad men were standing outside the boarded-up tube station on Candle Lane. There were so many lights shining down on them that they cast no shadows on the empty street. There were more Division Eleven officers stationed at either end of Candle Lane and at intervals along its length. Nobody had tried to enter the lane for several hours, not since the strange men had been turned away. There had been no repercussions from the earlier events, despite the men asking too many questions, but Franks still didn't like it.

"It's just Sweeney, sir," said Beecham.

Sweeney was on the rota for the belowground shift from ten until two, and his main duty was to make hourly situation reports.

Beecham pulled a slim, black notebook from a breast pocket and opened it.

"Twenty-three hundred hours. Sitrep logged at twenty-three-zero-four, sir," said Beecham.

"It's not good enough."

"There's nothing down there, sir. One way in, one way out. And nothing and no one has got past us, sir."

"He's ten minutes late for his zero-hour sitrep, and it's me who'll have to answer to command," said Franks. "It's just not good enough."

Franks turned and began to walk away, talking into his comms unit.

"Franks to Sweeney. Sitrep required. Franks to Sweeney...Franks to Sweeney. Shit!"

Franks walked briskly to the end of Candle Lane. He keyed his comms unit again and spoke into it.

"Franks to Sweeney. Sweeney?"

Franks keyed an open link and said, "Roll call." The names came back one at a time in alphabetical sequence.

"Adlard."

"Beecham."

"Corbett."

"Chandar."

"Franks," said Franks when it was his turn.

"Heggarty."

"Jaganathan."

"Millward."

...

"Sweeney? Are you there, Sweeney?" asked Franks. "Okay, continue roll call."

"Tyson."

"Watkins."

"Watson."

"Thank you, gentlemen. That will be all," said Franks. He keyed the command channel.

Three minutes later, Division Eleven reinforcements were on their way, and Franks was restructuring his group on the ground in Candle Lane.

"Heggarty and Jaganathan, cover the north end of the street, armed," said Franks. "No one enters the restricted area. Chandar and Millward, cover the south end of the lane. Same applies. The rest of you are with me."

"Permission to speak, sir?" said Watkins.

Franks nodded.

"Is this search and rescue, sir? Or something else?"

"Buggered if I know," said Franks. "We treat every situation as if it's hostile. Sweeney might have banged his damned head for all I know, and be lying unconscious down there. But we don't walk in blind and stupid. We assume we're entering a hostile situation."

"Right, sir," said Beecham.

"Heggarty, when reinforcements arrive, fully secure the street and send the rest down to us," said Franks.

"Understood, sir," said Heggarty.

"Right," said Franks, arming himself with his baton, "let's do this. Remember, no ballistics at any time."

"Bring Baris," Vata said to his bodyguard, "and follow me."

The three men left the fighting behind and wove their way through the site in search of the Dornier.

"Miss Croft has eight of the canisters. Denny Sampson had one. A full payload could contain up to thirty-two canisters. You two will retrieve the remainder," said Vata.

"If there's a gun battle?" asked Vata's bodyguard.

Vata glared at him.

"I have set an example," said Vata, "and I have given an order. You are a Wolf-Head. Would you disobey an order?"

"No, sir," said the bodyguard. "But what if the canisters are destroyed? What if the gas is released?"

"It cannot happen," said Vata. He was dismissive. "The men have their orders."

"You saw the woman fight—"

Vata drew his gun again and put it to his bodyguard's head, wrapping his arm tight around the man's neck.

"Do you want to die, Rugova?" he asked.

"No, sir," said Rugova. "I want to do what is right."

"Is it right to follow your commander's orders?" asked Vata.

"Yes, sir."

Vata let go of his bodyguard, straightened his suit, and holstered his gun. Rugova said nothing, and he did nothing. He had misspoken, and he would not make the same mistake twice.

"Over here," said Baris, holding the torn end of a piece of hazard tape and looking through a hole excavated in part of the wall close to where Vata had subdued Rugova.

Vata was first through the gap and into the chamber that housed the Dornier.

"Up, up," he said. "Empty it. Find everything."

Rugova and Baris climbed the ladder onto the scaffold boards and began to inspect the wrecked airplane. They did not have the skill or the finesse of archaeologists, but they knew planes and they knew weapons, and it didn't take them long to locate the payload bay. They worked their way to the rear of the bay and found the cradles into which the canisters had been loaded.

"You were right, sir," Rugova called down to Vata. "There are more canisters...many more."

"Retrieve them," said Vata.

Baris had been first to climb the ladder, so he was in the best position to unload the canisters. He took them from their cradles one at time, handling them carefully and giving them to Rugova to inspect and line up on the scaffold board. From there, they could be bagged and carried down to Vata.

It took only a few minutes for the first seven canisters to be removed, checked, and lined up. The next rack of eight was situated behind and above the rack that Baris had just emptied. He had been squatting; now, he stood and leant in. His position was awkward, and it took him longer to empty the next set of cradles. Four canisters came out.

"What's wrong?" asked Rugova when Baris failed to hand him the fifth canister from its cradle in the rack.

"It will not come," said Baris. "The canister is stuck."

Rugova cast an eye along the row of canisters on the scaffold plank next to him.

"We have eleven," he said. "It is enough. We take them down."

The two men filled net bags with the canisters, five in one and six in the other, working their way along the row, back towards the ladder. Then they descended to Vata, who had been watching their progress intently.

"You have them?" asked Vata.

"Yes," said Baris.

"All of them?"

"Eleven, sir," said Rugova.

"All of them?" asked Vata again. "That makes only twenty in total."

"There are more in the wreck," said Rugova.

"Then retrieve them," said Vata. "Do you know what this means for our cause? Are you a patriot? Is it right to follow your commander's orders?"

"As you command," said Baris.

He laid the net bag that he'd been carrying at Vata's feet and strode back across the chamber. Rugova hesitated.

"You are waiting for what?" asked Vata, glaring at Rugova.

Rugova followed Baris, and within moments they were back on the platform.

"You did not say that the canisters were stuck," Rugova said to Baris, quietly so that Vata could not hear them.

"So, I try harder," said Baris. He adjusted his position and put his arms back into the wrecked fuselage. He grabbed the end of the canister, wedged tight in its cradle. He pulled, but nothing happened. He tried to rotate the canister, first anti-clockwise. Nothing. He adjusted his hold on the canister and tried turning it clockwise. There was a grating sound of metal on metal, and the canister moved an inch.

Baris turned to Rugova and smiled, his hands still buried to the elbows in the fuselage. He rotated the canister back and forth, pulling as he went. The grating sound continued, but the constant, even pressure paid off, and finally the canister was free of the cradle and nestling in Baris's hands. He held it out for Rugova to take.

Rugova looked at the thing. The cylinder was no longer true, and clean, bright metal showed where layers of dirt and paint had been scoured away by the action of removing it.

Rugova took it carefully in both hands and placed it on the scaffold board, close to the top of the ladder. When he returned to Baris's side, he could hear the same ominous scraping sounds coming from inside the payload bay. He held his breath while Baris worked the next canister free.

Franks and his men made their way through the underground station and down onto the platform. They checked and covered at every touch and turn, completing the patterns and formations that they had drilled. Division Eleven worked by the book.

Any combat would be close combat. They were armed with knives and batons and with flash bangs. They had all been issued protective eyewear, ear defenders, and body armour, although not all chose to wear some or all of their gear. Some specialised in stealth and agility, and they trusted their skills more than they trusted their equipment. There was always a compromise, always a price to pay. Some preferred to keep their senses intact; they'd be at a disadvantage if the flash bangs came into play and they weren't prepared. But the alternative was to be permanently compromised. They trusted each other.

They heard the first shot as they reached the platform.

Franks gave the signal, and they dropped down onto the tracks into the lee of the platform, where they could not be seen.

Another signal, and the men made their way along the tracks in the direction of the site.

The second shot came soon after the first. No one spoke, and no one signalled. They didn't need to. They knew that Sweeney was not in a firefight. They had been ordered not to use ballistics, and they would not disobey an order.

The situation was hostile.

Franks's next signal was for the men to put on their gas masks. Word had not come back from command

verifying the contents of the canisters or the lethality of
the gas. They did not even know how effective the gas
masks would be, but they had been issued masks, so
Franks gave the order.

All but one of the men put on a mask.

Progress through the site was slow, and it was Adlard
who gave the next signal. He was not wearing protective
eyewear or ear defenders, and he'd taken point. He was
the first to spot Sweeney.

Sweeney was conscious, but when Corbett removed
the ropes and gag and performed a quick exam, it was
clear that Sweeney was concussed. The medic put his
patient in the recovery position with the last gas mask
securely in place and reassured him that they'd return.
Then he rejoined the group.

The signs were clear. Fresh footprints, broken hazard
tape, equipment shifted and knocked over: a number
of people had passed through the site, heedless of
disturbing it.

Franks signed for a halt, and the men took cover.
Franks removed his ear defenders at a sign from Adlard.
There was considerable noise coming from the oldest
part of the site, from the ancient chamber where
the historic finds had been made: shouts, scuffles. It
was physical. This was not a raid, a burglary. This
was combat.

Franks replaced his ear defenders and spoke.

"Ear defenders and eye protection, everyone, now."
Then he signalled the same command. When everyone
was kitted out, he gave the attack signal and started
the countdown.

CHAPTER TWENTY-FIVE: THREE FACTIONS
The Chamber

Two Wolf-Heads charged Carter. He shot once, into the chest of the man to his right, throwing him off his feet. The second shot thudded into the mulchy ground, as Carter's aim was deflected by a kick from the second assailant.

The kick was followed by a second that came in higher and harder, against Carter's armpit, throwing him off balance and sending the gun spinning out of his hand. The canisters in the knapsacks on his chest and back clanged ominously together, and their weight shifted, changing his centre of gravity.

Carter stumbled and took several staggering steps to his right, kicking up earth and leaves. The momentum turned him, and he finally crashed into a mossy tree trunk, jarring his left shoulder and falling to his knees.

The man he had shot got back to his feet. Body armour had saved his life, but the point-blank shot had knocked him onto his back and pissed him off. He kicked out at Carter, but missed as Carter turned, stepping onto one foot to stand. The Wolf-Head went down for a second time, under his own momentum.

His other assailant was faster, getting Carter in a headlock as he tried to get to his feet, but his grip was compromised by the bulk of the canisters. Carter grasped the Wolf-Head's hand in both of his own, locked it at the wrist, and twisted it, breaking the choke hold. An elbow to the Wolf-Head's gut dropped him, for the moment.

Carter turned his attention to the man he'd shot. They squared off against each other. The Wolf-Head had pulled a knife and was making fast, jabbing movements at Carter's body, trying to get in below the knapsack that covered his chest and belly. Carter reached for his own blade.

It was a standoff. Both men were armoured.

Another Wolf-Head began to circle Carter, and another. The man he'd just dropped came in low, slashing at Carter's legs, making him dance from foot to foot. Another produced a telescopic baton, which he flicked out to its full length and tried to deploy, swinging it at Carter's right arm.

It was chaos.

The Wolf-Heads were tripping over each other to do battle with Carter and Lara, but they were getting in each other's way, and the strange atmosphere and the morphing landscape felt like another adversary.

Lara was deep in the old English woodland, breathing the smells of the land and the air, hearing the creak of the trees and the rustle of the leaves in the wind, seeing the changing light in the dappled spots on the ground. The animals, too, smelt of musk and warm fur, of the cycle of life and death, and of the wild, savage lives they lived. Breathing them in was a heady sensation.

The snuffles of the boar, the howls of the wolves, and the roar of her beloved bear spurred Lara on, and the gleaming obsidian blade in her hand did the rest.

She felt as if she had come home. This was her place, her time to shine, to thrive, to show the world who she was and all that she could be.

Wolves circled her, wild boar stood guard, and men fell at her feet, not in fealty, but in death.

The sword swung again, as if of its own accord. It crashed against some weapon, a blade that it locked with, bit into, and twisted away. Lara's wrist turned, and Gwynnever's sword crossed in front of her body in another perfect arc, smashing the blade out of the Wolf-Head's hand, sending it spinning into the canopy. Her grip altered, as if the sword required it, and she was thrusting down, driving the obsidian blade into her combatant's belly.

Lara was ready when another Wolf-Head attacked, and another. They breathed hard and sweated. They exerted themselves, spent their energy. They grunted and spat. They groaned and fell. Lara's battle was a dance, her breathing light and sweet, her heartbeat slow and steady.

But there were so many of them!

Lara felled three Wolf-Heads...four. She caught sight of Carter as she circled with her latest attacker, waiting for another long swing of her sword. He was surrounded. She frowned, confused, afraid for a moment.

Lara blinked and glanced again, worried that Carter would be gone, disappeared beneath a pile of Wolf-Heads baying for his blood.

He was there...and gone. In his place, standing a head and shoulders taller, was her bear, soft eyes looking at her across the void, huge paws flailing, swiping at the nearest Wolf-Heads, maw wide open in a great roar.

Lara did not hesitate. She swung the sword, letting its weight and momentum do its work for her.

Beecham deployed the first of the flash bangs into a tightly packed group of Wolf-Heads. He could not see into the chamber, and Franks did not want to get any closer. There were seven of them, and there was a risk of being heard.

The rearguard of Wolf-Heads dropped to the ground, disorientated. Others, further into the chamber, tried to fight on, despite the instant deafness, disorientation, and visual impairment.

Carter dropped hard to a low crouch, wrapped his arms around the canisters strapped to his chest as best he could, and tucked his head low. He hoped that none of the canisters were damaged. If they were, he prayed for a quick and painless death.

A moment after he went down, Carter felt a weight drop onto his shoulders, and a moment after that he felt a tugging on the strap of the knapsack on his back. He reached around, blind, and grasped the knife that was sawing through the strapping. Part of the exposed blade cut deep into the flesh between his thumb and forefinger. Instinctively, he let go and threw back his head, hard. It connected with the Wolf-Head's face with a crack, breaking the man's nose and sending him reeling.

As the rearguard of the Wolf-Heads peeled away, towards the Division Eleven squad, Beecham deployed a second flash bang. It penetrated deeper into the chamber, momentarily pausing the skirmish.

With fewer bodies between him and the entrance, and the burst of bright light, Beecham also got a good view into the chamber.

"Bloody hell!" he said, as he took in the scene, as if it was some fantastical tableau. He was rooted to the spot for a moment, as his colleagues surged towards him, weapons raised, ready to take out the Wolf-Heads.

Having removed the four remaining canisters in the rack and placed them on the platform, Baris and Rugova set to work on the final rack of canisters. It was below the last batch and to the rear of the payload bay. It was the most difficult to reach, in the tightest space.

"It's enough," whispered Rugova.

"Nothing's enough so long as there are canisters in the plane," said Baris. "We do what the boss tells us."

"And we die."

"So we die for the cause," said Baris. "It will happen anyway, one day." He beamed at Rugova, and put his hands back inside the crushed fuselage.

He reached for the cradle furthest from him in the top row of the rack, put both hands around the nose of the canister, and pulled. Nothing. He tried turning it anti-clockwise, but it wouldn't move. He adjusted his grip on the canister and tried again, this time rotating clockwise. The canister moved a few millimetres, metal squealing on metal.

"Stop," said Rugova. "You have to stop."

"It's moving," said Baris.

"No."

Baris took his hands out of the payload bay and turned to Rugova.

"What?" he asked. "You want to do it?"

"If it breaks, we die," said Rugova.

"Easy ones first?" asked Baris.

Rugova wiped a bead of sweat from his brow.

"Okay," he said.

Baris put his hands back inside the airplane and tried the canister to the right of the one he'd just been handling. After some manoeuvring, it began to make the scraping sounds that had signalled the removal of the last four cylinders, and it was retrieved after a couple of minutes. The other two in the same row were collected in a similar fashion.

Baris turned his attention to the row beneath. The first two canisters barely moved, and when they did, they squealed horribly. Rugova insisted that he stop, but Baris became impatient. So did Vata.

"What are you doing? What's going on up there? Where are my canisters?" he called out to them.

Baris turned and waved to his boss.

"You see?" he rasped at Rugova. "Coward!"

He plunged his hands back into the broken plane and went straight for the canister on the top row, furthest from him, the first that had squealed, the first that Rugova had rejected.

He took the nose firmly in his hands and rotated it a few millimetres anti-clockwise to its original position. It squealed exactly as it had before. Then it stuck. He adjusted his grip and rotated hard in the opposite direction. The shriek of metal on metal was appalling.

Tugging and twisting, Baris wrestled with the canister, wiggling it a centimetre or two in either direction, exerting as much lateral and forward pressure on it as he could to try to free it from the constricting cradle. His bared teeth were gritted, and beads of sweat gathered on his forehead from the exertion. The last squeal ended in the sound of tearing metal and a faint hiss.

Baris pulled his hands away, his face turning to Rugova in a wide-eyed stare. Rugova's mouth dropped open.

A great ball of lightning and a crash of thunder filled the forest.

Lara's senses were almost overwhelmed by the majesty of it. The Wolf-Heads fell away around her, blinded, deafened, disorientated. Lara was no longer under attack. It was a sign. This was only the beginning. The battle would begin again, and it would rage more fiercely; her adversaries would grow in force and numbers. She needed to redouble her strength, to grow in might and vigour. She must prevail.

There was another great crash of thunder and another bolt of lightning.

Lara stood tall, feet shoulder-width apart, firmly planted in the rich sod, her home soil. She threw back her head, her hair swinging in the breeze, and cast her eyes up into the canopy and the sky beyond. She raised her arms at her sides, Gwynnever's sword...*her* sword...extended wide, the blade gleaming in the unearthly light.

The words came from somewhere deep in her heart. She did not think them, she only felt them, and they poured from her lips without her bidding.

Right must be done for the good of the world. Peace and order must be restored and preserved. She did not seek the fight, but when it was laid at her door, she would defend tolerance, compassion, and peace. There was no room for the ambitious, the ruthless, the unforgiving in her world.

After the words came the energy. It drove out of the ground and infused everything it touched, everything from her world.

Lara's beloved wolves stopped circling, sat, and looked up at her, their paws reaching into the sky. Then they began to stretch and morph into the air, becoming one with it and with each other, forming two dense clouds, one grey, one tawny. They were the very essence of wolves, their claws and teeth, their savage, carnal rage.

The wild boar stopped snuffling and gazed at Lara. Their eyes fixed on her, their forms began to mingle and shift with the breeze around them. They grew into one great, airy beast—broad shoulders, a massive hump, and great, gleaming tusks—ready to defend its mistress. It was as light as air, there and gone in an instant.

Lara turned to her bear and smiled. He dropped from his full height on hind legs and shambled over to her. She placed a hand on the top of his head, and he cast his soft eyes up to meet hers. She glanced past him at Carter, crouching, doubled over on the ground.

Her family would defend him now.

Division Eleven were already upon them when the Wolf-Heads were able to defend the attack. The rearguard had not gained entry to the chamber, but had been jostling in the space outside, trying to get in and join the fray.

They were being beaten and subdued with coshes and batons, but they were tough, battle-hardened soldiers, and they would not give up without a fight. Many of them had also come prepared, well-equipped with partial body armour.

Franks soon wished he had been able to give the order to fire, but ballistics were out of bounds for this engagement, for any engagement at the Candle Lane site.

Despite Division Eleven going in hard and fast, the Wolf-Heads were beginning to get up and fight back. They fought hard and dirty.

Franks allowed one of the Wolf-Heads to drive him back, away from the chamber into more open space. He ducked a blow to his left shoulder and swung his baton in a horizontal arc at hip height, coming in under the Wolf-Head's body armour and hitting him hard in the hip joint.

Off balance, the Wolf-Head made little impact with his next attempt, and Franks was able to parry and then drive the end of his baton hard into the man's groin, felling him. The Wolf-Head reached, instinctively, for the pain, dropping his weapon, which Franks kicked away. It took him mere moments to put a knee in his victim's back, cable-tie his hands and ankles, and move on to the next.

The rest of his squad followed Franks's lead, drawing the fight out into the areas around the crowded chamber, turning the battle into a series of hand-to-hand combats instead of a free-for-all brawl.

Watkins went down hard, caught by a baton to the kidneys by one Wolf-Head, and then punched hard in the sternum by a second. He was laid out by a second punch to the head. The second Wolf-Head drew a knife to finish him off, but Corbett tripped him, straddled him, and got in two good punches to the man's face before he could slit Watkins's throat. Watkins recovered, shook his head, and then reached out for a leg that was inching close to his position. He grabbed and pulled hard, tossing another Wolf-Head to the floor.

Division Eleven worked together and separately, fighting their own battles, but taking any opportunities they saw to attack the opposition.

Watkins was back on his feet, lunging, head down, at the next Wolf-Head, and the fight went on.

There were more Wolf-Heads than there were men in Franks's squad, and he was the only one who had taken a man out of the battle.

There was not a third bolt of lightning nor a third crash of thunder. It didn't matter. Lara's work was done.

The Wolf-Heads could rise again, and she was equipped for battle.

They did rise.

The Wolf-Heads got to their feet, before her, and then they divided. To the rear, they no longer tried to enter the chamber. She could see them, turning, fleeing.

Those who were left kept coming, bearing down on her.

The mist wolves reared and spun through the air, stalking their prey and pouncing. The horrified Wolf-Heads froze or tried to back away, terror written all over their faces. There was no mercy. The mist wolves attacked with claw and tooth, ripping throats and tearing limbs.

The cloud boar tossed its prey on shredding tusks until they were torn to pieces, and then grunted and snuffled through the remains of the Wolf-Heads it had destroyed.

The bear shambled over to Carter, shielding him from the Wolf-Heads, looming over them, swiping its great paws at heads and chests, snagging its claws in their flesh if they tried to attack Lara's friend.

Gwynnever's blade yet sang, cutting the air with impossible agility, defending attacks from two more Wolf-Heads brave or foolish enough to think they could take on this woman and defeat her.

They came together, wielding knives, ducking for cover behind the stone that had housed her sword, circling the great tree where the obelisk had once stood. They tried to evade her blade, and failed. The tree shifted its roots to trip one of the Wolf-Heads, and then curved a branch to throttle him as he fell forwards.

The second man had a cosh in one hand and a stiletto in the other. He bounded onto the altar to fly at Lara. The rubber soles of his shoes melted instantly to the molten-hot surface of the rock as the enemy's weight landed on it. The Wolf-Head lost momentum and balance and wheeled his arms frantically as he tried to free his feet.

Instead of the flying tackle, the Wolf-Head fell off the stone, collapsing onto Lara's outstretched sword, and another of Vata's men was dead.

He was the last.

Lara looked around at the devastation. The bodies of the dead Wolf-Heads, and of Florence Race, were strewn on the forest floor. Only Carter Bell sat, unharmed, a few metres to Lara's right.

The air trembled. Thunder spoke.

The pair of mist wolves flew around Lara, weaving between the trees, dancing an elaborate pattern midway between the ground and the tree canopy. The cloud boar joined the dance, and Lara's bear rose on his hind legs, turning circles and swatting playfully at them.

Lara sheathed her sword, strode over to Carter, and offered him her hand.

Rugova knew that the canister had broken. He had heard the sound of metal tearing and splitting, and he had heard the hiss of the gas escaping from a pressurised container. He would be sick or dead in moments. Worse, he would be insane.

Rugova strode with a purpose back along the narrow platform, past the row of canisters that he and Baris had already collected from the plane, and towards the ladder.

"Where are you going?" shouted Vata.

Rugova did not answer. Baris stood up beside the payload bay and turned to face his boss. Vata glanced at him, and Baris shrugged.

Vata slid his hand into his jacket and pulled out the Glock 42.

"Stop right there," he shouted. "You bring me the canisters, or you die."

"I'm already dead," said Rugova. "We're all dead. We have to get out. Now!"

Rugova did not wait for his boss's assent. He turned his back on him to descend the ladder.

Vata aimed the compact squarely at Rugova's back, following his progress down the ladder, his aim never wavering. He could have shot him dead at any moment. He wanted to punish him. He wanted to kill him for insubordination. Rugova was useless to him now, and useless to the cause.

Vata knew that he could not fire his weapon. While the canisters were believed to be intact, firing guns was a risk. Damaging a canister by accident was a risk, but there was also the danger of a slow leak, of toxic gases already being present in the air.

Foolishly Vata had taken that risk once, already. He could not take it again.

Baris waited for his commander's instructions. When Vata made one of his micro-gestures, he knew exactly what to do. He pulled two more net bags from a pocket in his pants, walked along the platform, and began to gather the remaining canisters. The ones still in the payload bay of the plane would not be recovered.

Rugova had to walk past Vata to leave the chamber where the Dornier was situated. He hesitated in front of his commander, and stopped. The two men looked at each other.

"We're all dead, now," said Rugova. "A canister is broken. The gas is in the air."

"You disobeyed a command," said Vata.

"So, kill me," said Rugova, raising his arms at his sides to show that he was defenceless and that he didn't plan to attack his boss. "We're all dead anyway."

"We die for our cause. Others will take our places," said Vata.

"What others?" asked Rugova. "We are few. Times change. I am here for my grandfather, but old hatred dies."

Vata said nothing.

Rugova bowed his head slightly and walked around Vata.

The clamour of fighting nearby meant that Rugova did not hear Vata turn. He did not hear his commander reach for the stiletto in his boot. He did not hear him take the two long strides that separated them.

Vata lunged at Rugova, the stiletto held high above his head, and plunged it deep into the back of Rugova's neck, leaving it there so that he didn't spray his suit with blood.

Rugova saw, heard, felt nothing. He fell to his knees, his mouth dropped open, and his eyes closed. He knelt on the clammy duckboards for a second or two and then fell dead onto his face, with a clatter.

Vata turned back to meet Baris, to check the net bags and count his haul.

Two additional eight-man squads of Division Eleven finally arrived at Candle Lane. The first squad was deployed to secure the street aboveground. The second gathered at the station entrance.

"Squad eight to command. Jenkins reporting. Request latest on hazardous materials."

Jenkins looked at the members of his squad while he listened to command's reply. His expression was serious, and he was nodding.

"Please verify. Repeat, verify HAZMAT update," Jenkins said into his comms unit. He listened again for several seconds as command repeated the information.

When the report was repeated and verified, Jenkins said, "Understood. Deploying squad eight, Candle Lane underground site. Stand by." He clipped his comms unit to his jacket.

"This is it," he said. "Formation B. Remember our men are already down there. Let's give them a hand and show them how it's done, shall we?" He beamed, and his squad let out one hard, short roar.

They went in hard and fast and were onto the platform and down on the tracks in less than half the time it had taken Franks and his men to deploy.

When they reached the site, Jenkins gave the signal, and four of the men peeled off in the direction of the Dornier while the remainder went on to the main chamber.

"Put the canisters down and step away," said the Division Eleven man, pointing his 9mm Sig Saur semi-automatic at Vata's back. His colleagues all had weapons drawn and were covering the group.

Vata turned. The expression on his face might have been a smile.

"The gas is released," said Vata.

"Do I look like I care?"

"You're not wearing masks," said Vata, shrugging and turning back to the canisters.

"You could just shoot him, Bhaskar," said one of the other men.

"I could just do that," said Bhaskar. He aimed his gun again and fired on auto, blasting a flurry of shots.

Vata fell hard, facedown, on the duckboards, and Baris flopped over onto his commander's back. A rain of dirt fell on them from the damage done to the ceiling where Bhaskar had fired into it.

"Do you want to do the honours, Taylor, as the shooting was your idea?" asked Bhaskar. "You, too, Bacon."

"It'll be my pleasure," said Taylor, shouldering his gun and walking over to the prone bodies, pulling cable ties from a pouch.

In one last-ditch effort, Vata rolled free of Baris and tried to pull the gun from the holster under his jacket, but Taylor saw the move and stomped a booted foot down hard, trapping Vata's hand on his chest and winding him at the same time.

"Too slow," said Taylor. He patted Vata down, took his concealed weapons from him, and then turned him back onto his belly and tied his hands behind his back. Bacon had already secured Baris.

"Was that too easy?" asked the fourth Division Eleven soldier, his gun held casually at his side.

Lara raised her arms above her head and circled with Gwynnever's sword. She could hear the fray in the corridors and chambers outside, and she still had work to do. She would follow the battle.

The mist wolves and the cloud boar circled once more in their triumphant dance and then followed Lara's command and ducked out through the portal and into the fray. They strafed the combat, snapping at heads and limbs, tugging at shoulders, nipping at ankles.

The beasts did not discriminate. Every combatant was a threat to their mistress.

Lara stepped out of the chamber and took up a fighting stance, sword raised, braced for action.

She would take on all comers.

She looked out into the fray. Battle lines were clearly drawn between the Wolf-Heads and the men whom she assumed were Division Eleven.

Lara stood for a moment, watching the action.

She caught the eyes of a man in black swinging hard with a cosh, trying to subdue his bigger, faster, balder assailant. The Wolf-Head badge on the bigger man's jacket flashed in the hard halogen light, and Lara knew what she had to do.

Suddenly, the tawny mist wolf swung through the air, carving a swirling figure of eight over the heads of the combatants. The air resonated with the sound of its howl as it flexed its jaws and then dived. Its jaws connected with the back of the Wolf-Head's neck. Then its front paws landed on his shoulders, and its hind feet powered into his thighs as it curled its body up.

The mist wolf's momentum pulled the Wolf-Head off his feet, flipping him end over end. The mist wolf flew free under the Wolf-Head's body, which completed a full rotation in the air. The man landed on his back, his neck broken, blood pouring from the tears left by the mist wolf's teeth.

Beecham rose out of his defensive stance, his cosh still gripped firmly in his fist. The man he'd been trying to fend off had been torn away, somersaulted backwards, and was lying, dead, several metres away. It had all happened in a blur.

He looked for the cause and saw again what he thought he'd seen when he'd deployed the second flash bang. He saw the air, golden and glowing, shaped like a vast wolf, but flying through the air, somehow part of it.

Beecham was mesmerised, fixed to the spot. He blinked and glanced back to where he had last seen the woman. Who was she? What was she? He had seen her first in the chamber, standing regal, commanding, apparently unaffected by the light and sound of the flash bang, despite having no obvious protection from it. He had shared a look with her moments before his attacker had died, and there she was still.

Lara nodded at Beecham and then gasped and pointed.

The first gunshots were fired over the men's heads, into the mist wolves.

Ballard had never seen anything like it. He was a seasoned soldier, had seen combat in two war zones. He had killed men before. He had seen buildings brought down by missiles. He'd seen civilian casualties. He'd taken friendly fire and survived, but nothing had prepared him for the apparitions of the two mist wolves making figures of eight in the air above the fight, pouncing at intervals on the bodies below.

Jenkins had not given the order to fire. Ballard didn't need an order. He saw a threat, and he responded. That was his job. It had been his job for a decade.

Lara winced. She wanted to act, but all she could do was watch as the mist wolves began to disintegrate, losing, for a moment, their bright, light forms, dissipating back into the air around them. They swirled a little faster, grey and tawny balls, like comets nestled head to tail around each other. Then they broke and returned to their figure of eights, coalescing once more into their proper forms. They crossed each other's paths and then met, side by side, and drove towards Ballard, snapping and snarling.

"Call them off," said Carter.

He had come up beside Lara and was watching her reaction to the battle.

Lara looked at him. There was more gunfire as Ballard let loose once more. This time, the mist wolves were impervious.

Carter's eyes shone with the warm, soft light that she had seen in her bear's eyes. They were Carter's eyes, big and round and impossibly dark, but Lara saw something there.

She looked out at the mist wolves, about to attack the defenceless man. She drew Gwynnever's sword towards her until the grip was tight against her stomach, held firmly in both hands, the tip pointing skywards. Then she lowered the blade to her side.

Inches from Ballard's head, so close that he could see the individual drops of spittle glistening on their teeth, the mist wolves suddenly turned and resumed their figures of eight.

Carter took Lara by the arm, turned her, and led her back into the chamber.

The forest was vast and spread all around them. Carter walked Lara to the great tree, where once the obelisk had stood, and he sat down among its roots, gently tugging on her hand to persuade her to sit beside him.

"It's over, Lara," said Carter. "That's Division Eleven out there. It's their job to deal with Vata, now. They're not the enemy."

"No," said Lara.

"It's you, isn't it, Lara?"

"What's me?" asked Lara, as if she didn't already know.

"There have been so many stories, but we rationalise. We explain what we cannot understand. I've seen things today. Is all of this about the canisters? Has the gas leaked? Is this a hallucination? Because it feels pretty damned real."

"It's old technology," said Lara. "Who knows what the Nazis were capable of?"

"Look where we are, Lara! Look at the artefact." Carter gestured at the sword, still held firmly in Lara's hand. "You're holding Gwynnever's sword. We're surrounded by an ancient English forest. I've seen beasts that haven't been seen in a place like this for a thousand years. All the things Florence Race talked about."

"Florence Race was a deluded, power-crazed maniac," said Lara.

"It's about you, now," said Carter. "If there's anything you can do. If it's possible that you can change what's happening here. If you can put it back the way it was... You should do it. Now's the time to do it."

"I know," said Lara. "You don't need to tell me, Carter. I know it."

There was a soft shuffling sound and a throaty rumble as the bear emerged from between two trees close by. He sauntered over to where Lara was sitting and flopped down in front of her, his head on the ground by her feet. Lara reached down and placed a hand on his head. He tilted his eyes up to look at her, and she ruffled the fur on the top of his head and stroked his nose.

Then Lara stood. She walked around the tree to the great boulder that stood next to it, and had once been the elegant altar with the long groove in it, which had so neatly fit Gwynnever's sword.

The stone was just that now, a large rock that had stood on the forest floor for millennia, bedded into the ground with clumps of moss, so that it was impossible to tell where the stone ended and the earth began.

Lara raised the sword for one last time and looked at it. Then, holding the grip in her right hand, she slid Gwynnever's sword into the slot on the top of the stone. It went in easily, almost to the hilt. Lara stood for a moment, and finally let go of the grip. The sword dropped a few more millimetres into the slot with the merest sigh, and Lara stepped back.

She looked down at Carter, sitting on the stone floor, the obelisk rising up behind him, and she glanced over at where Florence's body lay crumpled in a heap, dead and broken. The floor was littered with the bodies of the Wolf-Heads who'd been killed in the fight, their blood soaking into the pale stone. The chamber was, otherwise, exactly as it had been the first time Lara had stepped into it.

Not quite exactly. She turned back to the altar. Gwynnever's sword lay in the groove on the altar. It fit so perfectly that it looked like part of the structure, as if it had been laid there millennia ago and had, somehow, become one with the stone slab it lay upon.

The halogen lights suddenly shone brightly throughout the site. The grey, misty atmosphere dissipated instantly, as if it had been sucked away in one great breath.

The mist wolves were gone. Ballard wondered whether they had ever been there. But not for long. There was a battle to fight, and win.

Having subdued Vata and Baris, the Division Eleven men heard shots fired.

"Maybe not so easy, after all," said Bhaskar. "Since you're so cocky, Rowles, you can guard the prisoners. With me," he said.

Bhaskar, Taylor, and Bacon joined the fray in its final minutes. Franks's squad had done a thorough job of keeping the Wolf-Heads busy until the reinforcements had arrived. There were injuries, and the reckless gunfire had made some of the Wolf-Heads nervous.

One or two gave up the fight, others were subdued, three had to be shot.

Soon, it was all over.

"What about the woman, sir?" Beecham asked Franks, once all the surviving Wolf-Heads had been relieved of their weapons and cuffed with cable ties.

"What woman?" asked Franks.

"We should check out the chamber, over there," said Beecham.

Jenkins picked his way through the bodies to Franks's position.

"Problem?" Franks asked.

"There may be more combatants in the next chamber," said Jenkins.

"I'm sorry, sir," said Beecham. "It's a woman. I'm not sure she's a combatant."

"Was she armed?" asked Jenkins.

"She was carrying a sword," said Beecham. "Wielding it, I guess."

"Then she's an armed combatant," said Jenkins. He drew his Sig Sauer.

"Updated ballistics policy?" asked Franks.

"We're good to go," said Jenkins. "Fire at will. You want to do this together?"

"Let's do it," said Franks.

Beecham took one step back to allow his bosses to do their jobs, but he stayed close. He didn't like them going in after the woman. It didn't seem right.

Franks entered the chamber first, his gun on Lara and Carter. Carter raised his hands immediately. Jenkins was right behind him.

"Are you armed?" asked Franks.

"Yes," said Carter.

"What's in the bags?" asked Franks, gesturing at the orange, nylon rucksack still strapped to Carter's chest.

"Canisters from the airplane," said Carter.

"Take them off and put them on the ground. I want to see your hands at all times."

Carter began to do as he was told.

"Hands up, lady," said Jenkins, approaching Lara. Lara raised her hands slowly, Jenkins standing over her, the barrel of his gun less than a metre from her head. "Are you armed?"

"Yes," said Lara.

Jenkins took a step to the side to give her room to move, but never shifted his aim.

"On your bellies, hands on your heads," said Jenkins.

Carter and Lara did as they were told. Jenkins covered Franks while he cable-tied their hands together behind their backs. Then he patted them down and removed their weapons. When he was done, Franks helped Carter to sit, and Jenkins helped Lara.

"What's a woman doing with these goons?" asked Jenkins.

"We're not with them," said Carter. "I'm Carter Bell. I'm an archaeologist. This is Lara Croft."

"You're an archaeologist," said Jenkins, "and you're packing? Pull the other leg. It's got bells on."

"You're Division Eleven," said Lara. "You have a file on me. You should check it out. We're not with Vata, and we're not goons. This is about the site, the finds."

"Let's get them out of here," said Franks.

CHAPTER TWENTY-SIX: DEBRIEF
The Houses of Parliament

Dressed for the occasion in a skirt and jacket with a crisp, white shirt, her hair in a ponytail, and a small handbag hanging from one shoulder, Lara made her way to the Palace of Westminster. She passed swiftly through the security checks, and made her way to the office of the 6th Viscount Stowe.

"Miss Croft," said his secretary, "it's good to see you again."

"Thanks, Stephanie. You, too," said Lara, smiling.

"He'll be right with you," said Stephanie.

With that, the inner door opened and a well-groomed, but casually dressed man stepped across the threshold.

"I thought I heard your voice," he said, opening his arms to take Lara in a light embrace, kissing both cheeks.

"It's lovely to see you, Charlie," said Lara.

"Likewise," said Charles. "It's been too long."

They stepped into the elected life peer's office, and the Viscount closed the door behind them.

"What can I help you with, Lara?" asked Charles, ushering her into a chair and taking one for himself.

"This could be about what I can help you with," said Lara. "You were on the Crossrail Select Committee?"

"I was," said Charles. "It's a necessary innovation, of course, and you know I believe in supporting business, but I wanted to ensure that the city was taken care of and that our heritage was preserved. Is there a problem, Lara?"

"How much do you know about Candle Lane?"

"Probably not as much as you," said Charles. "Why don't you tell me about it?"

"You could say that I made some unauthorised visits to a restricted site, three unauthorised visits."

"After it was shut down?" asked Charles. "So you do know more about it than I do. Why doesn't that surprise me?" He smiled.

"I know almost everything there is to know about it," said Lara, "which is why I'm here. I need you to make a call. Can you get the Minister of Defence into this meeting?"

"No problem," said Charles. "Do you need someone from Heritage, too?"

"I don't think so," said Lara. "Not for this one."

In less than half an hour, Theresa Johnson, the Minister of Defence, walked into Viscount Stowe's office.

"Good morning, Charles," she said. "Can we make this quick? The PM's got me on something very time-consuming."

Lara turned in her chair as Ms. Johnson took a seat.

"Ah, Miss Croft," said the Minister.

"How long this takes rather depends on you, Minister," said Lara.

"You're here about the Candle Lane site," said Ms. Johnson. "I heard about your involvement in that little fiasco."

"A little fiasco that doesn't appear to have made the papers," said Lara.

"It's not considered to be in the public interest."

"There's a great deal that *is* in the public interest, though," said Lara. "The Dornier, the payload, the contents of those canisters, Dritan Vata... Shall I go on?"

"Miss Croft," said the Minister, "the contents of the canisters were examined and found to be inert."

"The closure of the dig and the site? The nerve gas? My friend Annie Hawkes? People were hospitalized, and you're going to fob me off with no explanation?"

Lara had an explanation. She also knew how to play the game. The establishment was not comfortable with many of the aspects of Lara's life and work that were very real. This time she had a scapegoat for the events that had unfolded, and she was going to use it.

The government would be comfortable believing that the Nazi weapon was responsible for the mass hallucinations that had stricken down the dig teams. It was something they could recognise, believe, and deal with. It was real to them, and that was the way that Lara Croft wanted it to stay.

Ms. Johnson coughed.

"Further investigations are, of course, underway to determine the exact contents of the canisters and how they were weaponised. There is speculation that the contained nature of the site created an environment that stored some of the chemical, which was released into the atmosphere during the dig."

"Further investigations?" asked Lara.

"That's as much as I can tell you," said Ms. Johnson.

"You know the effects of the weapon?" asked Lara.

"Of course," said the Minister. "Our Division Eleven operatives are being debriefed as we speak."

"Okay, then," said Lara. "Perhaps when you have collated their statements, you'll see the necessity of locking down the site and burying it."

"That would be your recommendation?" asked Ms. Johnson.

"It would," said Lara. "I would also recommend that you lock up Dritan Vata and throw away the key."

"I cannot comment on Mr. Vata's involvement, nor on any crimes he might have committed," said the Minister.

"Of course you can't," said Lara. "But I can. He's dangerous. He's dangerous to the world. He knows of nothing but conflict and war. He's utterly ruthless. He wanted those canisters, at any cost. He wanted Nazi weapons, and he didn't know what they were or what devastation they might cause, but he wanted them."

"I understand your concerns, Miss Croft," said Ms. Johnson.

"I'm not sure that you do, Minister," said Lara.

"You understand why the site was opened up?" asked Ms. Johnson.

"Crossrail?" said Lara. "Of course I understand why the site was opened up. Are you seriously going to talk to me about money?"

"Commerce is a consideration," said Ms. Johnson. "If your recommendation is that we bury the site, by implication you are suggesting that we reroute Crossrail, and that is going to cost a great deal of money."

"It is," said Lara. "It will cost less than the alternative, and I'm talking in terms of money, since that's what matters to you."

"How so, Miss Croft?"

"Have you considered the archaeological value of an historic site, Minister?" said Lara. "Of this historic site, in particular?"

"Touché, Miss Croft," said Ms. Johnson. "What do you consider the findings might be with regard to the national importance of this particular archaeological dig site?"

"I think it could be argued that Candle Lane is, perhaps, the most important site that has been uncovered by archaeologists in Britain...I don't know... ever!" said Lara Croft. "I imagine a site like that would be preserved indefinitely, would possibly become a World Heritage site. I can't imagine the cost of processing a site like that, of making it available for study by historians and archaeologists, internationally.

"Then, of course, there's public interest. Imagine if this site became as popular as, say, Stonehenge. Of course there'd be the cost of access, of making the site safe for visitors, of building a visitor centre. This is

London, after all. The costs would run to billions of pounds. I wonder if this government has that kind of money in its budget."

"You think that might be a possibility?" asked the Minister.

"I could almost guarantee it," said Lara. "Of course, the investigations would take a great deal of time. Archaeology is a slow science. The dig would have to continue for two, possibly three years. Studies would have to be made. There would be answers, eventually."

"You're holding me to ransom, Miss Croft."

"I have concerns, Minister. Of course, even if the site didn't prove to be as important as I believe it is, the Crossrail schedule would be compromised, and it would still have to be diverted."

"Indeed," said Ms. Johnson.

"You could look at it this way," said Lara. "If you bury the site without further delay—if you do so on the grounds of hazard materials with respect to the Dornier—you'll be saving yourselves and the taxpayer a vast amount of money."

"At this time, there is no way to know the composition of the chemicals in the weapons, how they escaped, or how they were released into the atmosphere," said Ms. Johnson, almost to herself. "There is no way to know whether there is a reserve of the chemicals, or whether they might continue to be a danger."

"More money," said Lara. "Science doesn't come cheap. How long is it going to take for your scientists to answer all your questions? Then how much longer to make the area safe for machines and a workforce? How long to do the risk assessments? How long to comply with the health and safety regulations? What happens when the unions get involved?"

"I'm not sure that's any concern of yours, Miss Croft." Ms. Johnson frowned at Lara.

"Maybe not," said Lara, sitting back, relaxing in her chair. "I was down there, though. Remember? I had that experience. I have no idea how this is going to affect me for the rest of my life. I saw Annie Hawkes in that facility. Am I going to turn into that? If that happened to an entire workforce... Wow! That wouldn't just cost you money; it'd be a national scandal. That could cost the government an election."

Lara was suddenly hungry. All the tension she'd felt knowing that she'd have to go head-to-head with the government had dissipated. She had Ms. Johnson in her pocket, and she knew it. She'd left the Minister of Defence with only one choice. They would shut the site down, and they'd do it fast. Crossrail would be rerouted, and the entire episode would be over.

Ms. Johnson gathered herself together and stood, reaching out to shake hands with the Viscount.

"Thank you for arranging this meeting, Charles," she said. "And I'm sure I needn't tell you that everything you heard stays in these four walls."

"Of course, Minister," said Charles.

Theresa Johnson turned to Lara, and they, too, shook hands.

"Thank you, Miss Croft," she said. "This conversation has been most enlightening."

"I'm happy you think so, Minister," said Lara. She didn't stand.

As the door closed behind the Minister of Defence, Charles looked at Lara, wide-eyed, and let out a long breath.

"Wow!" he said. "That was pretty impressive. Do you realise you just influenced government policy?"

"No, Charles," said Lara. "I just got the job done, and I got it done fast. Thanks for your help. I appreciate it."

They both stood.

"No, thank you for the lesson in firm negotiating," said Charles, embracing Lara again before showing her out.

CHAPTER TWENTY-SEVEN: LARA CROFT
London

"You did what?" asked Carter. He put his cup down and dropped his head a little, aware that people were looking at him. He hadn't intended to cause a scene, but he was clearly horrified.

"Why are you the only one not smiling?" asked Lara, sipping from a large cup of coffee, a lovely pattern drawn in the foam on the top. "Have you noticed how relaxed and cheerful everyone seems to be?"

"I just..." began Carter, putting his hands around his coffee cup. "I just don't understand what you're saying, Lara. I was there. We were both there. I really need you to explain what happened."

"I told you," said Lara. "I got it shut down. Candle Lane is being buried, and Crossrail is moving on."

"But why?" asked Carter. "What about the chamber, the obelisk, the sword, Lara? What about Gwynnever's sword?"

"London really does seem to have turned around, doesn't it?" said Lara. "Everything felt so grim, so vicious and despondent. Look around. There's hope in the air again."

"I don't want to talk about a change in the weather," said Carter. "People are always in a good mood when it's sunny. I want to talk about why you'd want to bury an important site like Candle Lane. There's never been anything like it found on British soil, and now, no one will ever study it. The public will never get to see those finds."

"You don't get it, do you, Carter?"

"I don't, Lara. I really don't get it at all."

"I'm not talking about a change in the weather," said Lara. "All the misery up here, in London, all over the country, it was because of what happened at Candle Lane. It was because of what Florence Race did in Nefertiti's tomb. It was because Gwynnever's sword was disturbed, stolen, and abused."

"And that's why you shut it down?" asked Carter.

"And that's why I shut it down," said Lara. "Some things are just too precious, too important. Gwynnever's sword is one of those things. There's no place for it on earth, no museum, no glass case where it would be safe."

"It was safe in your hands," said Carter.

"Even if that's true," said Lara, "that's too much responsibility for one person. Besides, you know what they say: 'Power corrupts; absolute power corrupts absolutely.' We might not live in a perfect world, or a perfect country, but in Gwynnever's time there was no such thing as democracy. They needed great leaders then. Gwynnever was the right woman, in the right place, at the right time. I'm not interested in replacing her. The country doesn't need another Gwynnever, and it certainly doesn't need me. It needs a compassionate society and a working democracy."

"But what about the archaeology? What about the work? You didn't want to study the chamber, find the connections to other sites?" asked Carter. "I'd have killed to work on that stuff."

"More than we killed already?" asked Lara. "I think there's been enough death, don't you?"

"More than enough," said Carter, slumping back in his chair and taking a long sip of his coffee.

"Gwynnever's sword is back where it belongs. You saw it. You saw how the sword fit the stone. It couldn't have been more perfect. That's its home. If it has a job watching over the good of the nation, it will do it from there. We've been more or less okay for millennia. I think we can trust the process."

"I can't say I'm not disappointed," said Carter.

"Me neither," said Lara. "But at least we had something that a lot of other archaeologists didn't have... Talking of which, drink up. It's almost visiting hours."

"Lara Croft and Carter Bell to see Annie Hawkes," said Lara at the reception desk. The nurse checked a list and smiled at Lara.

"Of course," she said. "It's room 307. That's the third floor. You'll find the lifts at the end of hall, on the right. Ms. Hawkes will be delighted to see you."

"Thank you," said Lara.

"It doesn't look as if we'll be chased out of here this time," she said to Carter, as the lift doors closed and she hit the button for the third floor.

"Lara!" said Annie, almost before Lara was in the room. She got up from her chair and met Lara in the middle of the room with a warm hug. "And Carter!" she said, hugging him, too. "How lovely of you to come. Take the chairs. I'll sit on the bed. They don't like visitors sitting on beds. I'm sure they think I'm going to be contaminated with something or other." Annie laughed.

"How are you?" asked Lara. "You seem much better than the last time I saw you."

"You were here?" asked Annie. "Nobody told me."

"I did pop in," said Lara.

"It was pretty dreadful," said Annie. "But, honestly, I don't remember much about any of it, except some of the dreams. Bloody Nazis."

"They told you what happened to you?" asked Carter.

"They must have told you, too," said Annie. "You were there. I assume they 'debriefed' you. Didn't you sign the Official Secrets Act? Of course, I'm not supposed to talk about it, but I imagine it's all right to talk to you, since we're in the same boat."

Lara cast a warning glance in Carter's direction.

"I guess they put us through the same process," said Carter. "I'm not sure we're supposed to talk, even among ourselves."

"You could just tell me if there's much to talk about," said Annie. "They say it was all hallucinations. The site... In my mind it was fascinating, important, but they say it was all in my imagination because of the gas."

"That's about the size of it," said Carter.

"They're shutting everything down and burying it," said Lara, "because of the toxic gas. So I guess that's the end of that."

"Of course it isn't," said Annie, almost indignant.

Lara and Carter shared another glance.

"What do you mean?" asked Carter.

"Have you any idea how bored I am in here?" asked Annie. "I'm over the worst, and they've reduced my medication. My GP will be able to monitor my recovery. I'll be home in a couple of days."

"That's great news," said Lara.

"I can't wait to get back to work," said Annie. "As soon as I get the all clear, I want to get back on the Crossrail project."

"Are you sure?" asked Carter.

"Do you know of anyone who's better qualified?" asked Annie.

"Absolutely not," said Lara. "Are you sure you'd want to do it, after all you've been through?"

"Of course I'd want to do it. It's my job. How many times do you suppose we're going to dig up and disturb Nazi weapons of mass hallucination, Lara?" Annie Hawkes laughed. "Crossrail is a godsend."

"How do you work that out?" asked Carter.

"How often do we get an excuse to go under London and dig around?" asked Annie. "How often do we have this kind of access to the millennia of history buried under our city? This could be a golden age for British archaeology, and I don't plan to miss that boat."

"Well, then, I hope you'll make me part of your plans," said Carter Bell.

"I wouldn't have it any other way," said Annie Hawkes.

"As a door closes, somewhere a window opens," said Lara as she and Carter left the hospital.

"Waxing philosophical?" asked Carter.

"I'm just saying you get another bite of the cherry," said Lara. "I know how disappointed you were that I let the Candle Lane site go."

"You were probably right about that," said Carter.

"I know I was right about it. Annie's right, too, though. There's a lot of history under London, and Crossrail has still got a long way to go."

"Maybe I should thank you for shutting down Candle Lane. Rerouting the line could open up a whole swath of new possibilities for archaeology."

"It certainly could," said Lara. "And you should definitely call me the next time something weird and wonderful happens."

"This couldn't possibly happen again," said Carter. "You heard Annie. This was a one-off."

"I agree," said Lara. "You're unlikely to find another downed Nazi airplane carrying a payload of weapons of unknown, possibly lethal, hallucinogenic gas. And if you did, you're not going to find it at an ancient Egyptian site."

"It does sound fantastical when you say it like that," said Carter.

"That should tell you that just about anything's possible," said Lara. "That's the wonder of archaeology, Carter. That's why we do what we do."

"So I should call you," said Carter, "the next time I find something interesting or hazardous or dangerous? I should call you the next time someone goes mad, or something gets stolen...or the next time the M.O.D. storms onto a site?"

"You should definitely call me," said Lara. "You'll know when."

ABOUT THE AUTHORS

Dan Abnett is a multiple New York Times bestselling author and an award-winning comic book writer. In comics, he is known for his work on the *Guardians of the Galaxy* for Marvel and *Wild's End* for Boom! Studios, and is currently writing *Aquaman*. His 2008 run on the *Guardians of the Galaxy* formed the inspiration for the blockbuster movie. He is a regular contributor to the British 2000AD, with series including *Kingdom*, *Lawless* and the classic *Sinister Dexter*. He also writes screenplays, and has written extensively for the games industry, including *Alien:Isolation* and *Shadow of Mordor*. Dan is published in well over a dozen languages and has sold millions of books worldwide. He was educated at St Edmund Hall, Oxford, and lives and works in Maidstone, Kent. Follow him and Nik Vincent on Twitter @VincentAbnett

Nik Vincent began working as a freelance editor, but has published work in a number of mediums including advertising, training manuals, comics and short stories. She has worked as a ghost writer, and regularly collaborates with her partner, Dan Abnett, writing novels and in the games industry. Nik was educated at Stirling University, and lives and works in Maidstone, Kent. Her blog and website can be found at www.nicolavincent-abnett.com

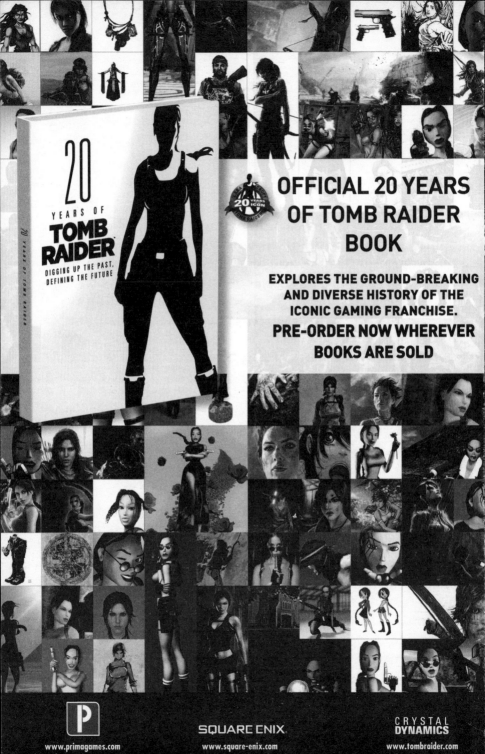